Queen of the Road

'Tell me what you're doing here, honey, all alone in a trailer in the desert. Are you all wired up and waiting for your pals to come arrest us?' He pushed Toni's dress up under her throat. 'Oh no. Nothing here –' his huge hand felt her breasts, '– only some firm little titties.' He pushed another finger inside her and Toni sucked on it greedily. 'You must be just another horny slut looking to get laid. Well, you've come to the right place. I hope you like it rough and ready 'cos that's all you'll get around here.'

Neb unplugged his fingers and Toni fell back on to the bed as her legs gave way. 'Slip those panties off and open wide for the biggest Cobra of them all.' He unbuckled his leather chaps and slung them across the room. Then he unzipped his oily jeans and pushed them down his hairy thighs. His tats ran down into his pubic hair.

Toni's eyes widened. It wasn't an empty boast. They could have named the Cobra gang after him for all she knew.

Queen of the Road
Lois Phoenix

BLACK LACE

Black Lace books contain sexual fantasies.
In real life, always practise safe sex.

First published in 2002 by
Black Lace
Thames Wharf Studios
Rainville Road
London W6 9HA

Copyright © Lois Phoenix, 2002

The right of Lois Phoenix to be identified as the Author of
the Work has been asserted in accordance with the Copyright,
Designs and Patents Act 1988.

Design by Smith & Gilmour, London
Printed and bound by Mackays of Chatham PLC

ISBN 0 352 33731 1

*All characters in this publication are fictitious and any resemblance
to real persons, living or dead, is purely coincidental.*

This book is sold subject to the condition that it shall not, by way
of trade or otherwise, be lent, resold, hired out or otherwise
circulated without the publisher's prior written consent in any form
of binding or cover other than that in which it is published and
without a similar condition including this condition being imposed
on the subsequent purchaser.

1

Al Bertorelli pointed a fat, nicotine-stained finger at Toni and grinned around his cigar. 'You drive one hard bargain, lady. I'll tell her she's fired as soon as Simon's done his money shot.'

'You're all heart, Al.'

'Hey, you know I didn't want to part with this one. She has the cutest pussy I've seen in a long time.'

Toni did know. It had cost her just under a thousand bucks to get Al to release Kim from her contract and that had stung because, as far as Toni was concerned, if Kim wanted to suck dicks in front of a camera for a living, that was her choice; she was certainly old enough to look after herself. But Kim's dad thought otherwise. He was willing to pay big bucks to get her home and Toni never argued with a five-figure fee.

'Come and have a look at one of the older mares in the stable.' Al slid a massive picture to one side, revealing a window on to the studio. He propelled his huge bulk forward in his office chair until he got a good view of the action being filmed. A blonde girl dressed in a skintight pink dress and thigh-high black plastic boots was being felt up by a unbelievably good-looking 'fireman'. Toni guessed that the only hose he'd ever been near was the one filling out the front of his fake black waterproofs.

'Ten out of ten for originality, Al.'

'Guys don't want originality – they just want to see big tits.'

'Clearly.'

The fireman was behind the blonde now, nibbling along her neck. He ran his tanned hands up over her breasts, squeezing them until she squirmed in feigned pleasure, and slowly pulled down the front of her dress until her tits sprang into view. Toni thought that they actually looked real but kept her mouth shut; she knew Al could wax lyrical about boob jobs for hours.

As the blonde writhed expertly, the fireman crouched behind her and, as he rose, pushed her dress upwards, revealing her neatly trimmed thatch.

'You won't shock me, Al; I've seen it all before. When they call cut I want Kim out of here. We're meeting her dad at six.'

'OK, OK, I hear you.' Al didn't turn around and puffed hard on his cigar.

Toni sighed and checked her watch; she could murder a cold beer. The blonde girl bent forward so that her tits dangled. Behind her, the fireman was losing his uniform with the ease of stripper, revealing a massive erection. The director was motioning to the girl to turn so that her ass was exposed to the camera, and not through coincidence, Toni knew, Al's window. She obliged, maintaining the same pout through over-applied lipstick the whole time. Toni felt a flush creeping up her neck, and looked at her feet. Nevertheless, she felt her eyes pulled back to the blonde's tanned buttocks and the nest of hair peeking out beneath them.

An assistant wearing a baseball cap came forward to say something to the director and they stood there for a while discussing positions while the girl remained bent over, her tiny dress rumpled around her waist. The director said something to the girl before parting her legs slightly further. More discussion, then the blonde shook her head and tousled her long mane while she waited. The director reached between her legs and gently parted her sex. Toni thought that her slit looked very pink between her brown thighs. They still weren't happy, however, and someone was called over with a bottle of water to spray her pubes so that they glistened under the bright studio lights. The director then arranged her pussy lips so they pouted neatly from within the nest of her bush. Once they were happy they stepped back, allowing the fireman and his huge cock to advance.

Toni coughed. The office was filling with cigar smoke but she didn't complain; the smell of expensive cigars was preferable to the stench of Al's body odour.

The fireman caught the girl around the waist but, instead of pushing his cock into her as she expected, he crouched and pulled her back on to his tongue. She was clearly surprised, her practised pout slipping into a start-led O. It wasn't long before she started enjoying it, Toni noticed, recognising the glazed expression and drooping eyelids of someone who was genuinely aroused. Toni shifted slightly in her chair, feeling her crotch start to twitch and willing herself not to become excited. She did not want anything connected with Al Bertorelli to turn her on.

Nevertheless, Toni couldn't take her eyes off the way the fireman was tonguing the girl from behind, running it along her sex lips to her clit and then back again. The girl was lost to it now, pushing herself back on to his face and moaning out loud. Toni noticed that the hand-ful of male technicians on set were sporting uncomfort-able looking lumps in the front of their jeans. Toni's eyes swooped involuntarily to the fireman's cock, stand-ing rigid between his muscled thighs. She crossed her legs and squeezed her thigh muscles around her clit. Out of the corner of her eye she noticed that Al had left the office. She guessed that he'd gone to whack himself off in the men's room and was relieved that he was no longer in the room with her.

The fireman was now rimming his tongue around the girl's anus. Toni shifted so that she could get a better view and saw that the girl's pussy was dripping with a combination of saliva and love juice. She was oblivious to the cameras and was groaning, 'Fuck me, fuck me.' The fireman rose up and traced the cleft of the girl's butt cheeks with the tip of his cock. As he was about to enter her, the director stopped him and motioned to him to move out of the way. The fireman looked confused but did as he was told. The girl looked up at the fireman and shouted, 'Will someone just fuck me!'

To her horror, Toni saw Al appear on set, still puffing on his cigar and struggling to release his cock from under his huge gut. Toni could see the looks on the faces of the others; they weren't sure how the girl was going to react, but she was too far gone to care who fucked her as long as someone did.

Al stood admiring her dripping pussy framed by the V of her tanned thighs as he groped beneath his stomach to pull a condom on to his flabby cock. His lurid Hawaiian shirt sported large sweat rings and flapped around the girl's splayed buttocks.

'Get on with it,' she yelled at Al. Al clamped his teeth around his cigar and pushed his cock inside her. The blonde pushed back against him, arching her back and moaning. Toni watched as Al ground himself into the girl. He was a disgusting sight with his pants around his ankles and his meaty fingers groping for a feel of her breasts as they swung below. He came quickly, squeezing his eyes shut and gripping the blonde tightly around the waist. When he was done, he withdrew and tucked himself back inside his trousers with his condom still on.

As he slunk out of the studio, the blonde stood upright, hands on hips, breasts jutting proudly, and commanded, 'On your back, Simon, I have got to get a proper fuck.'

The fireman was only too happy to oblige. The cameras still rolling, he lay on his back and watched her shimmy out of her pink dress. Still wearing the boots, she lowered herself on to his enormous cock. Oblivious to anyone else in the studio, the blonde fingered herself as she rode his cock hard, banging herself on to to him so that her breasts bounced. The blonde soon climaxed, her hair tumbling over her bobbing jugs as she arched her back and ground her pussy on to him. Simon waited until she had finished before withdrawing, flipping her on to her back, taking a beat to make sure the cameras were still running, and only then allowing himself to come in huge hot spurts all over her breasts. Finally finished, the two of them grinned at each other.

'Great stuff, guys,' the director called out in a shaky voice. 'That's a wrap.'

The fireman held out a hand to help the blonde up and someone rushed forward with two dressing gowns.

In the office, Toni stood on trembling legs, aroused and disgusted by what she had just witnessed and praying that she wouldn't have to face Al again that afternoon. The sight of him always filled her with revulsion and she knew that she would have to work hard to stave off the image of him with his cock wilting inside a used condom. She guessed that he had fucked the actress to let her know that, despite their deal, he was in charge here. Toni shivered. The thought of Al's slimy cock inside her own pussy repulsed her, and yet her clit was twitching like crazy.

In disgust, Toni slid the picture back over the window and stormed out of the office, her lace panties damp and uncomfortable between her legs. In his haste to get to the actress, Al had left the security door unlocked and Toni marched up the corridor in what she hoped was the direction of the dressing rooms.

'Kim Le Brock!' Toni barked at a minion who was making hard work of pushing a trolley loaded with equipment.

'No unauthorised personnel beyond this point, lady.'

'Don't give me that bullshit, I'm not in the mood.' Toni flashed her ID; it was surprising the number of people who assumed it to be a police badge, especially if they were working without a visa.

'Straight ahead.' The minion suddenly found the trolley easy to push after all and disappeared up the corridor.

Toni took a deep breath and forced a maternal smile on to her face before entering the dressing room. Four girls dressed in G-strings sat in front of the mirrors. They stopped talking as soon as Toni appeared and she wondered if they had heard about what had just happened on the set.

'Kim Le Brock?'

Lipstick and mascara wands hovered momentarily. 'Who wants to know?'

Toni took a chance. 'Her dad actually.'

'In that case, you better get your ass up the corridor before Al gets his hands on her.'

'Thanks.'

Cursing under her breath, Toni kicked open every door on the corridor, convinced that the double-dealing son of a bitch was extracting last-minute favours, when a tearful redhead nearly knocked her flying.

'Kim?'

'Leave me alone!'

'Hey, come on.' Toni held tight until the girl collapsed against her, sobbing. 'What did he do to you?'

Kim Le Brock looked up at Toni through eyes smeared with mascara. 'The fucker just sacked me!'

Toni stroked her shaking shoulders and smiled.

2

On the sidewalk outside Piedro's, Toni Marconi shook hands with a balding, middle-aged salesman.

'Thank you for finding my little girl, Ms Marconi.' He was slowly turning pink in the LA heat and reminded Toni of a hog roast.

'Pleasure.' It took every ounce of Toni's willpower not to wipe her palm on the skirt of her new linen suit.

Mr Macmillan dug inside his jacket and groped for the envelope containing the remainder of Toni's fee. 'It's all there, and a little extra.' He meant for confidentiality and shuffled his feet in embarrassment.

Toni smiled coolly and checked the contents; some people got mean once they got what they wanted. 'It goes without saying, Mr Macmillan. Pleasure doing business with you.' Toni turned to the young redhead at his side. 'Good luck in stage school, Kimberly.'

Kim Le Brock was hiding behind a pair of shades and curled a disdainful lip at Toni before following her daddy towards his station wagon. Toni waved as they pulled out of the restaurant car park and smiled a bright, insincere smile.

Taking a deep breath, Toni spun on one kitten heel and headed for the cool, dark interior of the bar.

'Afternoon, princess.' Piedro grinned mischievously from behind the bar. 'Snatched another budding actress from the welcoming arms of fame?'

'She seems to think so.' Toni perched herself on a bar stool. 'Usual please, Piedro.'

'Of course.' Piedro pulled a tall glass of cold frothy beer.

Toni took a long, deep swallow. 'Bliss.'

'Takes away the bad taste, no?'

'Sure does. Daddy's taking her home and enrolling her in stage school but some girls just don't need to be taught how to act, you know?'

'Sure, princess, I know.'

'Still, not for me to criticise.' She slipped a small wad of notes across the bar to Piedro and winked. 'Thanks for the tip.'

He slipped the money into his apron pocket. 'My cousins can find anyone in this town.'

'Not surprising when they run half the seedy joints in it.'

Piedro feigned hurt, his black eyes twinkling. 'But not this one. This is one clean operation.' He waved his hand at the empty bar.

'Only because the table dancers don't come in until eleven.'

'No drugs though, Toni, no trouble. The boys see to that.' Piedro pointed a finger at the ceiling.

'You didn't say they were in.'

'Sure they're in. They were asking for you.'

Toni drained her glass. 'I'll pop up, then. Gimme a bottle of Jack.'

Piedro eyed her long thighs as she slid off the stool. 'You know, princess, you don't need to pay Piedro for this information. A little bit of loving can go an awful long way.'

Toni took the bottle and laughed. 'You don't need my loving, Piedro. Not with all the girls in here who are falling over themselves to get to you.' She headed for the stairs, swinging her hips and throwing him a kiss over her shoulder.

'Only one princess though,' Piedro muttered to himself as he watched Toni shimmy upstairs. He felt a stirring in the front of his Calvin's. 'Piedro's gonna get himself a piece of you one day, princess, just you wait and see.'

The upstairs room was full of cigarette smoke and an eclectic bunch of police officers. Toni took a deep breath of good old-fashioned testosterone and grinned. Four male uniforms were playing pool and Toni took a stool to watch. Legs crossed, tumbler of Jack in one hand, she began to unwind. The guy leaning across the table to take his shot had the most exquisite butt, and Toni licked her lips. Most of the men had their sleeves rolled up to reveal muscular forearms, and their collars undone to reveal a hint of chest hair. Their jackets were slung over the backs of chairs but they kept their shoulder holsters on. Toni sipped her drink and thought it was a pity they weren't allowed to keep their radio belts on off-duty. She could feel a good night coming on. Who needed fetish bars when she had the real thing?

'Bit early for you, Toni.' Inspector John Bradley slid his stocky frame on to the bar stool beside her.

'I'm celebrating closing a case.' She lifted her glass in salute and pushed the bottle towards him; she didn't want to be too hammered to enjoy herself tonight.

'Well, us too. Cheers.' John Bradley clinked glasses and smiled, his dark shadowed eyes crinkling at the corners. 'I don't know why a nice girl like you chooses to deal with the scum that floats through this town.'

Toni quickly dismissed an unwanted image of Al Bertorelli's slug of a cock slipping in and out of the blonde's damp pussy. 'Same as you, John, it pays the rent.' She toyed with her glass and watched John's huge hand close around his. 'Anyway, how do you know I am a nice girl?'

John smiled over the rim of his glass but took her comment with a pinch of salt. Toni had been gently flirting with him for two years now, but as far as he was aware none of the boys had had her yet. John knew that every hetero male down at the station got a hard-on when they saw her walk in the room, but she still remained off limits.

Toni was leaning forward to tell him something, her cleavage flashing milky white in the deep V in the front of her suit. John shifted uncomfortably, wondering if her nipples were brown or pink. A roar of laughter from the other side of the room drowned out Toni's words.

Detective Ray O'Connor shouted from his seat. 'Oh, John, Toni! Get your asses over here. The bet is on for the best come story.'

John raised an eyebrow at Toni, who grinned. 'Come on, should be fun.' She led the way over to the table where four of LAPD's finest were belly laughing around a low table.

'Come on, you two.' Ray signalled with his cigarette to a pile of bills in the centre of the table. 'Twenty bucks a piece. Winner takes all.'

Toni squeezed on to a chair and grinned at Detective Jan Green, the only other woman there. 'Best come story? Not sure I qualify.'

Jan grinned and tucked a stray dark curl behind her ear. 'Apparently orgasm stories will suffice.'

'Really? Still, I don't think I'll bother. Us women are at such a disadvantage when it comes to props.'

'That's crap, Toni, and you know it.' Ray pointed to the pile again. 'Come on, pay up. You in, John?' John shook his head and took up a position behind Ray, sipping his drink and trying hard not to sneak glances down the front of Toni's jacket. She was used to men gawking down her top, and it usually repulsed her, but John Bradley made her clit twitch. She'd been toying with him for some time now and perhaps the time had come for her to have him; she'd see. Pretending not to notice his furtive glances, Toni shrugged out of her jacket, revealing a tight black vest top underneath. She knew full well that her push-up bra was making her breasts spill out over the top of it.

'OK, OK.' Toni flipped a twenty on to the table and grinned at Jan. 'Whose ref?'

'Has to be John.' Jan bit her bottom lip, sensing the sexual tension rising in the air. The crowd was thinning out now; the married officers were heading home, others going downstairs for food.

'Aren't you hot, Jan?' Toni was enjoying baiting the boys tonight.

Jan followed her lead. 'Now you come to mention it.' She slipped out of her sensible work cardigan; underneath she wore a tight red blouse, which accentuated her dark hair beautifully, and she undid the top few buttons. 'There, that's better. What's it to be? First? Worst? Best?'

Ray had gone unusually quiet. He was leaning forward with his elbows on his knees, Toni knew that he had the hots for Jan and would have bet any money that he had a hard-on right now.

Ray's eyes seemed very dark in the dim light of the club as he ground out his cigarette. 'Most unusual. Who's first?'

'I'll go first if you like,' Toni volunteered innocently. She had a strong suspicion that the men only got her and Jan to play this so they could hear them talking dirty. 'You know I grew up in San Francisco ...' Toni sat back and glanced around the table. She eyed a rookie called Matt, a tall, lean young man whom she'd met a couple of times before, and Ted – who was married and shouldn't be there at all. Both men pretended nonchalance, their faces half in shadow. '. . . well, I used to date a guy called Sammy Leibowitz. He was only young but had a great body from lifting meat carcasses in his folks' slaughterhouse. Anyway, after dark, when my stepdad had finally passed out from his quart of rum, I'd sneak out down the fire escape and make my way over the rooftops to Sammy's place. My pussy would throb just at the thought of it.'

Toni noticed Matt taking nervous sips of his beer.

'It must've been the danger more than the sex though. Sammy was gorgeous but he never did get me over that hill, if you know what I mean. It wasn't at all romantic; the garbage stank in the alley below and sirens wailed up and down on Main but Sammy's bedroom was heaven. We never had sex, but under those covers, boy could Sammy use four fingers.

'This one night, we must have fallen asleep because when I opened my eyes it was getting light. Sammy always helped out first thing unloading the wagons, so I knew we'd be rumbled.

'I managed to pull on my vest and was just zipping up my denim miniskirt when she appeared in the bedroom doorway. Mama Leibowitz! Two hundred and fifty pounds of rippling indignation. Boy, was I out of there! I grabbed my underwear and leapt out of that window, still pulling on my sneakers. I could hear her screaming, "You get in that bathroom, Samuel! I can smell that whore's cunt on you!"

'I didn't want her to see my route so I took a detour. I was soon well away and breathless. Being alone in the early morning with no one to hassle me was bliss. The whores were heading for bed but the rest of the 'Loin was just starting to come alive. Stalls were being set up, the ancient Vietnamese guy was pulling up the grubby shutters on his food store, and vans rumbled in with deliveries.

'The sun was just breaking through and I didn't want to head home. Mamma Leibowitz bursting in on us had given me a buzz and I knew I'd carry the frustration around with me all day if I didn't burn some of it off. I decided to take a ride on a cable car; they were quiet that time of the morning. I could be alone to think about Sammy, maybe ride out to the wharf.

'I caught a car at the turnaround. The interior was cool and shadowy. I assumed it to be empty. The pull and rumble of the cable car always felt good. I didn't care where I was going as long as I was moving. I grabbed a pole and rested against it, closing my eyes as the air rushed in at me. I thought of Sammy and his smooth, work-honed chest. His white biceps bunched up hard as he lay back on his elbows to watch my tongue flicker over him. I loved the way his battered hands pushed at my hair so he could watch me suck his nipples into tiny nuggets. His nails were ugly, chewed into stumps and stained from the bloody carcasses he lifted every day, but they fluttered over my cheeks like insect wings – until my teeth sunk into his white flesh and his hands fell away, clutching the rumpled sheet in pain. I remembered the taste of his pale stomach. He had a sprinkling of hairs running from his navel down to his glorious cock.

'The pole was hard and smooth and I wrapped myself around it. It was cold between my thighs. My belly lurched as the street rose and dipped beneath the car. People must have boarded because the car stopped and pulled away again. I didn't care. Sammy was there with me. I thought of him working, lifting meat, and I bet he had a boner like iron from thinking about me.

'I wanted to pee. Mama Leibowitz had kicked me out before I'd had chance to use the bathroom. My bladder was heavy and painful. I pressed harder against the pole, surreptitiously hitching up my skirt. My clit was throbbing and my full bladder was sending darts of agony into my belly. I bit my lip to muffle my groans and clenched my thighs tight around the pole as the car rumbled on.

'My tongue flickered onto cold metal but it was Sammy's cock I could taste, its pink, circumcised head bobbed against my lips. I grazed my teeth over it before probing the slit with my tongue. Sammy's head fell back and he writhed beneath me. My hot mouth enveloped the cool shaft and Sammy groaned.

'Someone bumped me from behind, bringing me back to reality. The car was crowded and I hadn't noticed. My pussy was bursting with frustration of two kinds. Dampness was oozing out of me. The pain was sharp and electric, sparking between belly button and clit. I pushed against the pole. It was like stabbing a cut. Pain then relief then pain again.

'One last tease, I told myself, not wanting to dispel the memory just yet. My eyelids flickered shut and in my head I traced the seam of Sammy's balls with my tongue. They were hard and tight. I reared over him. I wanted him inside me now. My teeth found one puckered nipple. I bit it hard just to take the edge of his excitement. He groaned the word "bitch" and flinched but his boner didn't waver.

'Someone bumped me from behind again. It must have been deliberate. I was pressed against the pole, hard. My skirt had risen right up. My eyes were shut tight. I didn't care if people could see what I was doing.

My clit was throbbing and my bladder was about to burst.

'It happened in one hot rush. On a crowded cable car with someone's hot body pushed up hard behind me. My clit pulsed against the pole and hot pee ran down my thighs. I shivered as my belly tingled with shards of relief. Whoever was behind me must have soaked up the warmth of my pee too. I couldn't stop.

'I clasped the pole tight for support as the cable car swayed and dipped and I shuddered with pleasure. Next stop I jumped off without looking back. It was a long walk home.' Toni reached out for her drink, allowing her breasts to hang precariously close to tumbling out of her top.

Ted scraped his chair back and slung his jacket over his shoulder. 'Well, you get my money, Toni. I'm out of here and the wife had better not try telling me that she's got a headache.'

Jan watched him go. 'My, some men are easily pleased. I bet it takes more than that to get you going, Detective.' She arched a provocative eyebrow at Ray.

'Oh, I don't know. That pretty much did it for me.'

Jan leaned forward and whispered something in his ear. Whatever it was, she didn't have to ask twice.

'It's all yours, Toni. We're off for something to eat.'

Toni grinned. 'I bet.' Turning to Matt, she asked, 'What about you? Got anything you'd like to tell us?' She could see him blushing despite the dimness of the room.

'I don't think he's had much experience in that department,' John spoke for him.

'Well, that's a downright disgrace.' Toni let her gaze linger on the rookie's long legs and smiled. She could see that he was probably just starting to grow into his angular features. 'We'll have to see what we can do about that, won't we, John?'

John grunted noncommittally, his face settling into frown lines.

'Hey, don't be a grouch.' Toni stood and traced a finger along his bottom lip. 'You and I can show him how it's really done. And this –' Toni scooped up the kitty '– can pay for the cab.' Stuffing the bills into her handbag, Toni strode out of the room, confident that the two men would follow.

3

Downstairs, the restaurant had filled up. Through the curtain into the back room, Toni caught a glimpse of a stripper gyrating perfectly formed buttocks in a man's face. Piedro was schmoozing a table of celebrities and waved to Toni as she left. Toni got to a cab first – she wanted a five-seater and didn't want any of John's chauvinistic good manners tonight. She'd been wound up since that prick, Al, had deliberately shagged the blonde in front of her this morning, and she needed to let off steam.

The cab driver was middle aged and tired. He turned bored, disinterested eyes on her as Toni leant in the cab window brandishing a twenty. 'I need to know how broad-minded you are.'

'I've seen everything in this town, lady. You want me not to see you, jump in the back, no problem.' He took the note without looking her in the eye.

'Just keep driving around, OK? I don't care how long it takes.' And she didn't care if the driver did see her; she just didn't want him doing an emergency stop and causing someone grievous bodily harm. Toni checked her reflection in her compact as the two men got in. 'You sit by me, John. Matt, you sit over there.' Toni motioned to a jockey seat opposite, where she knew Matt would get a good view. As the cab pulled away, Toni crossed her legs and watched the nightlife glide past. Without looking at him, she commanded; 'Take your tie and jacket off, John, for chrissakes. You're all trussed up like a Thanksgiving turkey.'

Matt flicked a worried glance at his superior officer and felt his erection twitch as the man did as he was told.

'Do you want to know how to fuck a woman, Matt?'

Matt swallowed nervously.

'Well, do you?'

'Uh, yes.'

Toni shot out a hand and caught Matt's face a good ringing slap, so hard it hurt her palm. John jumped in surprise.

'That's yes please, ma'am, to you, Matt.' Sitting back, she continued in a more reasonable voice. 'If you can't speak civilly to a lady, we can stop the cab here and we can say good night. What's it going to be?'

Matt held a long, shaking finger up to his bleeding lip. 'I can learn to speak civilly, ma'am.'

'You better, Matt, or it's going to be a painful learning process. Now clean yourself up, and stop acting like a girl or I'll smack the other side for you. And you know what Matt?' Toni blew on her palm. 'You really hurt my hand then. It's stinging. I was going to let you suck my titties but I'm not going to now. John is going to and you're going to sit there like a good boy and watch.'

'What do you say?'

'Th-thank you, ma'am.'

'You're a fast learner, Matt. I like that.'

John shifted in the seat beside her. 'Toni, I –'

'Shut up, John. You are not to speak or I'm stopping the cab. Got that?'

Toni looked John in the eye. He was clearly aroused but not a little surprised by Toni's commands. Toni was pulling her top down to reveal her nipples. The combination of T-shirt and push-up bra bunched beneath her breasts was erotically constricting, her breasts bouncing enticingly with the movement of the cab.

'Lick them, John.'

Whatever reservations John may have had, they disappeared at the sight of Toni's breasts pushed up towards him. He felt as if someone had a tight grip on his balls. He lowered his head and traced his tongue lightly over the very tips of Toni's nipples, aware that at any time he may meet with her disapproval.

Toni drew a deep breath; the sensation of John's tongue sent rivers of arousal straight to her pussy. She reached out a kitten heel, her skirt riding towards her waist, and rested it on the seat between Matt's thighs. His eyes were locked on the movement of the detective's tongue on Toni's nipples and he gasped when Toni pressed her shoe tight into his crotch.

'Are you watching, Matt?'

'Yes, ma'am.'

'Harder, John,' John started to suck at each nipple in turn.

'Does that hurt, Matt?' Toni pressed her shoe hard into his balls.

Matt winced but kept his gaze steady. 'Yes, ma'am.'

'What do you say then?'

'Thank you, ma'am.'

'Good boy. Ah.' Toni bit her lip as John sucked a little too hard. 'Now I can see that you and I are going to get on just fine.' She released the pressure of her shoe. 'Look at me, Matt. Would you like to kiss me? Like this?' Toni clasped John's head and brought it up to her face. Watching Matt the whole time she kissed John hard on the lips, opening her mouth wide and swirling her tongue around his. John groaned and Toni was aware that the cab had slowed just enough for the driver to snatch glances in his rear-view mirror. Matt watched as she kissed his Inspector, watched her working her lips over John's. When she had finished, she pushed John away from her and let him catch his breath.

'Would you like to kiss me like that, Matt?'

Matt's chest was rising and falling quickly now and he was struggling to hide his arousal. His answer thrilled her. 'I don't deserve to, ma'am.'

'No, you're fucking right you don't deserve to, Matt.' She ground her kitten heel back into his balls again. His erection pressed hard against the sole of her shoe. 'But that's not for you to say. Don't presume anything with me, Matt.'

Matt was eager to make amends. 'Sorry, ma'am.'

'I should think so. I know what you do deserve to do. I've had these lace panties on all day, they're creamy and damp and they've been riding up my ass. I'll tell you what you can do to make amends, you can lick the gusset for me. Would you do that, Matt?'

Toni heard a muffled 'Fuck' from John. 'Shut it, John, or you won't lay another finger on me tonight.' Toni placed her other foot in the V of Matt's thighs. 'Take my panties down, Matt. Slowly.'

Tentatively, Matt reached out for her, feeling underneath her skirt for the elastic of her panties and slowly drew them down past her knees. His fingers and the delicate material traced a path like butterfly wings over her skin. Toni watched them slide down her legs, her clit throbbing with excitement, until they reached her ankles. 'There's something incredibly erotic about the juxtaposition of damp panties and expensive shoes. Take them off.' Matt gently slipped her panties over each foot in turn, handling her shoes as if they were made of the most delicate china. 'Now lick them clean.'

Matt held the panties to his mouth. She could see his nostrils dilate as he breathed in the warm creamy scent of them before sticking out his tongue and licking the gusset as if it were smeared with the most delicious ice cream.

'That's good, Matt, very good. John, I want you in the other seat over there where you can see me.' Clearly embarrassed, nevertheless John slunk into the other seat and watched as Toni placed her feet on Matt's spread knees and wriggled down so that her skirt rode her waist. 'Can you see my pussy from there, John?' She knew that Matt could see her splayed open and it excited her. She also knew that the cab driver couldn't and that amused her. 'Get your cock out, John. I want to see you wank over me.'

John was only too happy to obey, by now he was desperate for relief of any kind. Watching Toni reach down and rub her clit with long slow movements, John pulled at his cock, trying not to rush, sweeping his hand over the swollen purple head in steady, slow strokes. Toni stroked herself, teasing her clit, her fingers slipping between her lips as she watched Matt eagerly tonguing her panties.

'I'm just debating whether or not to let you fuck me, Matt. Or whether I should just get my vibrator out of my purse and do the job myself.'

In response, Matt very slowly and deftly ran his tongue along the entire length of her gusset from front to back.

'OK, but only because you've been a good boy. You can lick me out first.' Toni's quim was twitching with the effort of not being filled. Turning sideways, Toni lay back on the seat, legs spread for Matt to tongue her. He was good, using long, consistent strokes until Toni started moaning in pleasure. Her bud blossomed and ached beneath his tongue. Bringing her knees together, Toni pressed her feet on to the cab roof so that all her pleasure zones were presented to Matt. He knew what to do. He thrust his tongue inside her as far as it would go, the soft sensation of it driving her wild because it aroused yet failed to satisfy. 'Hold my ankles steady for me, John,' Toni commanded. John knelt at her head and held her ankles. As he swayed above her, Toni flicked her tongue against his bobbing cock. John groaned and lowered himself slightly so Toni could reach it better. Matt was now tonguing her ass, pushing it into her. Toni cried out in erotic torment, the whole of her sex slippery with love juice. The sight of Matt rimming her proved too much for John and he came in hot, hard spurts over her breasts.

Pushing Matt away with her foot, Toni positioned herself on the edge of the seat, legs spread. Matt knelt in front of her. 'Clean your mess up, John,' she barked, and John hastily mopped at her still bouncing breasts with his handkerchief before he even had chance to put his dick away.

Toni unzipped Matt's fly and pulled at his cock unceremoniously. 'Put it in slowly and then I want it hard and high until I say stop.'

'Yes, ma'am.' The veins on Matt's neck were standing out as he tried not to wince at her rough handling. Ripping his shirt open, Toni used a corner of it to wipe his face clean of her love juices. Digging her nails into his clenched buttocks, she drew him into her until she was filled, holding him there with just the rocking of the cab pressing them together. Then, twisting his nipples sharply so that he cried in pain, she commanded, 'Fuck me!'

Matt had her ass in his big, strong hands and drove himself into her so high that her head fell back, gasping with the intensity of the sensation. Supporting herself on her rigid arms she surrendered herself to the pleasure of it. Matt dipped his head and sucked at her nipple as he held her on to him, driving himself into her, higher and harder. Toni ground her pelvis against him, her clit rubbing against him with each thrust as her climax mushroomed. As she came, Matt pushed himself hard into her and she throbbed around him before collapsing back against the seat. Matt buried his head in her neck, pulling her top back up over her breasts.

Toni shivered at his tenderness. 'You haven't come,' she whispered.

'You didn't say I could, ma'am.'

Sated, Toni had momentarily forgotten her game. Pushing him away, she pulled herself off his still hard cock and snapped at him, 'You can come in my panties, Matt.' Pulling at her skirt she watched Matt wrap her panties around his slick cock and finish himself off. Eyes shut tight, he came silently into the lace.

Toni's pussy was aching pleasantly. As Matt and John tidied themselves up and tucked in their shirts, careful not to look each other in the eye, she counted out enough bills to cover the fare and shouted to the driver to pull in.

'Next time, I want it done properly, good and hard up the ass as well. I'll be reprimanding you for that. Now out of my way.'

'Goodnight, ma'am,' Matt murmured.

John didn't speak. He just glowered at her. Toni slammed the door behind her and the cab sped off into the night.

4

Private Detective Toni Marconi spun her chair towards the window and stretched in the peachy afternoon sun like a cat.

'Hey, Josh,' she called through the open office door. 'If you're banking tonight don't forget the Adams' cheque.'

'I won't.'

Toni slipped her feet into her stilettos and made her way into the miniscule reception area.

'There you go.' Toni put the cheque on Josh's desk and perched on the edge. 'Is that it for today?'

Josh flicked through the diary. 'You've got a four-thirty.'

'What is it?'

'Missing person.'

'It's like taking candy from a baby. Coffee?'

'Thanks.'

'Have we eaten all those bagels?'

'You have.'

'Damn.' Good sex always gave Toni a roaring appetite. She handed the mug to Josh, who was intent on examining a collection of photographs. Toni sipped hers for a while, scanning the grainy black-and-whites which were going to be used in a nasty divorce settlement.

'Out with it.' Toni spoke to the top of Josh's blond head.

'What?' Josh didn't look up.

'When you pout like that you look the same as you did when you were five years old.'

Josh unfolded his lanky frame and cupped his hands behind his head. 'Why are we doing this shit, Toni?'

'Because it's better than working in a canning factory?'

'I just feel so shitty charging such huge amounts for finding these missing kids.'

'What do you know? You're nothing but a kid yourself.' It was her usual response but even as she said it, Toni knew it wasn't true. Her little half-brother had done a lot of growing up just recently.

Josh rocked back in his chair. 'Take a good look, Toni, I'm not your baby any more.'

Toni examined him over the rim of her coffee cup. He certainly was not. Not with the way his chest filled out his shirt and the way his biceps bunched up either side of his ears. 'You're still one big bleeding heart though.'

'At least I have a heart.'

'So go and work in an orphanage already. But excuse me if I've got a business to run.'

'Now who's the childish one?'

'Those cheques mean you and I don't have to suck dicks down on Sunset Boulevard to pay the rent.'

Josh glared at her, a muscle jumping in his jaw. 'Don't speak like a whore, Toni.'

'Listen, if those parents don't want to get their hands dirty trailing through bars and brothels looking for their little runaways then they have to pay someone else to do it for them. That's you and me, kid. We wade through pond scum every day looking for Papa's little budding movie star. And what happens when we find them, Josh? We find some kid with an expensive coke habit willing to spread their legs to pay for it.'

'Shit, do you have to talk like that?'

'Yes I do, to get you to understand that this isn't a charity. You and I are running a business here. Do you know why they pay us so much? It's because once they get their babies back, we've prettied them up all nice and tidy. Those cheques mean you and I get to go home to a nice clean apartment, sit on the balcony and sip a cold glass of Chardonnay away from all that filth out there.'

'Except that maybe you actually thrive on all that filth out there, don't you, Toni?' Josh's calm accusation stopped her in her tracks. He rose from behind his desk and pinned her against the filing cabinet, one hand either side of her. 'I do wonder if our Ms Marconi doesn't get off on all that lewd and depraved behaviour down on the Boulevard.

'You can pull the self-righteous shit with everyone else but it doesn't wash with me. I know how you get your kicks, Toni. I remember the way you had all the boys in the neighbourhood treating you like you were some four-star general. I remember the summer Danny Goodman moved into the building. I spent hours on the stairs acting as look-out for you and him just so you could tie elastic bands around his balls and make him stand naked in the corner.'

Toni ducked under Josh's armpit and dumped her mug in the sink. She checked her reflection in the tiny mirror. 'Josh, if you want to give half your money to charity then that's fine by me, but I prefer to make a living.' She stalked back to her office and hesitated in the doorway. 'Remember, honey, you and I spent years drifting and there was no momma or poppa to come looking for either of us.'

'That's not the point, Toni, and you know it.'

She closed the door between them.

Toni paced the floor in her office, fighting the slow churning in the pit of her stomach. She knew Josh must be really pissed at her to make reference to their past like that; it was an unspoken rule that they never looked back, only forward. Toni had the growing suspicion that Josh wanted to move on, away from his big half-sister who had taken care of him since they were kids. As usual, Toni suppressed the thought, telling herself that he was too naive to manage all on his own. She was, and always had been, in charge and whether Josh knew it or not, he needed her.

Toni's four-thirty sat in the chair opposite. Layla Crossley perspired gently under a layer of expertly applied Lancôme. Her thin fingers displayed rocks, which would have been in danger of slipping off if it weren't for arthritically swollen knuckles.

Toni examined the photos in front of her and looked up into Layla Crossley's troubled eyes. This was one lady who had gone digging already and knew perfectly well how deep her missing person may have sunk.

'And this was the guy your niece was last seen with?'

'Possibly. It's the same make of bike, a Harley-Davidson FXRT – they stopped making them in 1992. He's sporting the same Cobra legend on the jacket. My neighbour says he saw Caron jump on the back of this motorbike, or one very like it, about twelve thirty p.m. June seventeen.'

'And no one's seen her since?'

'No one's seen nor heard of her since.'

Layla Crossley sat bolt upright, patiently answering questions which no doubt the police department had asked her many times, the fingers of her right hand rotating the rock on her left, over and over.

'And these photos?'

'I found the camera in her bedroom and had the film developed. I hadn't seen her hardly at all in the last few months. She was out much of the time. She has always been a wild child; my brother found her nigh on impossible to cope with, which was why she had come to stay with me in the first place. The police found small quantities of drugs in her room, speed or some such. They seem to think she's nothing but a wayward socialite, having a bit of fun.'

Layla Crossley took a deep breath, her ingrained reserve would not allow emotion to break through. 'She wouldn't have disappeared this long without letting me know how she is. Something has happened to her and these biker people have hidden the fact. I won't let it rest until I've found her. Whatever you need, anything, it's yours.' Her grey eyes shone with unshed tears.

Toni admired the old woman's strength. 'Don't worry, Ms Crossley. Caron will be my top priority.'

And she meant it.

Toni lit a Marlboro Light and inhaled deeply, dropping her eyes to the photos of the missing girl, laughing, dancing, drinking; she certainly looked as if she knew how to enjoy herself and it seemed that she had the money to go with it. Her attention kept being drawn back to the photo of Caron Crossley and the mystery biker, both sitting astride the Harley. He was tall, well built and dark. Toni curled her lips around the filter as she examined his long straight nose and full lips. He was definitely fuckable. But there was one other thing about the photo which really made her pulse race: Caron's biker jacket, on which she could make out the legend, 'Property of California Cobras.'

Toni asked herself what would make a reasonably intelligent, wealthy, attractive girl like Caron end up considering herself the property of a biker chapter? The way the girl had slid her hands under the biker's T-shirt said it all. Sex. Toni ground her cigarette in the large ashtray on her desk and felt her nipples pucker beneath her blouse. There were certain types of privileged girls who went crazy for a bit of rough. She guessed it was their chauvinistic, domineering attitude. Toni didn't know a lot about biker culture yet, but she guessed it was chauvinistic to the extreme.

She admired the curved muscle on the man's arms and smiled to herself; he looked as if he could really take care of himself. She knew from experience, however, that no matter how tough a man was, they all responded to a bit of pussy whipping now and then.

After taking a large magnifying glass from the desk drawer, Toni examined the tattoo on the biker's right bicep. It was of a giant cobra twining itself around an Eve-like figure. Toni felt the old familiar throb start in her crotch. 'I don't know where you are, Caron Crossley,' she muttered to herself, 'but I'm going to have some fun finding out.'

Matt rose to his feet when he saw her enter the restaurant, his blue eyes wide and eager to please, and Toni's heartbeat dropped straight to her crotch. He was immaculate in a dark suit and neatly pressed shirt and tie. Toni had a fleeting vision of his mother spit-combing his hair before sending him out on a first date. As he pulled her chair out for her, Toni smelt his excitement doing battle with his aftershave. He was outwardly composed but Toni could sense the coiled anticipation in him.

She watched him as he returned to his seat, one hand on his tie to stop it dangling as he stooped to slide into his chair. He was tall and handsome, good old-fashioned husband material and, judging by the glances he was getting, there were a few women in here who thought so too.

Toni slid her briefcase underneath her chair and crossed her legs. 'I hope you're not presuming to fuck me, Matt.'

Matt's colour rose but he kept her gaze. 'No, ma'am.'

'Because if you are I'll have that tie around your assets so tight it'll sever the blood flow.' She fished in her purse for her Marlboros.

Matt swallowed. 'Yes, ma'am.'

Toni sat regally and lit a cigarette, blowing the smoke across the table into Matt's face. In LA she couldn't have been more offensive if she'd jumped on the table and pissed in his soup, but Matt didn't flinch. He just kept on looking at her with those puppy-dog eyes, begging to be kicked, and Toni's heart constricted with lust.

The waiter appeared and Toni ordered a vodka martini, waving away a menu in the knowledge that she couldn't wait that long before smacking the sweet look off Matt's face. He must have known this too. She noticed him shifting slightly as his arousal tightened the front of his trousers.

'Business first,' Toni said. 'What did you come up with on that biker for me? Did he have any form?'

Matt cleared his throat. 'Some. Drugs possession, assault and battery, the usual biker stuff. According to the jacket in the photo, he belongs to the Cobras. They're pretty notorious all over California as one of the wilder motorcycle clubs.'

'Do you have an address?'

Matt shook his head. ''Fraid not. He was last picked up near Death Valley. Gave his address as Oakland, California. I've had a colleague check it out but there's a family of five living there now. These bikers can travel thousands of miles a year and this guy has disappeared off the map as far as we're concerned.' Matt cleared his throat. 'If you can get a lead on these guys I'd appreciate it. We think that they may be one of the gangs into drug running. The Big Four outlaw gangs control three-quarters of the North American methamphetamine market.'

'Are the Cobras one of the Big Four?'

'Not quite, but that doesn't mean they're not danger-ous. I take it you're not investigating these guys on your own?'

'Of course not.'

Matt opened his jacket to slip an envelope from an inside pocket. Toni noticed his shoulder holster and hid a smile; she did so enjoy making big boys cry. He pushed it across the table to her. 'It's all in there.'

Toni opened the envelope to glance at the police file on one Alfred 'Red' Angelo, looking suitably menacing in his mug shot. It was the same guy that was in the photo with Caron and he didn't look as if he took orders from anyone. Toni's quim felt hot and heavy as she looked at him; she loved a challenge.

'You sweet boy, Matt.' Toni sipped the drink which had appeared at her elbow. 'I think a celebratory fuck may well be on the cards. First, I need to go and powder my nose.'

Matt stood as she left the table and Toni floated through the dining room feeling like a queen. She had the lead she needed and her clit twitched in antici-pation; like good sex, it was all in the chase.

She loved the bathroom in the Wyatt; its quiet opu-lence always made her pulse race. Toni's pupils were huge and dark in the gilt mirror and she smiled to herself as she reapplied her lipstick; it was a long way from the shit-hole she and Josh had had to wash in all those years ago.

She was alone. Tipping a bottle of Chanel on to a

forefinger, she gently dabbed it behind each ear. She twisted in front of the mirror, holding in her stomach and pushing out her breasts, admiring her new shoes and the way they made her calves curve. She had spent an entire month trailing a husband on the bidding of his jealous, psychotic wife for these stilettos; but the extra inches they gave her were worth every minute she had crouched in the back of the van with her camera. And later, if Matt was very naughty, she may be forced to fuck him with the heel of one.

Reaching into the waistband of her skirt, Toni pulled the front of her thong up tight between her sex lips, it rode uncomfortably high up and she throbbed with excitement.

Leaving the bathroom, admiring her ass in her tight silk skirt, Toni walked smack into Inspector John Bradley.

'Evening, Toni. You're looking exceptionally pleased with yourself.' His stocky frame blocked her exit and Toni felt herself pressed very close to him. He was the negative to Matt's positive; his five o'clock shadow was dark, his suit crumpled and Toni could smell whiskey on his breath.

'Excuse me.' Toni attempted to swerve him but John stood fast and reached a large hand out to stroke her neck, his thumb rubbing the underside of her chin. 'I haven't been able to get the other night off my mind, Toni. You were magnificent.'

'Thanks. You too.' Toni gave him her best ice queen smile. 'Now I said excuse me.'

John gripped her arm tight, 'I'm not a fucking poodle to be told how to jump through hoops,' he hissed.

'No and you won't be a fucking police officer much longer either if you don't get your hands off me.'

John backed off, slapping his hands on his head in frustration. 'Please, Toni, you're driving me insane. I've got a permanent hard-on just thinking about you.'

A frisson of excitement rippled through Toni and her nipples hardened at the memory of his thick hard cock and the way his eyes had fixed firmly on her the other night.

'I'm with Matt,' she snapped, but her clit tingled against her thong at the possibility of being with him as well.

John Bradley knew what she was saying. He rubbed his stubbled chin with one hand and drew a deep breath, scowl marks digging deep into his forehead. He leaned in close to Toni's ear. 'Can I come, too?'

Toni pretended to think about it. 'OK, but we play by my rules.'

John's grizzled jaw set hard. 'I don't think I can.'

'Your choice.' Toni dodged him and weaved her way elegantly between the tables of chattering diners back to Matt. She stooped for her briefcase. 'We're leaving.'

Matt almost fell over himself in his eagerness to follow her out of the door. From across the room, Inspector John Bradley watched them leave, his eyes black with hopelessness and lust.

The perfect gentleman, Matt walked on the outside as they strolled down Melrose Avenue. Toni had told him she wanted to walk a while and, of course, he complied. It was a beautiful evening and Toni loved the feel of the warm breeze on her skin. The roaring traffic, neon lights and expensively dressed people made her as horny as hell. She knew that the town's glittery, shiny veneer hid an unforgiving, stony heart and it made her own heart race faster. Toni had no time for her mother's drippy hippy sentiments; she had tried to maintain a sixties dream and all it brought her was a string of failed relationships and a shabby apartment. Toni understood Tinsel Town – like her, it worked hard and it played hard, and tonight, she was going to have herself some fun.

A car roared to a halt at the curb. Matt's reflexes sent him reaching straight for his gun but Toni laid a placating hand on his arm. John Bradley leant out the window. 'Can I give you a lift?'

Toni raised an eyebrow. 'That's very kind. We're going to the Plaza, you can join us for a drink if you like.'

Matt opened the door and Toni slid in. Matt struggled to fit his lanky frame in beside her and John sped off towards the hotel in stony silence.

Toni's thong was digging uncomfortably tight between her legs and rubbed taut against her clit. She turned to examine Matt's profile; he was one of those guys who spent their childhood looking like a geek but grew more and more handsome as he got older but would probably never realise it. John, on the other hand, looked decidedly seedy and lived-in; he was just on the cusp of a paunch and jowls but had the innate sexiness of a man who had seen and done it all.

And here they both were, all hers for the taking.

'Show me how you kiss, Matt.'

Matt hesitated, half expecting a slap, but Toni knew a good mistress was never predictable. She reached out one hand and gently turned his face to hers. He dipped his head and placed the sweetest, gentlest kiss on her mouth she had ever tasted. Toni's quim grew heavy. Matt kissed her again, so gently that Toni's limbs turned to mush, and she sat there dumbly, her lips parted and her heartbeat drumming a tattoo in her throat. Matt shifted in his seat and held her face in his hands as he worked his mouth slowly over hers, even daring to dip his tongue between her lips. It was too soft and too good. Toni suppressed a moan, which threatened to escape, and caught his lower lip between her teeth. He froze and she released him.

The car had stopped.

John turned in the driver's seat to look at her and Toni leant forward, grabbing the back of his head in one hand and kissing him savagely as she erased Matt's sweet saliva from her lips on to John's rough, unshaven mouth. She worked her mouth on his until her lips were raw.

'Let's fuck,' she muttered, and clambered from the car, dizzy with lust and anticipation.

5

The corridor seemed endless before they found their room number. She let them in, trying not to let them see her hand shake; she wanted sex so badly she was afraid that she would lose control of the situation. She knew John was a huge risk; he wasn't a natural submissive like Matt, and she needed every ounce of willpower to maintain her command. She took deep breaths and gripped her briefcase as the door swung open. The room was plush; she never cut corners when it came to business or pleasure, and with her tastes she often mixed both. She swept her eyes over the room, quickly learning the layout before shutting the door with a soft thud. There would be no danger of irate neighbours hearing her moans through the thick walls at the Plaza.

She felt John tense as soon as they entered and knew that if she didn't take charge he would soon be attempting to pull rank on Matt and ruin the whole scenario. She willed her voice to sound calm and smooth.

'Matt, be a good boy and fix us all a drink.' She took John's hand and led him to a love seat, which she had spotted, on the far wall. He moved like a wary panther and Toni knew he was ready to spring at any moment. She placed the briefcase on the floor and smoothed his jacket off his shoulders, letting it fall. John went to kiss her but Toni placed a finger on his lips. 'Sit down and don't worry, you get to go first.' John lowered himself slowly on to the love seat, distrust bright in his eyes;

she knew he wanted to fuck her badly and he wasn't going to be humiliated this time.

Matt placed three drinks on the dressing table and Toni swallowed hard; her throat was dry. She circled John, slipping her buttons through their holes and looking him straight in the eye. She slipped off her blouse and unclasped her bra, careful to keep just out of his reach. Her nipples were tight and sore and Toni rubbed them hard.

'Watch me carefully, Matt,' she commanded, hoping she could trust in his obedience. 'John, they're so tight for you, I want you to suck them hard like you did the other night.'

Slowly, Toni moved to the back of the seat until she was directly behind John. Pulling his head back, she dangled her tits in his face and John groaned, chasing her nipples with his mouth like a baby bird. 'Oh yes, that's good,' she moaned encouragingly and unbuttoned his shirt to stroke his broad hairy chest, scraping her nails over his nipples. When she was sure she had him fully occupied, Toni looked up at Matt, who was hovering by the drinks, unsure of his role, and pointedly looked at the briefcase. Like a true submissive, Matt was quick and eager to serve and he moved towards it. Toni mouthed 'open it' and gasped as John bit a little too hard on her breast. 'Now!' she mouthed, and Matt clicked the briefcase open. Toni felt John stiffen beneath her but Matt's reactions were alert and very fast – as soon as he saw the handcuffs, he guessed Toni's intention and had John cuffed to the metal arms of the love seat. Toni rapidly withdrew her nipples from John's teeth.

'You fucking bitch!' John rattled his cuffs furiously, nearly lifting the seat off the floor in temper. 'I'll have you thrown out of the force for this, Matt, you prick.'

Matt's colour drained but Toni patted him for reassurance. 'Have a drink, Matt, and don't worry – the Inspector here will soon realise that it's only for his own good.'

Toni slumped on to the bed in relief and held out a hand for Matt to pass her vodka, which she drank greedily. 'Good, I needed that. Matt, you are such a good boy.' Toni fished out two ice cubes and held the empty glass out for Matt. 'Another. That was perfect.' Toni rose and rubbed the ice cubes over her nipples, droplets of water dripping on to her flat belly. She stood in front of John, who glared venomously back at her; she noticed that the cuffs had already carved red marks into his wrists.

Toni smiled down at him. 'I told you, John – my rules.' John bared his teeth, too angry to speak. Toni sucked on an ice cube, her breasts standing pert, just inches from John's face. 'I knew you couldn't be a good boy like Matt. I knew you wouldn't play things my way. So lets get things straight. Matt, come here.' Matt appeared at her elbow, drink in hand, which she took. 'Lick all this icy water off me, Matt, it's making me cold.' Matt dropped to his knees and complied, licking her breasts and belly as gently as if she were made of spun glass, while Toni watched John and sipped her drink. 'Now, John, do you see what a good boy he is? He listens to what I say,' Toni pouted patronisingly at John, who glared back, dragging his eyes away from the sight of Matt, still immaculate in his suit and tie, running his tongue over Toni with the most tender, gentle touch. 'If you don't play this my way, I will leave you there all night.'

John's erection was hard and painful and Toni had a very cold glint in her eye; he didn't doubt her for one second.

'Stop it, Matt.' Toni drained her glass and Matt stopped immediately. 'So what do you say, Inspector?'

John's wrists ached and so did his cock; his balls felt as if they were in a vice. 'I'm sorry.'

'Excuse me?'

John hung his head, defeated, 'I'm sorry, ma'am.'

Toni grinned and handed Matt her glass. 'Good boy. Now we can have some fun. Matt, remove my skirt.'

John's head snapped back up. Matt stood behind Toni and slowly undid the zip before sliding it down to her ankles. Toni stepped out of it and Matt folded it neatly on the bed. John gasped and rattled his cuffs, his eyes pleading for release, as he gazed at Toni's quim lips jutting either side of her thong.

'I think we ought to set you free now, John, you look very uncomfortable.'

'About fucking time, this has gone beyond a joke!'

Toni grabbed his face tightly with her right hand, her fingers digging into his cheeks. 'It seems you won't learn. Perhaps we'll just set you free a bit at a time.' Toni pushed his face roughly away and thought that perhaps he was going to cry; he bit his lip and rolled his eyes upwards, muttering under his breath. Toni knelt and undid John's trousers. His cock sprang out, thick and stout, and Toni grazed its weeping tip with her tongue. John groaned deliriously, his fists clenched tight. Easing his trousers under his awkwardly raised buttocks, Toni pushed them down to his ankles and spread his knees.

'Matt! Ice cubes!' Toni demanded and, popping two ice cubes into her mouth, she moved down on him, moving his cock into the contrasting hot and cold inside her mouth. John rolled his head and cried out loud, lost to anything but the sensations surrounding his desperately swollen rod. Toni tormented him a while longer before spitting out the ice cubes into her palm and rubbing them into his balls. John was trying to push himself into her roaming hand but was seriously impeded by his trousers. His wrists looked red and sore. Toni dipped her head and moved her tongue slowly up the crease of his scrotum.

'So sweet,' she tormented. 'Just like kiwi fruit.' She backed away. 'Matt, let him have a sip of his drink.' Matt moved forward, offering the crystal glass to John's lips. John wet his dry lips greedily, gulping the icy vodka and eating Toni's quim with his eyes.

Pushing Matt away, Toni licked the icy droplets from John's lips.

'Bitch,' he muttered, but Toni sensed the change in him. His anger had ebbed away as the waves of lust washed over him. She scraped her nails down his unshaven cheek.

She moved to the bed and sat on the edge, her legs spread wide so that John could get a good look at what he couldn't touch. 'There was no need for all this you know, John – Matt would have gladly played the part.' Pulling her knees together, Toni raised her legs and slipped her panties down and off. Her pussy ached from the chaffing of the lace. Standing, she dangled them over John's face, and he closed his eyes to drink in their scent.

'So near and yet so far,' she goaded, snatching them away and throwing them on to his cock like a hoopla ring. 'Well done.' She smirked. 'Wonder if that means you win a goldfish.'

'For fuck's sake, Toni.'

'Uh, uh.' Toni shook her head. 'I have to break you in properly, John, or you'll just never, ever learn.'

Matt was still perched on the edge of the dressing table, reflected from behind by an enormous mirror.

Toni walked towards him, dressed only in her stilettos, and picked up the end of his tie, drawing him gently towards her. 'Sweet, sweet boy,' she murmured, and lifted her chin to kiss him.

Matt kissed her back, gently at first, but Toni grabbed his face and moved her mouth hard over his, her mouth wide and her tongue forcing his to do battle. She felt his stiff cock pressing through his trousers for her. 'I want your hands all over me, Matt,' she commanded as they kissed. Matt obeyed, sweeping his long fingers down to squeeze her buttocks. From behind them, Toni could hear the rattle of cuffs, and John groaning incomprehensively.

For a while, Toni allowed herself to become lost in Matt, kissing him like a lover, not a mistress, pressing herself against his warm, exploring hands and relishing the sensation of his clothes against her bare skin. Pushing away his jacket, she withdrew slightly for him to shrug off his gun holster; it dropped to the plush carpet with a soft thud. She undid his buttons eagerly, raking her nails over the firm flesh beneath. She reached down and unzipped his flies, grabbing his cock and pulling his skin upward, like unsheathing a sword. She pushed his pants down over his taut buttocks, and Matt removed his shoes before kicking them both away.

Matt turned her, so her backside was pressed against the dressing table and her back was to the mirror. Her head fell back and she gasped with pleasure as Matt dipped his mouth to her breasts. Dropping to his knees he spread her legs wide. Toni was wet and aching for him, for both of them. Her spread pussy glistened in the soft light of the hotel bedroom, and all the while, Inspector John Bradley looked on; frustrated, hopeless and skewered with lust and this time not even able to bring himself release.

Matt raked her open sex with his tongue and Toni writhed her hips beneath his mouth until she could feel her climax dangerously close. Lifting her knee, Toni pushed her shoe sharply against his shoulder, sending him sprawling backwards on to the floor. Reaching behind her, she wrapped her fingers around a glass and threw its contents into Matt's shocked face, sending ice cubes skittering over the carpet.

'Hands, I said!' She was breathing heavily, her breasts rising and falling. 'Get on your hands and knees.' Matt complied, his balls dangling, exposed and vulnerable between his legs.

Toni knew he deserved some reward for serving her tonight and in her briefcase she had just the thing. Matt watched her pull the dildo from the case and she saw his prick bob with excitement. Picking up his tie from the carpet, Toni looped it over his head and into his mouth like a horse's bit, pulling it tight. She ran a hand down between his legs, smoothing his trembling balls and jutting cock. He quivered beneath her touch, bracing himself for pain should she wish to administer it.

'Isn't he beautiful, John?' Toni strapped the dildo on to her with a thin leather belt that ran around her waist and between her legs so that it jutted out in front of her. Next she reached for the gun holster and shrugged herself into it, pulling the soft leather straps tight around her slight frame and enjoying the sensation of the buckles biting into her pale flesh. She stood in front of her prisoner, the straps and stilettos accentuating the beauty of her otherwise naked flesh. Grabbing a handful of his hair, she jerked John's head roughly backwards.

'What do you say, Inspector? Should I get Matt to give you a blow-job?'

John's eyes widened in horror, but he was struck mute with the agony of his swollen cock. Toni laughed.

'I'm only joking. It's Matt's turn for a bit of fun now. You've earned it, haven't you, Matt?'

Matt didn't reply. He hung his head, but raised his buttocks a fraction higher in anticipation. Toni grinned, and took a tube of lubricant from the briefcase, which she applied to the shaft of the dildo and then smeared the lube around Matt's twitching anus. After throwing it back into the case, she grabbed the end of his tie with one hand and gently eased the dildo into his ass with her other. The tip was tapered, and Matt was accommodating. Toni pushed carefully until Matt felt ready to push back against her. On her knees, her thighs tensed, Toni began the slow rhythm of entering Matt with the dildo. Riding him like a cowboy, one hand jerking the tie, she drove the dildo between his taut buttocks; each thrust driving the dildo back against her aching clit and bringing the strap up tight between her legs.

Matt cried out, his mouth wide open as the tie pulled between his teeth, and Toni rode him harder, each thrust bringing them both nearer to climax.

From his vantage point, Inspector John Bradley moaned in frustration, twisting like Tantalus inches away from the source of his agony. His cock was swollen purple, quivering for some release and throbbing in envy as Matt spurted huge jets of white-hot come on to the carpet in front of him.

No sooner had Matt finished his quivering release than Toni was barking at him to clean it up. Her voice was thick with arousal and her eyes slightly glazed as she undid the straps of the dildo and used them to whack Matt a vicious swipe across both buttocks. Almost immediately a red welt appeared across his still throbbing ass.

'Clean that up, as well,' she ordered, slinging the dildo at the crouching rookie. 'You're going to use it on me in a minute.' Turning her attention to his senior officer, Toni straddled John on the love seat. His cock leapt towards the heat of her spread pussy as she hovered over him but John hung his head in submission. She had him beat and if she refused to let him climax this time, he felt that he would quite literally die of frustration.

Toni was throbbing in an agony of prolonged arousal, but she needed to be sure that she was still in control. She pushed John's lolling head backwards; he was weak with lust and longing, his wrists red and raw from the metal cuffs.

Toni pressed her lips on to his and whispered into his mouth, 'If you come too soon, I will punish you with the utmost severity. Do you understand me?'

John whimpered in reply and braced himself as she lowered herself on to him. Toni cried out as she allowed herself to finally be filled with his rigid prick. She knew that the pain in his wrists would hold back his climax and so she impaled herself on him to the hilt. She felt him inside her, hard and high, and withdrew almost to his tip before driving herself back down. He quivered beneath her, terrified to come, and with each thrust her jutting breasts flicked his face. She dug her fingers into his shoulders as she rose and fell, his rough chin grazing her nipples as she thrust herself on and against him.

She was almost there. Gritting her teeth against her impending climax, she forced herself to be still. 'Matt,' she groaned. 'Now!' As she hovered over John, his cock jammed halfway into her stretched pussy, Matt knelt behind her and offered the freshly lubed and rubbered dildo to her rosy anus, exposed between the stretched cheeks of her trembling ass. She didn't need much more than the tip. She felt complete and drove herself downwards on to John's cock, gasping in pleasure and pain as the dildo rode upwards too. She felt torn in two, her finger nails bit into John's flesh as the hot, dark waves of her climax crashed over her.

It was some time later, when the sweat had begun to dry on her cool flesh, before she realised that John had come too.

Toni's cell phone shattered the peace of her early morning slumber. She stretched her limbs along the expensive cotton sheets and winced at the ache in her thighs. A similar ache in her pussy brought a languid smile to her lips as she felt warm flesh press back against her. Clambering over the paraphernalia of last night's depravity, she rummaged for her mobile in her briefcase.

'Toni?' Josh sounded worried. 'I've been trying to reach you all night. I was just wondering if you were OK.'

Toni knelt at the bottom of the king-size bed and grinned into the mobile. 'I'm fine, Josh – just hooked up with a couple of friends that's all.'

'Who?'

'That's none of your business.' Toni's gaze wandered over the two sleeping men in the bed. The older man lay with his right arm thrown above his head to expose thick underarm hair. His other hand, still sporting the livid welt around its wrist, lay across his stomach where the sheet barely covered his half-aroused cock. The younger man, fair and rangy, lay with his back to her, with the sheets twisted around his long thighs, affording her a glimpse of white buttocks and the red whip mark across them. Toni's free hand dipped to her crotch.

'I have to go, Josh, expect me when you see me.' She cut off his protestations and slipped back into the warm gulf between the two men.

'Morning, Toni.' John's voice rumbled deep in his chest as he rolled towards her.

Toni's pussy dripped with early morning dew as she drew her smooth thigh up along his rough hairy one.

John's cock sprang to life beneath her searching fingers and he groaned. 'I didn't expect to wake up a free man this morning.' He grimaced as he flexed a wrist.

Toni nipped at his shoulder as he loomed above her. 'I want your hands free today.'

'So I can do this?' John dipped a long finger inside her and Toni's back arched like a cat's. 'Or this?' John held her arms above her head with one hand and stroked her clit tantalisingly slowly with the other. Toni squirmed beneath his touch. John's cock butted against her side as he slipped his finger into her wetness again. Her moans woke up Matt and he stirred awake, rolling towards them with his erection already quivering.

'Morning,' he mumbled, and stretched his sinewy arm out along hers on the pillow. 'Can I touch you too?'

Toni couldn't reply. Her throat was thick with arousal as she squirmed beneath John's probing finger. She tipped her chin up towards Matt and he bent to kiss her, his gentle lips moving softly over hers. She pushed both hands up towards the solid oak headboard and arched in pleasure, caught between the two men.

John continued his one-finger teasing and she moaned into Matt's mouth, wanting more. Matt used his left hand to draw slow sensual circles around her nipples, which were as hard as gumdrops beneath his touch.

She squirmed between them. Matt moved his mouth on to her nipples, flicking them with his tongue as she tried to press her breasts into his mouth. John kissed her then, his mouth harder, and she tongued him greedily. She gasped as Matt moved his hand down to meet

John's between her legs. She spread her thighs wide, silently begging them to frig her hard. She was lost to the sensation of the two men either side of her, no longer a free-thinking human being, merely a mass of tingling nerve endings desperate for their touch on her flesh.

Working as one, the men released her and she whimpered in frustration. Matt pulled her down the bed and flipped her over on to her belly, his hands sliding all over her. Her small breasts dangled beneath her as Matt pulled her pelvis up towards him so she was positioned on all fours. She felt as limp and pliable as a rag doll, willing to do anything to satiate the deep burning between her legs. John moved across the bed and held her head as he pushed his cock into her mouth. She sucked it willingly. Her ass felt cold stuck up in the air, legs spread as Matt held her tight around the waist and waited for her to suck the other man's dick. Matt teased her further, sliding one finger in and out of her cunt from behind as she moved her mouth up and down John's cock, mimicking her movements. She laved him with her tongue and took him deep into her throat, desperate for the reward of Matt's deft fingering. John wasn't afraid to come this morning and he was soon pushing himself into Toni's mouth, coming in short sweet bursts.

Matt didn't waste time, sliding his own cock into her slippery pussy from behind and jamming it into her hard, as she had done with the dildo the night before. Toni pushed back against him, gasping as his prick pushed up high inside her. John had fallen back on to the pillows and watched as Matt slammed himself into her, his balls slapping Toni's clit with each thrust. Her breasts danced and John reached out his hands under them, so her nipples grazed his palms each time Matt thrust her forward. Toni was moaning incoherently, her climax building. Matt released her waist with one hand and reached beneath her to rub her clit, smearing juices on to his finger before pushing it hard into her anus. Toni cried out with pleasure as her orgasm raced through her, held between the two men; Matt's cock and finger still buried deep inside her and John pinching her nipples hard. She rode the waves of her orgasm until they both released her and she collapsed, sobbing with pleasure, on to the unkempt bed.

6

A shower and a large breakfast later, Toni breezed into the office carrying the envelope containing 'Red's' criminal record. Despite the early hour, Josh was behind his desk.

'Morning, Josh. Anything for me?' She poured herself a strong coffee.

Josh didn't look up. 'Nothing new.' He looked like the one who'd been without sleep all night, but Toni was too fired up to notice.

'Well, I have something for you.' She dropped the envelope on to the desk in front of him. 'I think this guy is the biker Caron Crossley was last seen with. He rides with a club called the Cobras. I'm going to be checking them out.'

'Do you have an address?'

'No, I'm going to have to ask around.'

'It'll have to wait until I've cleared up this divorce.'

'Why?'

'So I can come with you.'

'You can catch up. I promised Layla Crossley top priority.'

'Why? Because she's loaded or because you fancy hanging about with bikers?'

Toni reached out and stroked Josh's cheek with the back of her fingers. 'You really are cross with me at the moment, aren't you, baby bro'?'

Josh jerked his head away. 'Will you stop calling me that.'

'Jeez, Josh. Asking around about some motorcycle club is no worse than going into porn shoots and dancing clubs. I'm a big girl. I can handle it.'

'How're you going to get to know them? They're not going to take kindly to some broad nosing around and you don't ride, so there's only one option left – you hook up with one of them...' Josh threw his pen down on the desk when he saw the look on Toni's face. 'I fucking knew it. You're like a bitch on heat.'

'Grow up. It's just another case.'

'Fine. Then we do it together.'

'How? You don't ride either.'

'I can learn. I'll get a bike, you can be my old lady, we'll hang out with the club, get friendly...'

Toni could feel a choking sensation in her throat. 'Oh *pulease*. How long is that going to take?'

Josh was standing behind his desk, the veins in his neck throbbing. He mimicked her. 'Oh *pulease*! You know it makes far more sense than you offering blow-jobs for answers. Fuck!' The force of her slap sent him falling back in his chair.

'That's really overstepping the mark, Josh, and you know it.' Toni's voice was dangerously calm. 'I'm good at my job and you've never questioned it before. Now, if you want out then that's fine – you don't need to pick a fight as a reason to leave.'

The two of them stared at each other, chests heaving, breathing shallow. Toni could tell Josh was already feeling guilty about what he'd said; she could still play the big sister card, but not for much longer, she guessed. She drew a deep breath.

'I can't do anything right with you at the moment. You've obviously got a bug up your ass about something so if I leave on this investigation for a while, perhaps the space will do us good.' Toni swallowed hard, fighting tears; Josh was the only male who had ever been able to penetrate her armour. 'You never used to argue with me.'

Josh came around the desk and hugged her. 'I just worry about you, sis. I know you've always taken care of us, and I know you like taking risks, but I'm all grown up now and I don't want you hanging out with a biker gang – the dangers are too great.'

Toni breathed in the scent of Josh's familiar after-shave, knowing that the risks were never too great as far as she was concerned. Josh was rubbing her back in slow circles, his head resting on hers, in the same way she used to comfort him when they were kids. Toni smoothed her own hands along the muscular planes of his back; he felt very, very different now. She could hear Josh's heartbeat start to quicken and her nipples tightened in response. She reached up to soothe the red mark where she'd slapped him but Josh was pulling away – but not before Toni detected the telltale bulge in the front of his chino's.

Mortified, Josh grabbed his camera from his desk. 'I need to go out,' he mumbled. 'See you later.'

Toni crossed to the window to watch him climb into his jeep. A pulse throbbed in her crotch. There was obviously more to Josh's mood swings than she'd realised and perhaps, she reasoned with herself, a time apart would help them sort themselves out.

Toni drove back to the apartment in a fit of temper, music at full volume, foot to the floor. What was it with him? He had never played the heavy in the past. He was acting like a little kid. She couldn't blame it on puberty; that was well and truly gone, along with an unfortunate assortment of air-headed girlfriends. She hadn't interfered with his love life. Toni chewed her lip. Well, maybe a little, but she was the eldest. Anyway, he needed a little guidance when it came to girls. Come to think of it, she hadn't met a girlfriend in a long while. Maybe that was it, he wasn't getting any.

Toni swung the Corvette into the driveway of her apartment building, and stared blankly at the sprinklers rotating on the communal lawn. There was no way a man with Josh's looks was going to have trouble getting laid, so maybe he was struggling with being gay? The movement in the front of his chinos would indicate otherwise and that was just too scary to think about right now.

Toni locked the car and headed up to her apartment. Boy, had Josh spoilt a fantastic day. She had been glowing from the three-in-a-bed and now he had her all tensed up. Where did he get off telling her how to run her investigations? If he was going to start that bullshit then she was better off alone. Toni's throat burned – she knew that wasn't true; for all her independence she had always relied on Josh as her one constant. Toni took a deep breath and enjoyed her view as she did every evening; the bobbing palm trees on the sun-drenched boulevard, the designer people walking their designer dogs. They had worked hard to get here. But she still had that itch, and she knew that Josh knew – now that she had it all, it still wasn't enough.

That was the trouble with domestic situations, they unfocused you. Which was why she had always avoided getting involved in relationships and not because she was a control-freak like that ass-wipe of a shrink had suggested. Toni shook herself. She needed to make a start on her case and find that biker. She had a name and she had a club, but if his record was anything to go by then he was something of a nomad, travelling all over the south west. She needed a more specific location.

There was one biker she knew she could approach without prejudice, in a town with a diverse biker culture. Sidney Cabe. And that meant going back home to SF. It was as good a place as any to start.

Toni needed to wash and glam up; she knew Sid had a soft spot for the feminine look and she didn't want to disappoint. A change of outfit and a dousing of Chanel later and Toni was regaining her composure. Toni blotted her soft coral lipstick and twirled in front of the mirror. Casual elegance. Perfect. Low sling-backs, bias-cut skirt and a sensual silk shirt, all had that feminine feel but would do as an evening outfit should the meeting go as planned. Toni grabbed her keys and her purse. It was time to quit joking around and get to work. Fuelled by anger, Toni was ready to go in under an hour. There was always an emergency suitcase packed under the bed. If she took the interstate, she could be in San Francisco by this evening.

The Corvette cut a groove into the corner of the immaculate lawn as Toni swung the car out of the driveway. Usually Toni was the perfect resident but this morning she didn't care. In her rear-view mirror she caught Mrs Carnegie clutching her poodle in horror but her numerous face-lifts prevented the old woman from any actual expression. Toni pushed in a tape and smirked; if that woman's face got any sharper she'd be able to carve wood with it. Fuck them all; she was cutting loose for a while.

Toni was glad to see that life in the 'Loin looked just as gritty as when she'd left it. Three trannies looked at the car and then dismissed it when they saw who was driving. The dusty awnings outside the Vietnamese food store made her heart lurch in memory. Living among such a large Asian community had given her a lifelong penchant for Eastern food. She cruised down Polk, observing the cheap hotels with their grubby, crumbling façades and remembering the afternoons spent behind tatty shutters with the young writer with a weakness for bourbon. Toni wriggled in her seat at the memory. Patti the hat-check girl had told her about this gorgeous guy who could only get it up for hookers. Toni never could resist a challenge. He had boned her all summer, thinking that she was a tart with a heart who was doing it for free. She had done it for the thrill of padding up threadbare corridors in her shabbiest coat and no underwear while the artists and drug-dazed rock stars cast lascivious glances her way, thinking she was a whore.

The Corvette drifted past brick apartment buildings, like the one she'd grown up in, where bored and grubby whores sat on the stoops in the shade. She passed converted theatres that were now flesh palaces promising untold delights both on stage and in private rooms. There was something about old-fashioned, rundown theatres that always gave Toni a little buzz. Streetwalkers and panhandlers, that was life on the edge, not her little forays down back alleys armed with a Gold Visa to bail her out. Little wonder the back streets of LA didn't scare her. Josh was making his bid for respectability while she ... She loved the sleaze. She had drifted away from the city with Josh but when you thought about what she did for a living – she hadn't drifted that far.

Toni swung the car into the back street and stretched. It had been a long day's drive and she was pooped. She was normally in control of her emotions but there was something about Josh which made her overreact. He would think she was losing it if he found out she'd driven here in a fit of pique. Was it spite that had brought her here without him? Or was she laying ghosts to rest before she moved on?

Whatever.

Toni flicked her cigarette butt out into the gutter. She hated all that psychobabble bullshit. She just hoped Sid was still living the same routine or she was in trouble. But thankfully the garage was there. The grimy sign read simply CABE's. The roller door was open and Toni could make out two boiler-suited figures working on an elevated bike. They were covered in grease and she was already regretting the sling-backs. Toni drummed her fingers on the steering wheel. Her heart was racing now; the last time Josh, Sid and her had met up they'd partied for a week and she felt guilty for not bringing him. Still, he shouldn't have been such an irritating shit this morning. Anyway, this wasn't a social visit. She had work to do. The thought propelled her from the car. Toni hovered in the doorway, preserving her sling-backs for a little bit longer. Music and the metallic tang of motor oil wafted out at her. A greasy well-thumbed Fog Hog calendar hung just inside the cubicle which was used as an office. Toni debated whether to enter and swivel provocatively on the seat but her skirt was too expensive to waste on such a trivial flirty gesture. She eyed the array of tanned tits and buttocks on an extensive collection of *Easyrider* posters. Very offensive to customers she would have thought; but then again – perhaps not Sidney's customers. Nobody brought the family station wagon here for its annual service. Not to this garage and certainly not in this neighbourhood.

'Toni?' She'd been spotted. A spanner clanged to the floor as Sidney came to greet her. She whistled through her teeth, 'What are you doing here? Hey, looking good, girl.' She nodded her appreciation.

Toni grinned. It had been a long time. 'You too.'

'You better believe it. Hottest goddam bitch-biker this city has ever seen.'

She shouted over her shoulder, 'Hey Arlene! Come and meet an old friend of mine.'

Arlene was wiping her hands on a rag and thought better of offering one to Toni. 'Lucky you.'

Toni winced, she was beginning to feel like the bimbos in the posters.

Sid misread her discomfort. 'I mean a friend, friend. We go way back. She's not one of us in either way; she's not a dyke and she ain't got a bike.'

Arlene's interest was fading rapidly. 'Thought not.'

Toni watched the girl's ample rear retreat back into the garage. 'Not the most flattering of outfits on her frame.'

'Still the bitch, I'm glad to say.'

'Of course.'

'You're OK though?' Sidney's green eyes flashed with concern. 'Where's Josh?'

'Working. He's fine.'

'Glad to hear it. If ever I went over the side it would be for that boy.' It was an old joke. Sidney was no bi. 'What brings you here? Business or social?'

'A bit of both, hopefully. I need some advice, on bikes and bikers, and I'd like to take you out if that's OK?'

'Sounds fantastic.' Sidney flashed a toothy grin, looking incredibly young and boyish under her buzz-cut. 'It's good to see you, Toni.'

'You too.'

They held the moment between them for a second. Sidney broke it first. 'Come and see the Panther. She's my new baby.'

Toni didn't know the first thing about bikes but it certainly was an impressive machine. 'She's great.'

'We've been fine-tuning her ready for the ride next month. She's going to eat the road.'

'It's big. Shit, Sid, how do you manage to keep it upright?'

'Small but strong, don't forget. Can you imagine what it feels like to have her purring between your legs for hours on end?'

'That's some vibrator all right.'

'You better believe it.' Sidney tore her eyes away from the bike. 'So, you taking me out or what?'

Toni nodded. 'Love to.'

'Follow me home then? This baby's not quite finished. I've got the old faithful Sportster out back. Do you want to ride?'

'Not in this skirt.'

'Pity. We could've cruised the streets. Give me five minutes?'

'OK. Well, nice to meet you, Arlene.'

Arlene cast a disinterested look. 'Sure.'

Toni was sitting in the Corvette by the time Sidney rounded the corner on her bike and her heart did a flip. Sid looked exactly the same as she had ten years ago when Toni had first spotted her out on the Bay. Toni had mistaken Sidney for a boy and had come on to her before realising her mistake. Sid had laughed it off and the two of them had become friends, but it still intrigued Toni how Sid could possess such smooth pecs and loud tattoos and still be such a sexy woman. Sexy to other gay women – that was – with her wide mouth and her nose-ring. Of course she did nothing for Toni. But she had to admit, as she pulled away from the curb and followed Sidney's bike home, that the girl did look pretty hot astride the machine.

Sidney lived in a converted lock-up on Avalon and shared her living room with her bikes. Toni stood back as she lifted the security shutter and edged the purring bike from the street into her living space. The brick walls had been painted stark white and covered with photos of bikes and more bikes. Her one concession to comfort was a huge sofa bed at the far end.

'Grab a drink, while I clean up.'

'My God, you've still got the chopper.' Toni had spotted Sidney's customized Harley, with its high bars, parked next to her Sportster.

'You can't buy bikes like this. I made the handlebars from the tubular arms of an old diner chair. She's the best chick magnet there is. You should see the business cards that get left on her. 'Specially after Gay Pride . . .' Sidney trailed off, realising her faux pas. 'Anyway, I've got to degrease.'

Toni headed for the fridge and found it packed full of organic food and bottles of Mexican beer. Toni grabbed one and sipped it while she examined Sidney's photo collection on the front. There were a lot of smiling bikers kicking back at cook-outs or looking spaced in clubs. She frowned at one of Arlene looking grim in black leathers and bearing more than a passing resemblance to a waiting-room sofa. There were quite a few of a scary Goth chick with bright red lipstick and dark-ringed eyes who looked as if she had a tendency to self-harm. Toni grimaced into her beer. Sidney loved to wrench and ride but she wasn't sure how much she would know about the whole male biker thing.

Bluesy music flooded the room and Toni turned. 'You look fantastic.' The words were out of her mouth before she had time to check them.

'Thanks.' Sidney padded toward her on bare feet, her long toes glinting with toe rings. Her pert breasts and hard nipples jutted out from beneath her tight vest and she wore baggy, silky trousers. Droplets of water glistened on her close-cropped hair. 'Let's get the business stuff out of the way so we can get down to enjoying ourselves, yeah?' She reached out a tattooed arm to open the refrigerator and Toni could smell soap on her freshly scrubbed skin

'Shall I whip us up some noodles?'

'Mmm, please.' Toni sipped her beer and watched Sidney move around her sparse kitchen. She had put on silver thumb rings now that she wasn't working and her ears were decorated with hoops of varying sizes. Toni wondered how many other piercings she possessed and her clit twitched at the thought.

'OK, shoot.' Sidney reached past her for the sesame oil, her hard breasts briefly rubbing against Toni's thin shirt. Her nipples puckered immediately and she cleared her throat before speaking.

'I'm looking for a misper. A society chick with plenty of cash who likes to party.'

Sidney dropped an uncooked noodle into her mouth. 'Aren't we all, sugar?'

Toni ignored the sarcasm and helped herself to another beer. 'Well, this one has disappeared. She was last seen riding two-up on a Harley FXRT belonging – possibly – to one Alfred Angelo, street name Red. His patch reads "Cobras". She stopped to draw breath. 'I'm looking for a place to start with this whole biker thing.'

Sidney gave the wok a shake and looked Toni straight in the eye. 'My advice to you is don't go there. Leave well alone, Toni. These male biker gangs are bad news. I know I'm not into the whole testosterone thing but, shit, they're tough mothers to deal with.'

Toni didn't answer; she raised her eyebrows and waited.

Sidney forked the stir-fry into bowls and carried them over to the sofa, indicating to Toni to bring the chop-sticks. The two women settled down with their food.

'But if you're still the hard-nosed chick who can enter a bar and hit on complete strangers then I guess you're still taking a walk on the wild side and won't listen to a word I say. What has Josh got to say about this?'

Toni swallowed a mouthful and pointed to her bowl with her chopsticks. 'This is gorgeous.'

'I asked you a question.'

'Same as you.'

'Thought so, and I bet he doesn't know you're here or he would have come too.'

Toni coloured guiltily.

'There are thousands of great bikers out there and hundreds of great clubs, but then you've got your outlaw gangs. They're not just about bikes; they're into organised crime; drug running, prostitution. You know you may never find her.'

'I'm being paid to try.'

'Well for fuck's sake be careful.'

'I'm an investigator for a living, Sid. These are the type of people I deal with all the time.'

Sidney shot her a disbelieving look but didn't argue further. 'I wouldn't know where to start. I only ride with chicks. But we could ask around town.'

'Thanks.'

Sidney stood up and took her empty bowl. 'You can meet the rest of the Vixens while we're there.'

'The Vixens?'

'The dykes I ride with.' She pulled Toni off the sofa. 'C'mon, we both better brush if we're going clubbing.'

7

It was too early for a club so Sidney dragged Toni into her favourite local bar. It wasn't one Toni remembered but she guessed some things had to change. Her shoes stuck to the bare wooden floor and the air was heavy with the waft of cigarette smoke, musk oil and weed. Toni took a deep breath. It was so not LA. The crush of bodies parted to let them through and Toni felt the old familiar rush. A battered Rockola cranked out some dirty rhythm and blues.

Toni surreptitiously studied her old friend. She was still wearing her vest but had changed into tight denims with a thick leather belt that showed off her flat stomach. Toni felt very femme in her silky outfit and regretted her choice. She was used to hanging out in gay bars with Sidney; you didn't live in the Bay area and not become used to alternative sexuality, but tonight she felt very self-conscious – very Vanilla Ice among the Ben and Jerry assortment. Sidney was confusing her, perhaps because she hadn't seen her for the longest time. Or perhaps LA had rubbed off on her more than she'd realised. She looked and felt like a tourist.

Sidney was perched, open legged, on a bar stool, ordering beers and flexing her pecs for the benefit of admiring onlookers, and in this confined sweaty space, Toni noticed, there were many. Sidney looked very butch; years of handling big, dangerous bikes had given her an edge, an aura of confidence that turned heads. And yet, when she handed Toni her drink and smiled, her green eyes twinkling, she was the prettiest girl ever. Toni gulped down her drink, her heartbeat tripping in uncomfortable paradiddles. She was used to being queen bee in a bar of men. Here, strong and horny women surrounded her and it was pretty damn unsettling. Sidney, however, was enjoying causing a stir, sipping her beer and pretending to ignore the curious looks.

She bent to whisper in Toni's ear. 'They're wondering who the new girl is because I've brought Lou in here a couple of times. I'll wind them up a bit first. They'll hate me when they find out you're straight.'

Jealousy tingled up Toni's spine. 'Who's Lou?'

'My wild new vampyre babe – you'll meet her later.'

Sidney's breath had caused goose bumps to ripple up Toni's neck. She had always been straight but tonight something different was happening. She took a look around her, fuck knew why when she was standing in a bar full of dykes. They certainly weren't all pretty either. She needed to get her mind away from her crotch.

Suddenly they were surrounded by a posse of mean-looking chicks high-fiving and drinking from their bottles of lager.

'Who's the doll, Sid?' They crowded round to look Toni up and down.

'This is Toni. She's an old friend of mine. Toni, meet the Vixens.'

'A very respectable-looking friend too.' A dark-haired girl hung her arm around Sid's shoulders. Her hands were strong, the nails painted black and she had a V tattooed on the apex of her thumb and forefinger.

'She was born and brought up in San Francisco so nothing you lot can say or do could shock her.'

'Bet Raven's tattoo would,' someone chimed.

'You Raven?' Toni asked the dark-haired girl.

The dark-haired girl grinned. 'Why do you say that?'

'Because of your lovely dark hair.' Toni smiled as the crowd wolf-whistled.

'Here we go, any excuse to show it off. Get your tits out then, Rave.'

Raven buried her face in Sid's shoulder.

'Don't pretend to be shy.' Sid bent conspiratorially towards Toni. 'She has the most amazing tats and she knows it.'

'What about you, Toni?' a blonde girl asked. 'You into body decoration?'

''Fraid not.'

The girl looked disappointed.

'That doesn't mean that I don't enjoy it on other people. When I was younger I used to hang out at Happy Jack's. Do you know it? It was incredible what that guy could do with a needle.'

The blonde girl beamed. 'He did this.' She pulled down the waistband of her jeans to reveal ivy, which curled around her navel and ran down on to her shaved sex.

'Wow.' Toni was speechless.

'It covers my lips as well. It's incredible watching someone eating me out. Two pleasures for the price of one.' She beamed innocently.

'For fuck's sake, Dale.'

'No, it's fine.' Toni looked at the blonde girl, who smiled shyly. 'It really is beautiful.'

Dale was warming to her subject now. 'My arms match –' she tipped each shoulder in turn to Toni '– and so do my breasts.' She pulled up her T to reveal high breasts with each dark-brown nipple circled in more swirls of ivy.

Toni admired the effect, envying her nipple-rings. She

bet the sensation of rubbing them against someone's chest was amazing.

'Put them away, Dale. Haven't you got a less obvious chat-up line?'

Dale reddened with embarrassment and tucked her T back into her jeans.

'Oh dear, the conversation seems to have wandered away from Raven,' someone quipped.

'These are my babies.' Raven whipped up her vest to reveal her namesake, its wings outstretched, emblazoned on her torso. Her nipples were tattooed as wheels on fire. 'So, why our good friend Sidney has to hang out with the freaks down at the Zone when she is surrounded by such beauty is frankly beyond me.' Raven jiggled her tits and kissed Sid on the top of the head. The others cheered.

'Come on, ladies. No lewd behaviour in the bar, please.'

'Fuck you, grandad. I didn't hear you complaining last week when you were watching me have my titties sucked by that cute redhead.'

The barman turned away, embarrassed.

'Shut up, Raven,' Dale admonished. 'Or you'll have us barred from this place too.'

She turned to Toni. 'So where do you live now?'

'LA.'

'In the music business?'

'No, I'm a private investigator. I'm looking for a missing girl and I was hoping for the inside track on a biker gang.'

'Name of?'

'The Cobras.'

The girls winced collectively.

'Not our scene, baby.'

'Not at all.'

'Redneck bastards.'

Toni shrugged apologetically. 'I know, but Sid's the best biker buddy I've got and I thought that maybe the friend of a friend . . .?' Toni grimaced. 'Of a friend?'

A tough looking little redhead spoke up. 'Hey, maybe I do know someone.'

'Who?' Raven asked accusingly.

'Couple of dancer friends of mine.'

'Strippers?'

'Erotic dancers at the Sapphire.'

'Oh, I remember. You were dating that weird one for a while.'

'Raven, will you shut up and let Cherry speak?'

Toni caught the barman's eye and signalled for another round, slipping a large tip across the counter. She turned back to the group. 'I'd be really grateful for any lead you can give me.'

'I know this one dancer, used to be into One Percenters. Travelled around with them a bit. Hitching rides and sucking cock for a free pass into biker parties and stuff.'

Raven pretended to vomit.

'Look, we're not talking about me here. It's a friend of a friend.'

Sid stepped in. 'I'd appreciate it if you could help Toni out.'

Cherry nodded. 'For a friend of the Vixens, sure.'

Sid raised her bottle. 'Here's to us then.'

Four of them left for the Sapphire. Raven stayed in the bar. Nubile dancers were too much like competition. Toni paid for them all to enter. It was a small grotty place, dark and seedy, but it didn't bother Toni; she'd been in hundreds just like it. They found a table.

'I don't want any of this getting back to Raven.'

Cherry was looking nervous. 'I'm doing this to help Sid, so I don't want any sly references made in the future.'

'You have my word, Cherry. No worries.'

Dale was looking pensive. 'I don't know, girls. Isn't this exploitation? Aren't we just like guys doing this?'

'Don't worry; it's not a real strip joint. There are no victims here.' Cherry thought about what she'd said and added, 'Only willing ones.'

A waitress approached. She wore a thick, spiked dog collar and an outfit that consisted mainly of straps. The studded straps just about covered her nipples and a thicker one covered her slit, but her ass was bare and wobbled as she walked on her high heels. Sid raised her eyebrows and winked at Dale.

Cherry looked up at the waitress. 'Hey, Lena, is Anthea in tonight? I'd really like to talk to her.'

'Hey, Cherry, I haven't seen you for a while. I'll go see. Do you want to order first?'

When they'd ordered, Lena strutted off. Toni looked around the club. She was surprised that they'd been let in. Normally these clubs had a strict dress code to deter voyeurs and tourists. Some of the drinkers were wearing fetish gear, but not all. There were a few girls dressed as guys, a lot in PVC and a girl in a see-through plastic dress. A pretty girl with dark lipstick and false eyelashes approached the table. She bit her thumb and looked round the table. 'Anyone want me to dance?'

Cherry looked embarrassed. She opened her mouth to speak and then shut it again.

Sid spoke for them. 'Sure, honey.'

The four women sat back and watched as the girl started to sway to the heavy bass that was pumping around the room. Their drinks arrived and strobe lightning gave the girl's movements a jerky, unreal sensation. Toni was mesmerised; she had always been fascinated by dancers, had always held a fancy for exhibitionism herself. When she was younger she had crept into the O'Farrell Theatre and watched the girls dancing there.

There was one particular Asian girl with a dragon tattoo around her calf that had really fascinated her. She would come down off stage and strut up and down the front row of men. Toni had loved the way she held all those men in thrall. She would bend and twist her incredible body in front of them, her long black hair swinging like a shiny curtain as she writhed. The men would steal a touch: a stroke of her buttocks, a tweak of a dark nipple, and once – the memory still turned Toni on – she bent in front of an old man to allow him to slip a finger inside her, albeit briefly, but the entire audience was in a state of rapture. She knew she was coveted, lusted after, adored. It was her body and she was parading it, rightly so, as a treasure. The men could gape, stiff cocked, and pant over it, strain for it and perhaps touch it – but they could never own it.

It was strange to be watching another beautiful body displayed in front of her now but with a group of girls. The looks on their faces were a mixture of embarrassment and lust. The dancer was wearing a tight PVC dress that had poppers running up the front.

She was undoing these slowly. She climbed on to the table in front of them, and four faces were automatically raised up to watch her. The dress fell away and Toni's mouth dropped open in surprise. The girl was a work of art. She dipped and rose on the table, allowing them to see her pussy, which were heavy with rings. Her sex looked so alien that at first Toni thought her quim looked more like a tropical flower than anything else. Her nipples too were pierced and held thick, gold hoops.

Her neck, wrists and ankles were all bound with studded straps. She looked like an exotic tribal warrior. As Toni examined her closer, she could see scarring covering her belly and breasts; patterns which had been cut into her flesh. Toni watched her dance, fascinated.

She was distracted by a voice in her ear and, for a moment, she was so caught up in the movements of the girl in front of her that she didn't immediately realise that Cherry was asking her to follow her. She led Toni down a staircase and they were permitted entry to the downstairs room after Lena the waitress had vouched for them. There was no way Toni would have argued with the dyke on the door.

Cherry turned to her. 'I didn't want the other Vixens to see down here; I think it's a bit heavy for their tastes.'

The long basement was split into small rooms. Toni peeked into each one as she passed and realised she had entered fetish heaven. The club's clientele came down here to indulge in their favourite fantasy or to be included in someone else's. In the first room a naked slave girl knelt before her mistress. Toni hesitated, the scenario making her pulse trip a little faster. Would she be allowed to watch? she wondered. Cherry caught her curiosity and nodded her approval.

On first glance it appeared as if the slave girl was holding up her hands in prayer, when in fact they were chained to her neck collar. Her face was red and Toni could see finger marks on her cheeks where she'd been slapped.

The mistress towering over her was a formidable sight. She must have been six foot tall and Toni coveted her incredibly long slender legs, which were encased in fishnet stockings. Her slim waist was squeezed into a tight black corset and her high breasts were pushed up so that their nipples were skimming the top of the bustier. Her pussy was exposed, the smooth pelt of dark hair accentuated by her suspender belt. Toni envied her outfit; she'd love to see the Inspector's face should she turn up at Piedro's with that lot on under her coat. She would especially like to see him crouched in front of her like the slave girl.

'Insolent bitch,' the mistress snarled. 'How dare you ask to relieve yourself!'

'Sorry, mistress.'

'Don't you dare speak to me, slave!' The mistress reached out a gloved hand and clamped a peg on to the girl's left nipple. The slave whimpered. 'Don't you dare make a sound. You will receive a just punishment for your impudence!' Another peg was clamped on, catching the tender white flesh of the underside of her breast. 'Stand. Stand at once! We have witnesses to your punishment.'

The slave girl struggled to her feet. Toni noticed red weals on her legs where she had been whipped. Her white sturdy thighs trembled as she stood. Her feet were bare, and her unpainted toenails looked naked among the paraphernalia of her punishment. The mistress grabbed a handful of hair and pulled the girl's head back, her eyes shiny with excitement. Toni's clit throbbed at the sight of the pegs quivering on her breasts. The mistress clipped more pegs on to the girl's body with her gloved hand, until the soft flesh was twisted and puckered. The girl whimpered in pain and excitement.

'Do you understand why I punish you, my precious?' the mistress purred, one gloved hand holding the girl's head right back, the other twisting a peg on her nipple. 'It's because you are my favourite slave. I have to teach you the correct protocol.' She lowered her blood-red lips on to the slave girl's naked ones and pushed her tongue into her mouth. The slave girl moaned and opened her mouth to receive the kiss. One gloved hand released the peg and slipped down on to the slave girl's belly. 'Still want to pee, my precious?' She pressed hard with the ball of her hand. The slave girl whimpered and nodded. The other gloved hand released her hair and pushed her back down on to her knees. 'Then you have my consent.'

Toni took a step back, aroused but ever protective of her footwear. The slave girl gave a cry of pleasure and relief, spread her thighs and a stream flooded from between her legs, splashing on to the tiles and spraying the mistress's black boots. The mistress laughed, watching the golden liquid pooling at her feet. The slave girl shivered, unable to stop, and Toni wondered how long she'd been prevented from relieving herself. The mistress caught the girl under her chin and tipped her face up, watching her expression as she pissed, stroking her red cheek with her thumb. The slave girl looked up adoringly, like a new puppy, as the final few drops sprayed from her.

Toni felt a dampness between her own legs and took a deep breath. The mistress was unclipping the pegs tenderly and stroking the slave girl's hair. The slave girl's cheek was laid reverently against the mistress's bush, her eyes closed in satisfaction. The pegs were discarded, the mistress unlocked the slave's wrists, and she slid gratefully into the puddle on the tiled floor. Cherry tugged at Toni's hand and Toni followed on shaky legs. In the next cubicle stood a nurse with a long plastic enema tube. A patient knelt on a trolley, her ass in the air. Toni quickly averted her eyes.

Cherry led her past the cubicles and through to a dressing room at the far end. Several girls were sitting around, drinking and smoking or dressing for upstairs.

Toni hardly dared look at the outfits; she was slipping into stimulation overload. Two women were sitting together in a corner and looked up as they approached. One had pale skin and platinum corkscrew curls, sharp little canines and crazy, reptile eyes. The other was dark, her lips and ears and eyebrows hung heavy with studs and rings.

Cherry spoke first. 'Hi, I've a friend here would like to speak to you.'

'Lena said. Are you making a booking?' Reptile Eyes watched Toni suspiciously.

Toni cleared her throat. 'No, no, I'm not. I'm hoping you can give me some information.'

'On performing?'

'No. Riding. Do you ride with the Vixens?'

'We don't ride. We're into the riders.' She looked pointedly at Cherry.

'May we sit?'

The girl shrugged.

'Have you heard of the Cobras?'

'Everyone's heard of the Cobras. One of the big outlaw gangs, yeah?'

'That's right. I'm looking for someone who was riding with them, a girl. Have you any idea where they hang out in the city?'

The dancers looked at each other. 'Did she run out on you?'

'I'm a private investigator.'

'Must be quite an important little miss to have you looking for her.'

Toni paused before answering. 'She's the only family her aunt has left. She's desperate to get in touch.'

Yellow Eyes tossed her curls. 'Shoulda tried Oprah.'

Toni leaned in towards them. 'Cherry told me that maybe you knew something about this male biker gang thing. I'm used to going undercover, and if I can find this gang then that's what I'll do. Only I've heard that they can be pretty rough on the girls who ride with them.' Toni pushed the photo across the table. 'She's got an aunt waiting for her. I just want to check that she's OK.' She turned the photo to show the wad of notes underneath. 'I'm not in the business of telling anyone how to live their life.'

Ms Pincushion shrugged. 'I suppose it's common knowledge that I used to be a bit of a biker slut. Turns out it was more of a fetish for the leathers than the man thing. Anyway, I woke up one morning after an all-night party and it turned out I was down Arizona way. I thought we were just passing through but the biker I was with said that the gang spent quite a bit of time down there. I'm a city girl at heart so I was a bit freaked. Camping out under the stars wasn't my bag at all. Turned out they were all doing business in this big club down there. Shit, what was the name? The Sphynx, that's right. Guy I was riding with got me some work dancing there and it was full of Cobras, the place was crawling with them. Reckon they owned it. Probably used it to launder money like the mob.'

'That's fantastic. Where was it?'

'Shit, it was a long time ago and I was doing a bit of speed back then. A shitty place with casinos and stuff. We all called it Smallville, but that can't have been its real name, can it? I really can't remember.' She looked questioningly at Yellow Eyes, who shrugged.

'Were you dancing there long?'

'Not too long. I've danced in a lot of clubs but yeah, the Cobras stick out in my mind. I hope your girl's a tough cookie.'

'Are you sure you can't remember the name of the town?'

'I'm sure. I had some pretty hot shit going on back then.'

'What happened?'

'A lot of the dancers were into each other rather than the guys. Made me realise what I was missing.' She shot a sly look at her friend.

Toni stuck out her hand. 'Well, I really appreciate you talking to me. I guess I need to head down that way.'

As they were leaving, Ms Pincushion called them back. 'Are you really going down there to look for her?'

Toni nodded. 'For sure.'

'Good luck. I hope you find her.'

Toni took a moment to enjoy the piece of information; the name of a club was a great start. She would take some time out to enjoy seeing Sid and tomorrow maybe head back to LA. She was beginning to form an idea about how she could get to meet Red.

Toni and Cherry made their way back upstairs. The girl in the enema room was having a dildo inserted into her rectum to prevent her evacuating and, in the punishment room, the slave girl was lapping eagerly between her mistress's legs. It made LA seem like a retirement village for gentlefolk. Upstairs the scarred warrior had left and Sid was looking edgy.

'Can we go now? I promised Lou I'd meet her at the Zone.'

'No problem.' Toni grabbed her purse. 'Let's go.'

Sid slipped her arm through hers. 'Any luck?'

'Yeah, good, thanks.'

She steered her through the packed bar. 'Does that mean we can party now?'

Toni nodded.

Outside, the street was buzzing; people were spilling out of every bar. The smell of garlic and noodles was sharp in the air.

Toni hugged herself. 'So, where are you taking me?'

'A new place – it's more Lou's place than mine but I said we'd call in.'

'Is this the vampyre babe you mentioned?'

Sid nodded.

'We're going back to meet Raven. See you tomorrow.' Cherry held out her hand to Toni.

'Thanks for your help, Cherry.'

Dale looked sorry to be leaving. 'When you've found the girl, come back to see us, won't you? You can't leave San Francisco without jamming some wind with us.'

Toni smiled. 'Sure.'

Dale looked back over her shoulder and then they disappeared into the crowd.

Toni hooked her arm through Sid's as they walked. 'Tell me about your new chick.'

Sid shrugged. 'It's a mixed marriage really. I don't fit in with her friends and she doesn't ride with the Vixens, but the chemistry's right, you know?'

'Please don't tell me that she's freakier than Cherry's mate back there.' Toni shuddered.

Sid laughed. 'She's a dark horse, that one. The table next to us paid the dancer to pee in their laps.'

Toni wrinkled her nose. 'I bet it gets a bit rank in there when it warms up.'

'I bet Cherry gets a right thrill when we're out on a run and we're all peeing behind bushes with our leathers around our ankles.'

'You promised not to give her a hard time, remember? She got me a good lead in there.'

'Don't worry, her secret's safe with me. It'll keep her quiet about my new girl anyway.'

'You're scaring me now.'

'Come on. You'll be fine.'

8

Toni had visited one or two Goth joints before and they never were her bag of pretzels. The Zone was no exception. She always felt like the freak in these places. The club was in an old converted church and Toni stuck close to her friend as they entered. The wooden floors shook with the vibration of a live band which was playing somewhere at the back of the building. The ultraviolet lighting was giving the whole place an eerie otherworldly glow, which was obviously the intention. It was a vampyre fantasy land – more New Orleans Mardi Gras than Hammer Horror – with a good deal of black rubber in evidence. Now that was her thing. A boy/girl with Edward Scissorhands nails caught her admiring his/her high black boots and winked. Toni smiled thinly and ducked into the bar behind Sid. She needed a drink to steady herself.

Sid amazed her. She moved through the crowd like she owned the place, despite her ordinary streetwear, and her confidence got her served almost straight away by a girl in a feather headdress and shimmering tight dress. Sid flashed her best smile and Toni rolled her eyes.

'You are such a flirt.' She had to lean in close to make herself heard.

Sid tipped her bottle to her mouth and wiped her lips with her hard mechanic's hand before leaning back to answer. 'Never got me anywhere with you though, did it?'

Toni could feel her heat all the way down her own

body. Sid's belt buckle grazed the flimsy material of her skirt.

'And about time!' A pale girl with crimson lips interrupted them. She kissed Sid hard on the lips and then wiped away her lipstick. She tipped her dark head close to Sid and gave Toni the eyeball.

Sid grinned. 'Lou, this is Toni, an old friend who's in town for the night.'

Lou's lips stretched briefly before she tossed her long hair and whispered possessively in her girlfriend's ear.

Toni sipped her beer. It was going to be a long night if she was forced to play gooseberry. Sid took her hand. 'C'mon, Lou wants to catch the show in the Red Room.'

A voodoo priest frisked them all before he allowed them to enter the door to the Red Room. He examined a small package of Lou's and handed it back with a warning. Toni couldn't make out the words against the blare of the band.

'Are you taking responsibility for her?' He meant Toni and Lou nodded. His eyes looked yellow against his white painted face as he watched them enter.

They passed through and Toni felt a flicker of panic. A naked girl with spray-painted gold skin and a gold strap-on bobbing at her crotch squeezed past with a tray of drinks.

'Members only,' Sid murmured in her ear, as if reading her thoughts.

'Member being the operative word,' Toni quipped back and Sid made a face.

Toni thought of her apartment and how she could be sitting on the balcony right now with Josh, sipping a cold glass of Chardonnay. She thought of her two detectives; how could she ever have imagined herself to be outré? Lou handed her a drink and Toni accepted it gratefully. Lou pointed and Toni turned to see what she was supposed to be looking at. A girl in a diaphanous pink negligee lay supine on a faded red chaise. She clutched a long-stemmed rose to her breast and her fair hair spilled over the edge. Toni halted and watched, transfixed, as what could only be described as a man with the head of a beast hovered over her.

Lou was watching too, her eyes bright with interest.

Sid was at Toni's ear again. 'They're all hardcore in here.'

Toni raised an eyebrow.

'We only got in because of Lou. This is like the inner sanctum. They perform cutting rituals in here.' Sid noticed the look on Toni's face. 'Don't worry. They wouldn't have let you in for that.'

A man with a shaved head signalled his disapproval and Sid shot a challenging look in return. Nevertheless, she fell quiet to watch the tableau.

The beast was moving his hands over the sleeping girl without actually touching her. His nails were long and sharp. Her sleep was growing disturbed. She stirred slightly in her slumber but didn't awake. Now he was sniffing her with his piglike snout. Her toes twitched slightly as he drank in the scent of her bare feet. He moved his head up her legs and the sleeping beauty began to twist in her sleep. The beast snuffled at her crotch and the girl arched her back, moaning quietly. With his talons, the beast grasped at the neck of her flimsy gown and pulled it down.

The sleeping girl's arm fell so that the hand clutching the rose touched the floor. The beast exposed her breasts, which were rising and falling as she grew aroused. His sharp nails scraped the pale skin on her chest and drew fine rivulets of blood. Toni gasped, the talons must have been razor sharp to have drawn blood so quickly. She sensed a rising excitement in the room. The beast dipped his head to the blood and lapped with his long tongue, chasing the thin trickles of blood over a breast and down the girl's ribcage. The girl squirmed. Her negligee grew bloody and tattered about her waist. The nails scratched and the tongue lapped. The girl's legs splayed, but it was the blood that fascinated the crowd, not her exposed quim. The excitement rose as her torso became a mass of red and bloody scratches. Toni winced as a nail caught a nipple, but the girl's pain was her pleasure too and she arched her back, offering the bloody nipple to the beast's mouth.

Lou had grown excited; she produced a razor wrapped in paper and looked at Sid expectantly. Toni was amazed to see Sid comply. They moved to a quiet corner and Toni followed. Sid sat, her arms stretched along the back of the sofa and her knees apart, and tipped her head back, watching Toni from under half-closed eyelids. Toni admired the white arch of her neck, the curve of her muscled arms, the strength of her wide shoulders. Lou knelt on the sofa next to Sid and stroked her lover's neck and shoulders, searching for the right spot. Satisfied that she had found the right place, she flicked her long dark hair out of the way and steadied herself before cutting into Sid's shoulder with her razor. Sid winced as the sharp metal sliced into her skin but she kept still. Lou massaged the skin around the cut, bringing the blood to the surface and letting it burst like a dark bud from Sid's flesh before lowering her lips to taste. Toni watched, aroused, as Lou sucked and Sid braced herself against the sharp pain of Lou's teeth. Lou sucked harder and Sid's eyelids closed as she fell into the rhythm of Lou's greedy, sucking mouth.

Toni watched in fascination. She knew about the underground bloodletting scene but hadn't witnessed a blood-sucking before. It was tender and erotic, the one girl taking and the other submitting. As much as it turned her on, Lou couldn't have shut her out more effectively. Toni drained her drink and went to the bar for another; the close proximity of so many fetishists was giving her claustrophobia. Toni made her way out of the Red Room and down a long corridor. She caught a slight breeze and sensed a door was open. Sure enough, the back door of the club opened on to a little courtyard. People were chilling out here. Despite the warm night air it was still cooler than the thick atmosphere of the club and Toni fell into a wrought-iron chair. She scrabbled in her bag for a smoke and, lifting a bent cigarette to her lips, was surprised to see a well-manicured hand offering her a light.

Toni accepted and sucked gratefully on the cigarette. A pair of exotic dark eyes watched her through the blue plume of smoke. Toni's head tipped back. She felt suddenly exhausted from her journey. The woman in the chair opposite puffed her cigarette elegantly. When Toni's lungs had begun to fill satisfyingly with nicotine she relaxed a little and adjusted herself in the chair.

The woman opposite rotated one expensively clad foot. Toni's eyes were immediately drawn down her long, well-curved leg to admire what looked suspiciously like a pair of diamante Manolo Blahnik spike heels. Toni's mouth watered.

'Aren't they just the best?' The woman grinned.

Toni nodded. 'They are gorgeous.'

'I can see you like shoes.' The woman tilted her head at Toni's own precious sling-backs.

Toni sucked on her Marlboro and lifted up her feet for examination. 'They've had too long a day. I doubt whether they'll ever recover.'

The woman sipped her Martini and Toni ran her eye over her tight red dress. A pale and buxom cleavage rose out of the button-through bodice but still Toni wondered if the diamante choker hid an Adam's apple.

'I just had to come out here and admire them. The masses have no respect for classic footwear.' She swapped feet to admire her other shoe. 'Have you ever been to Shoe Heaven?'

Toni shook her head.

'You must go. The assistants are all foot fetishists and the shoes are divine. You could lose days of your life just trying them on. It's tough leaving them behind but for those few hours...' She shivered. 'Bliss.' She pulled on her cigarette. 'And large sizes are no problem.'

Toni and the woman sat in comfortable silence for a while, happy with their own company and attractive footwear. Eventually a willowy girl who was dressed in a little black dress and long black gloves joined them. Over her gloved fingers she wore huge zirconium rocks. She smoothed a lock of hair away from her chiselled cheekbone and settled down gracefully. She removed the cigarette from her friend's fingers and put it to her own raspberry-red lips.

'Darling,' she purred though the smoke, 'I hope your friend here isn't easily offended but I have got to have some cock inside me. This place makes me quake all over.'

Toni swallowed, still unsure whether she was girl or boy. Either way, her friend would definitely find her pony-skin heels a turn-on.

The woman in the Manolos lit another cigarette. 'Help yourself, darling.' Then to Toni, 'Excuse us, won't you? But we do enjoy a little al fresco. And these shoes are making me burst with pleasure.'

Toni shifted but couldn't quite bring herself to leave.

The woman continued, 'By all means stay. An audience always adds a little spice. Rea, darling, blow me a little tune first. The sight of your mouth on my cock and a pair of Manolos on my feet sends me into orbit. After that you can ride me all night if you want to.'

Toni's hand was a little shaky as she watched the girl/boy in the black dress drop to her knees on the ground in front of her friend. Her black-gloved hands pushed up the red skirt until stocking tops and a fantastic erection were exposed. The woman puffed regally on her cigarette, holding it between long, manicured fingers as she watched the girl between her legs swallow her cock between her glossy lips.

'Oh, Rea, darling, you really are good at that.'

Rea's gloved hands held up the red dress gracefully as her head moved up and down the long shaft. Her friend's cleavage rose and fell in appreciation and her voice was deep when she spoke next.

'Best you climb on, sweetie, before I explode.'

The girl lifted her little black number to reveal a neat black bush. She obviously didn't require any first course. She moved to sit astride her friend, giving Toni a full-on view of her neat white buttocks. Before lowering herself she closed her gloved fingers on the cigarette and took a long deep pull.

'I'd like to burn you with it, sweetie, but I'm afraid I might singe your lovely dress.' She kissed the woman beneath her with a mouth full of smoke.

'Come singe your minge on me instead,' her friend replied with a deep chuckle.

Rea kept hold of the cigarette and lowered herself on to the rigid cock beneath her. The two of them moaned in satisfaction. Rea's buttocks tensed as she rose and dipped, swallowing the shaft and then withdrawing almost to its tip. She paused, puffed the cigarette and offered it to her friend's painted lips before dropping on to the cock again.

Her friend's red nails clasped into her buttocks, the cigarette was discarded and Rea rode the shaft more aggressively, pumping it hard and groaning in satisfaction. Toni watched in awe as the two best-dressed women in the club fucked good and hard on the seat opposite.

My, but she'd forgotten how much fun San Francisco could be.

Toni woke in the sofa bed with Sid and Lou. She'd slept top-to-toe with them but they could have been at it all night and Toni wouldn't have known; she'd slept like the dead. Sid and Lou didn't stir so Toni slipped out from beneath the covers and helped herself to some cold orange juice from the refrigerator. She would have liked to spend some time cruising the shops and maybe visit the Haight to catch up with some old friends, but there wasn't time. She had to move this investigation along. Toni stretched and set about retrieving her clothes. It was a long drive home.

9

'Make sure that you maintain eye contact at all times.' Shaylee snapped her chewing gum with her tongue. 'That way the suckers really think that you're dancing for them, not the money. If you don't look them in the eye, the tips won't be half as good because the men will think that you're either pissed at them or out of it on drugs – and they don't like either.'

Toni had come back to LA for the stripping lesson. The 'Loin wasn't her stamping ground any more. There was no one she knew at the O'Farrell whom she could ask for tips and she was beginning to wonder whether she could really carry this off; there was certainly more to stripping than she'd thought.

Shaylee was dressed in a baggy tracksuit which hid her voluptuous double-E cup and, without her make-up, looked like any other jogger on the streets of LA. 'Just pretend that the pole is a giant cock and you won't go wrong. Lick it, rub yourself on it, do it with enough confidence and you'll be fine; we all had to start somewhere. A lot of the girls do warm-ups before they go on because some of them get pretty athletic. But I don't suggest you attempt hanging upside down from it or doing the splits up it, not unless you're a pro.'

Toni took a deep breath; the air in the club smelt of stale beer and cigarette smoke. 'Going in as a dancer will mean I'll see all the faces.'

'And as long as you don't mind them seeing your pussy, you'll be fine.' Shaylee grinned.

The thought of strangers seeing her gyrating on stage was an old fantasy of Toni's and she wanted to get it right. She hadn't wanted to do it in this town and travelling south would be an ideal opportunity. 'There's more to it than opening your legs on stage, though,' said Toni.

'Sure, and if I knew the club, I could give you more help.' Shaylee counted on her three-inch-long nails. 'Firstly, if it's lap dancing, pretend you're fucking them and slowly rotate your ass in their face – they go wild for that. Secondly, if it's pole dancing, pretend that you're fucking the pole. Watch the other girls and copy them. It may be a good old-fashioned strip joint; if it is, have your own tape with some music that turns you on and have a short routine ready. It's all just a performance. You'll be fine.'

'Thanks, Shaylee, I appreciate it.' Toni glanced around the empty club; the window blinds cut the intruding sunshine into strips. She imagined herself dancing on one of the tables and a crowd of men gazing up at her, slack-jawed, slowly masturbating to the beat of her rotating ass. It would be more than a performance to her and her panties were damp at the thought of it. On her way out of the city she would call in the Honey Bee and pick herself up some costumes; she'd always had a penchant for black plastic dominatrix gear. She envisioned herself masturbating with the handle of a whip and jumped as Shaylee's hand gripped her shoulder.

'Hell, Toni, you haven't got to do this, you know; it's not for everyone.'

Toni smiled guiltily. 'I'll be fine.'

'I have to shoot. I'm picking the kids up from day nursery but I'm sure Piedro won't mind you using the place to practise before you hit the road.' Shaylee dangled the keys from her electric-blue talons.

'Thanks, I will.' A bit of practice would warm her up a little for the undercover work ahead.

'Help yourself to whatever's in there. The music is behind the bar.' Shaylee pointed to the back room. 'Take care of yourself, and come back safe.' She kissed Toni on the cheek. 'If you tire of detective work, Piedro would love to have you working here.' She grinned naughtily. 'Hey, he'd just love to have you.'

The two women laughed.

'See ya.'

'Bye, Shaylee, and thanks again.'

Alone in the club, Toni made her way to the back room, feeling aroused but self-conscious. She knew that she couldn't just walk into the Sphynx and demand a job there. She would have to prove herself. Reaching behind the bar, she popped in the first tape she could find and a loud bass filled the room. Trailing her hand along chair backs, Toni wove her way between the tables towards the mirror on the back wall and stepped up on to the small podium. Slowly she began to move her hips to the beat and she loosened up a little as she watched herself dance in front of the mirror.

Unlike Shaylee, Toni was dressed in her usual smart suit. Shrugging off the jacket, Toni undid the top couple of buttons of her blouse to reveal her cleavage and pulled her skirt up her tanned legs. She liked the way her thigh muscles tightened as she dipped and rotated her hips. Watching herself, Toni slipped off her panties, enjoying the sensation of her bush rubbing against the fabric of her skirt as she moved. Pushing her hair up on top of her head, Toni pouted into the mirror, tipping forward from the waist so that her breasts quivered, thoroughly enjoying herself.

When the music ended, someone clapped and Toni spun round, startled. Piedro was sitting on a chair in the centre of the room, legs spread, black eyes mocking, a bottle of beer on the table in front of him. He clapped slowly, seeing her shocked expression, but Toni soon recovered and, as the music started up again, she advanced towards him, her hands still holding her hair up and her hips swaying in an exaggerated movement as she sashayed across the room.

She raised one eyebrow as she saw how quickly his mocking smile faded to a look of arousal. He was the perfect practice audience and her quim pulsed heavily as she danced slowly in front of him, hiding her own nervousness and grateful that the loud music prevented speech. He swigged nervously at his bottle, his eyes sweeping from her face to her breasts to her legs. Toni's heartbeat raced; she was as horny as hell after her visit to San Francisco and didn't want the music to end.

She slipped off her blouse, threw it over a chair and danced around him, feeling her tightened nipples cutting into the lace of her bra. She slipped each strap over a shoulder. Piedro licked his lips, hypnotised by the promise of her breasts as she turned her back to him and undid her bra, holding it out before flinging it to one side. She tormented him by watching him over her shoulder as she caressed her tits out of his sight. He shifted uncomfortably in his seat, a massive boner swelling in the front of his jeans. He gulped at his beer in irritation as she teased him further, sticking her ass in his face and moving it in slow circles.

Eventually she turned and Piedro gaped at her tits as Toni squeezed her nipples hard and pulled on them, revelling in the look of stunned pleasure on his face. Her cunt was hot and creamy; she wanted fucking, but not yet. Turning her back to him again, Toni unzipped her skirt and pushed it over the swell of her hips, noting Piedro's gasp at her lack of underwear.

Naked except for her shoes, Toni swayed to the heavy, sensual music, running her hands over herself, feeling parts of her body that she knew he wanted to feel. Raising a shoe on to the arm of his chair so that her quim throbbed just inches from his face, Toni reached for his bottle and took it from him. Piedro watched, hypnotised as she sucked on his bottle of beer, allowing a dribble to run down her chin and between her breasts. Then, looking him straight in the eye, she rubbed the bottle against her swollen sex lips, revelling in Piedro's shocked expression. Toni tipped her head back in arousal, working the bottle backwards and forwards against herself, her hot quim moist compared to the cold, unyielding glass. Toni groaned, her self-pleasuring momentarily blocking out Piedro.

A warm hand crept up the back of her thigh and another pulled the bottle away from her creamy slit. Toni looked into Piedro's dark eyes, feeling dazed with lust and extremely pliable. Piedro was muttering to her in Spanish, beside himself with a desire to fuck her. He rose from his seat and kissed her hard on the lips, forcing his tongue into her mouth.

'My princess,' he was muttering, 'I never thought you would be such a dirty, sleazy tease.'

Toni felt drugged and rubbed her tits against his groping hands. Piedro pushed her back so that she lay on top of a table. Aroused, Toni arched her back but allowed her legs to splay wide open over the edge, inviting his touch.

Piedro stood between her legs, his eyes fixed on her sex, and he smoothed his hands up her open thighs, over her belly, squeezing her nubs once before gently enclosing her neck with both hands.

He was fully dressed, hands around her throat as she writhed naked on the table in front of him, and yet she felt that she had him in total control. His trousers bulged as he contemplated her. He swept his hands down to her tits, kneading them hard before stroking back down over her stomach and moving both thumbs down to rub her clit.

Toni moaned in pleasure, thrashing her head from side to side as he kneaded her clit hard with the balls of both thumbs. Toni threw her legs wider and grasped the table in ecstasy.

'You are a hot one, princess. You want me to fuck you, hard, yes? Like I never fucked a woman before?'

Toni moaned her assent and Piedro tore at his flies to release his cock. There was no finesse; he just wanted to fuck her now. He gripped her buttocks and pulled her towards him, jamming his cock into her hot hole. He felt good, and Toni tipped her pelvis so he could slip deeper inside her. Piedro rocked himself into her, working higher each time. He fucked her hard, so that her tits bounced with each thrust and Toni gripped the table to stop herself from falling off.

Still she wanted him deeper and she drew her knees up so that her shoes raked the shirt on his back and gasped as his thrust hit high up inside. Piedro rammed himself home, sinews straining in his neck as his balls slapped her ass and one thumb still worked her clit. Toni trembled and arched and cried out on the table in front of him as her orgasm ripped up inside her and almost tore her in two with pleasure. Piedro watched her come, overwhelmed by her appetite, and shot his load deep inside her.

When she was dressed, Toni sank into a chair, sated, and accepted Piedro's offer of a cold drink. His hand shook slightly as he passed her the glass and Toni smirked inwardly at his dazed expression. She sipped her beer, crossing her aching thighs. She could feel his come, sticky on the insides of her legs.

'Don't go looking for bad men, princess.' Piedro leaned across to smooth a lock of hair away from Toni's face; she could still smell her juices on his fingers. 'There's a job for you here. Piedro will look after you.'

'You know I only work for myself, Piedro.' Toni placed the beer carefully on the table in front of her. 'On second thoughts, I think I'll forget the drink. There is a lot I have to do.'

She rose, irritated. Why did men think that the only safe way for a woman was to be looked after by them? Toni knew that that was the most dangerous and insecure route of all.

'I'll catch up with you when I get back.' She forced a smile; Piedro was a good source of information and a pretty good fuck – she didn't want to freeze him out completely.

Piedro rose to his feet too. 'Take care, princess.'

Toni allowed herself to be kissed, eager now to get home and take a shower.

'Come home to Piedro soon.' He ran a hand through her mussed hair.

'Sure.' Toni blew him a kiss as she left.

Back home, Toni was pleased to see that the daily had left her apartment immaculate. Disorder annoyed her and she wanted a calm space to collect her thoughts before leaving for Arizona. She took a bracing shower and wrapped herself in a towelling dressing gown to raid the refrigerator. Satisfied that she had a suitably enormous collection of food, she settled on the sofa to listen to her answerphone messages.

There was nothing from Josh. Disappointed, she munched her way through a packet of salami while she contemplated what to do. Josh was working out his sexuality, she guessed, having always been overshadowed by her own excessive appetites. The longer she left it, the more embarrassed he would become. He'd only had a stiffy for goodness' sake. Toni rested her head on the back of her cream sofa and plunged her hand into a box of pretzels. Josh was all grown up now and she had no business keeping him tied to her either personally or professionally. If he annoyed her by worrying about her risk-taking then how much more annoying must she be, his bossy, older half-sister?

Toni chewed thoughtfully. She'd always loved Josh; he was the gentle, compassionate one. She pictured him in front of her now, tall and blond with fantastic cheekbones, just like the Scandinavian artist she remembered her mother living with the summer before Josh was born.

She would have to cut Josh some slack if she didn't want to lose him. Toni picked up the phone and started punching in numbers; she'd have to teach him not to be so uptight. But Josh wasn't answering anywhere. Toni left a breezy message at the office and hung up. She would have liked to have spoken to him before she left but he could suit himself – she was off to find Caron Crossley and hopefully realise a couple of fantasies along the way.

Toni had cancelled all deliveries to the apartment; you never knew how long these undercover assignments were going to take. Her suitcase was packed but she was missing a few extra special outfits. A trip to the Bee Hive was called for and then she would be ready to leave early the next morning.

The Bee Hive was ostensibly a bookshop, a good old-fashioned take-your-time-and-browse bookshop, suitable for tourists and locals alike. But for those with more specialised tastes in literature and fashion there was a discreet notice directing them upstairs and, for the cognoscente, the attic room. Deceivingly spacious and packed with fantasy paraphernalia, Toni often spent an afternoon browsing the shelves.

The place was also a superb pick-up joint for its owner, Jon, who knew that his shop's innocuous appearance attracted men who may not otherwise wander into sex shops.

The attic room was quiet today and Toni took her time. Her tastes were pretty simple and she didn't have much trouble finding what she'd come in for – a pair of long black boots, a black plastic bustier, long gloves and a black cap. She also threw in a couple of crops for good measure; if she was going to do this thing, she might as well ham it up completely and go for the full Miss Whiplash look. She was studying a case of unusual nipple rings – she loved them but had never had the nerve to have them done herself – when she realised that she wasn't alone. An extremely good-looking business type, dressed in a suit and tie, was rummaging among the crotchless panties, an embarrassed flush creeping up his freshly shaven cheeks.

Toni smiled to herself; it wouldn't take him many visits here to realise that frilly panties worn under business suits were pretty commonplace. She studied him surreptitiously, knowing it was bad form to make anyone feel awkward here but still wondering if she should come on to him. He looked clean-cut and wholesome and Toni's clit throbbed at the contradiction of him being here, among the nipple stars and flesh hooks.

He was glancing towards the staircase and flicking nervously at imaginary specks on his expensive suit when another man appeared. This one was far more confident; he brought with him a faint whiff of lemony designer aftershave, and Toni just had time to take in his starched white shirt and gorgeous blue eyes before she slipped discreetly into a changing room.

She hovered behind the curtain, unsure whether they knew if she was here or not. The electricity sparking between them led her to believe that they were so drawn to each other, neither cared. She watched them through the chink in the curtain, her clit pulsing just at the thought of the excitement the two men must be feeling.

The first man was clearly on edge and Toni wondered if he had ever been with a man before. His Adam's apple bobbed as he snuck glances at the man he had come here to meet. The second man planted himself in the middle of the room with his hands in his trouser pockets and his expensive leather shoes wide apart.

'You're not seriously thinking of buying those, are you, Tom?'

Tom dropped the panties he had been holding and let out a huge relieved breath. 'I thought you weren't going to show up.'

'I'd have been mad not to.'

Tom laughed nervously and ran a hand through his dark hair. Toni noticed a wedding band on his finger.

'Mal, I don't know whether I can, you know . . .'

Mal looked at his feet and cleared his throat before answering, obviously wary of frightening the other man off. 'It's OK, Tom, I'm not here to make you do anything you don't want to.' He adjusted the knot of his tie with a large-knuckled hand. Toni watched his square clean nails. He was obviously disappointed but reluctant to force the other man into anything.

Tom raked his hair again. 'Maybe another time, yeah?'

'Sure.' Mal took a step back towards the staircase. He clearly doubted it.

'Or maybe now?' Tom's voice was gruff with nerves and Mal didn't need to be asked twice. He closed the gap between them, his shoes falling heavily on the wooden floorboards, and as he clasped Tom's face in both hands he opened his mouth over the other man's lips. Tom groaned in relief as soon as Mal kissed him, running his hands into the man's hair as they kissed fiercely.

They worked their mouths hungrily, holding on to each other as if afraid the other would escape. Toni saw Tom's wedding ring glinting dully as his broad hands clasped the other man's head. She sagged against the dressing-room wall, transfixed by the vision of male mouth on male mouth, stubbled chin working against a clean shaven one, male tongue searching greedily for male tongue. They kissed long and hard, groaning into each other's mouths. Toni guessed that this had been coming a long time. Her nipples tightened in recognition of their arousal and her quim felt heavy with her own.

The two men pressed themselves hard against each other, searching now for each other's bodies beneath their similar jackets.

'You taste fantastic, Tom.' Mal held the other man's chin in his hand, his face stern with arousal. 'I can't wait to get your cock in my mouth.' He reached down to feel the other man's cock through his trousers, rubbing it against his palm.

Tom's breathing was laboured. 'Christ, Mal, the years I've wasted pretending I didn't want this.'

Mal grabbed the other man's hand and rubbed it against his own swollen cock. 'We'll make up for it. You'll never want a woman again by the time I've finished with you.' He bit his lip as Tom picked up the rhythm, pushing his hand hard against the straining material of Mal's trousers. They stood nose to nose, panting into each other's faces, rubbing each other hard.

Tom grabbed his friend's wrist. 'I'm afraid I'm going to come.' He looked about him, as if aware of where they were for the first time. 'Why did we have to meet here for fuck's sake?'

Mal grinned, showing large white teeth. 'Because you won't come to my apartment any more. Not alone anyway.'

Tom rested his forehead on Mal's. 'What am I going to tell Jessica?'

'Tell her she's had you for long enough and from now on you only fuck men.' He pulled him towards the dressing room and Toni froze. 'Come on, I'm going to blow you good and hard and show you how it's really done.'

Tom allowed himself to be led into the joining cubicle and Toni slumped in relief. She knew that she should slip discreetly away but she so wanted to see Mal's lips around Tom's cock. She slid further into the cubicle, knowing that Jon had designed their rough wood look with voyeurism in mind – the cracks between the planks were pretty good for spying through; she just hoped that Mal's mouth around his dick was enough to put Tom off noticing she was peeping through the gap.

She crouched and pressed herself against the joining wall until she had a pretty good view. Opening her legs, she delved into her panties with her right hand, parting her sex lips and pushing her fingers up inside herself as she watched Mal pressing his old friend up hard against the cubicle wall.

He kissed Tom again, feeling for his body underneath the suit jacket, running his hands over chest and stomach, still loosely covered by his shirt. 'I'm going to have you naked, Tom, really fucking soon.'

Tom was overcome with arousal – his head tipped back against the cubicle wall and his chest heaved as Mal dropped to his knees in front of him. Slowly he pulled down the zipper on his friend's flies. Tom looked down at him, excited and terrified.

'The number of men I've sucked off, pretending they were you, Tom, you wouldn't believe.'

Tom swallowed hard. 'I always pretended it was your mouth on my cock, not hers.'

'Well, I wish you'd told me that years ago.'

Tom gasped as Mal drew his trousers down. 'Fuck! So do I.'

Toni's fingers slipped in and out of her pussy as she watched Tom's thick cock spring into view. Mal ran his hands over the other man's hairy thighs and up between them, freeing his balls and stroking and lifting their weight. Above him, Tom gasped, concentrating on not coming too quickly.

His swollen cock strained for the other man's mouth, its purple head glistening with pre-come. Mal poked out his tongue and licked the droplet delicately from the tip. Tom groaned and clasped Mal's head in his hands, but Mal was not to be rushed.

He dipped his head and ran his tongue along the seam dividing Tom's balls so that they tightened with pleasure. He licked his balls all over, tasting him for the first time and wanting all of him. Tom's hold became lax but his fingers remained entwined in Mal's hair as his tongue lifted and rolled his balls.

Mal withdrew and looked up at Tom before opening his mouth over his friend's cock, teasing him with light brushes of his tongue. Tom looked on, weak with lust and arousal as his friend tormented him, torturing him sweetly for the years kept waiting.

Reaching behind Tom, Mal grasped his buttocks and

began to move his mouth up and down Tom's shaft, sucking him hard now, laving him with his tongue, licking his foreskin, poking it into the hole, working him hard.

Tom groaned and pushed his cock into Mal's mouth. The world was just his cock and Mal. He gasped as it plunged over and over between his friend's lips. Just the other side of the partition Toni was working her fingers to the same rhythm, ploughing her cunt hard and reaching for the spot high up which would bring her release.

'I'm coming!' Tom yelled and Mal shot a hand up to cover his mouth, aware that there may be someone in the shop to hear them. Tom moaned against Mal's fingers as he shot his hot come into Mal's throat, throbbing into the other man's mouth in hot hard spurts. Mal drank him up eagerly, savouring every last drop.

Three feet away, Toni came silently, shuddering against the cubicle wall in a secretive, compact climax, one hand pushed inside herself and the other braced to keep herself from falling.

Mal rose to his feet, grinning. 'It kills your knees.' He placed his hands either side of Tom's head, waiting for him to catch his breath before kissing him hard, allowing Tom to taste his own spunk, warm and salty on his lips.

'Get used to it,' he grinned against the other man's mouth. 'It's something that you're going to be tasting a lot of.' Mal pushed Tom down gently. 'Starting now.'

As quietly as she could, Toni tiptoed from the changing room, clasping her outfits to her chest. Downstairs, the bookshop was fairly busy and Toni had to wait a little while for Jon to discreetly bag up her merchandise.

'He's a fast learner that one.' Jon's almond eyes twinkled as he handed Toni her card and receipt. 'I hope he's not one of the monogamous ones.'

Toni frowned quizzically until she followed Jon's glance towards a small screen behind the counter. On it she could see Tom going down on Mal, relayed from a security camera in the changing rooms.

'I could see you enjoyed it.' Jon winked.

Toni blushed, she didn't often get embarrassed but she hadn't expected someone to be watching her frigging herself in the cubicle.

Jon leant forward and whispered. 'If watching men turns you on, you're welcome to come to one of my parties anytime.'

Toni smiled. 'I think I might develop a taste for it, yeah.'

'Well, he certainly is, sugar,' Jon tipped his head towards the screen. 'I'm certainly going to be asking them along.'

Toni dragged her bags off the counter. 'Count me in.'

The bell chimed as she let herself out of the shop.

Toni called into the office to clear up any loose ends before her trip. The door was locked and Toni felt a faint thud of disappointment. Everything seemed to be in order, Josh wasn't avoiding work, just her it seemed. She returned a few phone calls and informed Layla Crossley that she was heading for Arizona in the morning.

Josh's desk was neat and tidy; she perched on it and flicked through his diary. He was pretty tied up for a short while with his divorce case. Toni sighed; the people in this town had more money than sense. Still, it was her living. She pushed herself away from the desk. She could have made a killing as a lawyer too, but it wouldn't have been half so much fun. Toni scribbled a note for Josh. The office felt empty without him, and she didn't want to be here alone. She headed home for a good night's sleep.

10

Toni had her Corvette packed early. She had her shades on, her music up loud and she was feeling good. She had certainly covered some miles in her trusty old Corvette but she didn't mind being on the road. Maybe Josh was right; perhaps she would never settle and it was unfair to drag him around with her. It was just that somehow she had assumed that he would always want to. For fuck's sake! She really was starting to sound like a whiney brat. She overtook a truck in temper. Interstate 10 was a lonely stretch of highway and she wasn't going to stop until she got to Arizona. She nearly made it, too, except her old faithful decided that she really had done enough for one week and broke down on a deserted expanse of highway. There wasn't even the spectacular scenery of the Colorado plateau to look at, just miles of scrub and sand. Toni sat at the wheel of the silent car, dumbstruck. If only she'd ever taken car mechanics in night class she may have learned something about what went on under the bonnet of an automobile, but as it was...

A hysterical bubble of laughter caught in her throat. Josh would have a field day if he could see her stranded right now. She had her cell phone and insurance but how long would it take for a recovery vehicle to come? Toni tapped her fingers furiously on the steering wheel and told herself that she'd have to be stoical about it and maybe soak up some rays while she waited.

The road in either direction danced in the heat. Toni

took a slug from her bottle of water and tamped down her frustration. She'd look like a tortoise in no time if she spent too long stranded in this sun, and the silence was eerie. Snippets of disaster documentaries flooded her brain. She lit a cigarette and puffed on it angrily; it tasted foul and metallic. One thing was for sure, she'd burn all four tyres and scatter her clothes as an SOS before she'd ring Josh and ask for help. She hated it when other people were right. And if the bastard really cared about her as much as he said he did then he'd never have let her come on her own.

She was in danger of feeling really sorry for herself when she spotted a Highway Patrol car heading her way. She took a deep breath and smoothed down her skirt. Toni was always glad to see a man in uniform but today it was more than a fetish – it was love.

The car pulled up in a cloud of dust. Toni leant back on the bonnet and squinted at the driver as he approached. He was big and bulky and hooked his thumbs into his belt as he walked. His partner remained in the passenger seat.

'Good day, ma'am. Is everything OK here?'

Toni admired her reflection in his mirrored shades. 'I'm glad you stopped to ask, officer. My car's broken down and I'm stranded.'

The officer looked her Corvette over as if the cause of the breakdown would suddenly become apparent. The radio crackled in the patrol car.

'Where are you headed?'

'Smallville.'

'I know it. May I see your documents?'

The patrolman stepped back for her to retrieve her documents from the glove compartment. She handed him the papers and leant back on the car, so that her breasts jutted out, and examined his bulky torso crammed into his shirt. She wished she didn't like uniforms quite so much.

'Mind if I try it?'

Toni shrugged. 'Go ahead.' She moved just a fraction for the officer to lean into the car and turn the ignition. His hair was greying and cropped very short. His arm brushed her and sent goosebumps rippling along her skin.

'Flat as a pancake. Like us to get it sorted for you, ma'am?'

'That's very kind of you, officer.' She noticed the other patrolman getting out of the car. He watched them, shielding his eyes from the sun.

'I'll have to take a few insurance details.' He took a notebook out of his breast pocket and moved around the car, taking down the registration number. 'We'll have that fixed in no time. Where can we find you?'

'My address is in LA. Best you take my cell phone number.'

The patrolman removed his shades to read her card. He placed them on the bonnet of the car. As he leant behind her, Toni caught a whiff of musky aftershave. Toni gave him her best 'bring it on' smile. He gave her a cautious glance. His face had that lived-in look and deep laughter lines surrounded his eyes.

Toni's nostrils flared at his closeness. He didn't seem to be in any hurry to move on. Over his shoulder she could see his friend hovering nervously by the patrol car. She pushed her groin a fraction closer. His breath was heavy as he pretended to look over her documentation. She could smell the shaving soap he'd used that morning. His sleeves were rolled up and she admired the tough muscles on him, honed through work, not vanity.

'I bet you've seen and done it all, haven't you, officer?' she murmured.

He looked up. 'Not quite.'

'Ever fucked someone on the bonnet of your car while your partner watched?' What the hell, Toni thought, the worse that could happen would be that she'd be left stranded again. This opportunity was too good to miss.

He swallowed hard. 'I can't tell you how sweet that sounds, lady.' He glanced over his shoulder. 'But I don't know if I can trust the new boy.'

Toni's sex was throbbing uncontrollably. It seemed forever since she'd seen Matt and John and she suddenly realised how much she had been missing them. The patrolman was rooted to the spot. Time for her to take charge, she guessed. Toni signalled for his partner to come over. He was tall and blue eyed, and screamed rookie from every pore. Toni's sex fluttered hungrily.

'I've got a proposition for you. I want the officer here to fuck me but he doesn't know if he can trust you. What do you say? Is there anything you've always been too afraid to ask for? Think of it as a bonding exercise.' She started to unbutton her blouse slowly and the older patrolman shuffled his boots in the dust, waiting for his partner's reply.

'Well, ma'am, being as you asked –' he cleared his throat and stared at her cleavage '– I've always wanted to watch a lady urinate.'

The older patrolman muffled a shocked curse and stepped back, looking at his partner curiously.

The younger one looked scared, 'Well, she did ask.'

'So I did.' Toni licked her lips. 'Which one is first?'

'Me.' The older patrolman spoke decisively.

'Come on then, let's go behind the car.'

Toni moved around the car and opened the passenger door. There was shade here and they were glad of it. She sat on the passenger seat and signalled for the patrolman to kneel down. He looked around and cleared his throat before kneeling in the dust.

'Don't worry, officer,' Toni murmured, 'there's no one around for miles. It's only the three of us.'

The patrolman reached for her and brought his mouth down on hers. His tongue felt hard and warm in her mouth. They kissed, long and wet, before the patrolman dropped his mouth to her neck, licking and nibbling. Toni unbuttoned his shirt and pushed it aside to feel his muscular, hairy chest. She watched the rookie over his shoulder and the fact that he was there, watching, made her burn even more.

The patrolman in front of her was undoing her blouse. Toni chewed her lip in anticipation. Unhooking her bra, he exposed her breasts and enclosed them both in his big square hands, pushing them up so that Toni's nipples dug into his calloused palms. He stooped to suck each nipple in turn and Toni heard the rookie gasp. Toni's back arched in pleasure. It was awkward in the confines of the car. She was half in, half out, and the patrolman was kneeling uncomfortably on the ground, but neither cared.

It was hot and awkward and sexy.

He was reaching underneath her for her panties now. Toni shifted to allow his big hands to pull them down.

'I don't know your name,' she said.

'It's Stan,' he muttered, slipping her panties down to her ankles.

'And I'm Nick,' the rookie added eagerly.

Toni suppressed a laugh. He was so sweet.

Toni spread her legs and the patrolman bent his head to taste between her thighs. Shivers ran through her entire body as his tongue flicked tentatively. She pushed herself down on to his face and moaned as his tongue delved deeper. She couldn't wait any longer; she wanted it short, sharp and sweet.

'Come on, then, Stan.' She pushed his head away. 'Let's fuck.'

She watched Stan undo his belt; it hit the earth with a soft thud. He gazed between her spread thighs as he undid his zipper and released his cock. Toni reached out and stroked it, slowly, with one finger.

'Got a condom, Nick?' she asked. The rookie handed one over with a shaking hand.

She ripped it open with her teeth and rolled it down carefully. The patrolman's broad chest was heaving; droplets of perspiration sparkled on the greying hair. She ran her hand down to cup his balls just for good measure; they were full and heavy.

'Come on, then, baby.'

He didn't need to be asked twice. Toni slid down lower, pushing her legs further out through the door and Stan slipped in. She was moist and ready. Stan's strong hands were on her waist as he ground himself into her. She caught a fleeting glimpse of Nick's excited face before her head fell back. She was on the edge already. Toni felt for her clit and rubbed it. Stan's hands were gripping her tightly; he was panting hard, pushing himself higher. It was good. So good. Her tits danced as he ground into her, over and over. Stan called out and rammed in with one last push and Toni exploded around him.

Her elbows were killing her and she was covered in a fine sheen of perspiration but the patrolman had successfully doused the fire between her legs. She grinned down at him as he fumbled with the condom. Nick was hovering nearby, ready for his part of the deal.

Toni caught her breath. 'Still want to see me pee?'

He blushed and nodded.

Toni reached into the glove compartment and took out the bottle of water. She gulped at the cool liquid. Screwing in this heat was hard work. Stan was brushing sand off his trousers and buttoning himself back up. She wondered if he would watch too.

Nick was sweating with a fury. He was dabbing at his forehead with a handkerchief. Around them the desert lay silent in the searing heat. Toni pulled herself to her feet and, with her skirt still around her waist, crouched down low. Nick licked his dry lips. Toni spread her legs. The heat was pulsing off the sand. Nick was gaping at her pussy as he struggled to unzip his flies. His hand stroked along the length of his cock. Toni started to pee, sending jets of hot liquid spurting over the sand. Nick's hand flew up and down his prick, tugging himself off roughly as he watched Toni pissing hard on to the ground. Toni shuddered as she finished and Nick came, pulsing white jets on to the sand at his feet.

Toni stood and smoothed down her skirt. Stan was leaning against the bonnet of the car, arms folded. He had his shades covering his eyes once more.

'Well, there's no accounting for taste, boy.'

Toni buttoned up her blouse and grinned. 'Guess you can safely say you can trust him now.' She looked over at Nick, who was still admiring the dark tracks of her pee in the sand. 'You OK over there?'

He nodded. 'Awesome.'

Toni and her luggage were taken to a diner truck-stop, supposedly for her to meet up with her 'husband' (as if). As much as she had enjoyed the lift – being fussed over by two men in mirror shades and a radio crackling in the background was a definite thrill in her book – there was no way she wanted a police escort into Smallville, Arizona. Highway Patrol had kindly agreed to oversee the recovery of her Corvette and Toni was going to have to find a ride into the next town. She also had two new numbers logged into her cell phone.

She ordered a shake and sighed. She perched cross-legged at the counter and sipped on her drink, half aware of a trucker admiring her bare legs. The ancient air-conditioning just seemed to stir the desert heat inside the café and Toni could feel trickles of sweat between her breasts and under her arms. The waitress watched her suspiciously as she swabbed a greasy cloth over the Formica-topped tables.

The waitress poured the trucker another coffee, her mouth puckering like a chicken's backside, as he looked around her wide hips to try to grab another glance at Toni's thighs. Toni turned slowly on her stool to face the trucker, but directed her question to the waitress.

'Excuse me, honey, do you know if there's any work for dancers around here?' She batted her lashes innocently and slowly uncrossed and re-crossed her legs, affording the trucker a pretty good eyeful of pussy, if his eyesight was good enough. She smirked when he choked on a mouthful of coffee and she inched forward slightly, balancing precariously on her stool.

The waitress was unimpressed. 'No I don't. Can I get you something to eat or are you going to make that shake last all day?'

Toni baited her further. 'Only I heard there was a club around here called the Sphynx. A friend of a friend told me about it.' She deliberately ignored the trucker, although she knew full well that it was him and not the waitress who would have the low-down on the club.

'I have no idea what you're talking about, lady.' The waitress threw the trucker's dirty plates on to a tray and strutted out to the kitchen with it.

'Oh well.' Toni pushed her empty glass away and

climbed down from her stool. The trucker was beyond pretending not to ogle her now; his jaw hung slack as he watched Toni's body jiggle inside the new miniskirt and blouse which she had deliberately bought a size too small. Toni toyed with her purse, enjoying the attention. She was going to have some fun being a bimbo for a while.

Toni left a tip on the counter, despite the waitress's churlishness, and walked slowly towards the door, dragging her heavy suitcase. As she drew level with the trucker's booth she dropped her purse and the contents scattered over the grubby floor tiles. The trucker immediately leapt to his feet to assist but froze to a halt at the sight of Toni bending over in front of him to collect her make-up. Toni collected up loose change and lipsticks, knowing full well that the trucker was gawping freely at her ass under her short skirt. When she had finished, Toni straightened and smoothed her blouse over her breasts, blowing at her escaping hair.

'I guess it's just not my day today.' She looked up at the trucker who was pressing himself back against the table, his gut trembling with excitement. Toni swept her eyes up and down him – it was hard to tell whether he was aroused under his overhanging stomach but Toni bet he had a hard-on like a pool cue.

'I know where the club is, lady.' His voice shook. 'I could take you there.'

'Have you been there?'

The trucker's face turned puce. 'Only once.' He cleared his throat and bent forward conspiratorially. 'Do you know what type of dancing they do there?'

'The kind that pays the rent, I bet.'

'I was shocked.'

'Really?' Toni pulled a worried face. 'Only, I am pretty desperate.'

The trucker dropped his voice. 'I could take you there and if you don't like it, I could bring you back.'

'That's so sweet. But will I be taking you out of your way?'

'Oh no.' The trucker shook his head so fiercely his jowls shook.

'Well, that would be great. Thank you.'

The trucker stumbled after her.

The waitress returned from the kitchen to find the café empty. Through the flyblown window she spied the trucker lugging Toni's heavy suitcase across the dusty car park. Disgusted, she spat on Toni's tip, and then had to clean it off again because she was too short this month to be proud.

Toni was having trouble getting into the cab. The trucker was strong despite his flab and had easily thrown her suitcase into the cab – it was getting Toni up there which was the difficult bit. Or, rather, she was making it difficult. Torturing men whose normal sex life revolved around dirty magazines and their own right hand held a special little thrill for Toni. They were always so grateful and scared. She didn't want the trucker to know she was teasing him, it would scare him off, so Toni prayed that he was dense or too aroused to suss her out.

At first, the trucker tried being gentlemanly, afraid to touch her. He tried giving her a leg up but Toni pretended to miss her footing and ended up sliding down, giving him a face full of cleavage and a handful of moist pussy.

Toni pretended not to notice. 'It's no good. This skirt is too tight. Don't look; I'm going to have to jack it up if I'm going to get up there. No peeking.'

She knew only a saint or a homosexual wouldn't look at her ass wobbling as she climbed into the cab with her skirt around her waist. The trucker was sweating all over as she leant down to take her purse off him, her tits nearly spilling out of her bra. Toni grinned at her reflection in the visor mirror as the driver nearly broke his neck rushing around to clamber up into his seat.

The trucker stalled the engine three times trying to get the lorry out of the car park. Toni sat like a well-behaved schoolgirl, hands neatly folded in her lap until the truck was on the open road and throwing up dust as it headed east. The trucker's meaty hands were slippery on the gear shaft and Toni wondered whether she ought to leave him alone; she was probably putting both their lives in danger, prick-teasing the driver of a 20-tonne truck.

Her heel caught on the cover of a porn magazine, which had been pushed down into the footwell, and Toni imagined the driver jerking himself off during his breaks. She reached down to look at it, enjoying the driver's embarrassment as she turned the magazine around to examine the photos inside.

She turned in her seat and asked innocently, 'Do you think my titties are big enough to be a dancer?'

The driver swallowed and concentrated hard on the long straight road ahead, beads of sweat prickling his forehead. He nodded cautiously, flicking her a sideways glance.

'You don't, do you? I can tell. Have a look and tell me what you think.'

The driver clenched the wheel, his chubby knuckles turning white as Toni undid her blouse and front-fastening bra. She twisted in her seat until she was facing him, her tits bouncing gently with the movement of the cab. She knew they weren't huge but they were pert and men loved her enormous nipples. The driver was no exception.

'Fuck!' he exclaimed, desperate to ogle but forced to keep checking the road ahead.

Toni teased her nipples until they were erect. 'Do you think men will like looking at them?' She pretended to examine her boobs. This was even more fun than having him manacled; he was desperately trying to maintain a straight line at fifty miles per hour with a half-naked woman squirming in the passenger seat. He nodded, speechless.

'It's just that I've only ever been with my husband so I'm not sure if I've the type of body men like.' Toni bit her lip with mock shyness and pushed her skirt up around her waist. 'Will you take a look at my pussy and tell me what you think?' Toni's head came close to hitting the windscreen as the truck swerved violently. 'OK, I won't, I can see it's disturbing your driving.'

The driver managed to force himself to speak, croaking, 'It's not.'

'I'd be too embarrassed to show you if you weren't driving.' She didn't want him pulling over just yet.

The driver stuck out a pink tongue and licked his lips, flicking glances at Toni as she knelt up on the seat and pushed her panties down to her knees. She stroked her neatly trimmed pelt. 'Can you see it from there?' She knew he was having the greatest of difficulties watching the road and her bush; the best he could do was to snatch the odd tantalising glimpse. 'Do the women in your magazines have nice pussies?'

'Not like yours, lady.' He was nearly exploding with excitement, his face turning an unattractive shade of purple.

Toni stroked herself, his discomfort sending waves of arousal up her moist sex. 'Why not? Because this is real?'

The driver nodded.

'It's very warm, and wet.' Toni slipped a finger inside

herself and the driver's eyes widened in disbelief. 'Ooh, that feels good. Look.' Toni splayed her lips open so that her clit peeked out at him. 'I'm all excited now because you've been looking at me. Do you think other men will like looking at me?'

The driver nodded.

Toni held a finger under his nose. 'It smells like real cunt too, doesn't it?'

'Yes.'

'Tell me.' Toni slipped her finger over her swollen nub, back and forth, 'Tell me.'

The trucker was really struggling now, performing the incredible feat of keeping his truck on the road and trying to watch a half-naked woman, with her tits bouncing and her panties around her knees, fingering herself on the seat next to him.

He cleared his throat good and hard. 'You look good enough to eat, lady.'

'Do I?' Toni pressed a little harder.

'I ain't never seen a pussy as pretty as that one. That little strip of hair down the middle, all glossy like that.' He licked his lips and peeked over. 'And when you open up your pussy lips I can see you all pink and shiny and your clitty –' he swallowed hard '– I didn't know women's clitties got so big and puffy.'

Toni's fingers were slipping in and out of her now, slick with love juice. 'More,' she ordered. 'Tell me more.' She grasped the back of her seat with her left hand.

'I want to eat you all up. I want to suck on those cute titties and I want to lap up your creamy juices. I want you to sit on my face and ride me like a horse till I can't breath.'

'I bet you love it, don't you? I bet you could follow women round like an eager dog, sniffing up their skirts. I bet you could eat pussy for hours.' Toni could feel herself throbbing like crazy but she didn't want to bring herself off with her own fingers today. 'Pull over,' she ordered.

The windscreen was obliterated with flying dust as the truck swerved off the road. When it was safely parked the driver struggled out of his seatbelt, panting for her. Toni could smell his sweat, rank in the small cab; two huge stains were spreading out from under his arms.

'Have you got a bunk?' Toni had stopped fingering herself now and was slipping out of her panties.

He nodded mutely.

'Well, get on it then. I want you to eat me all up.'

The trucker squeezed himself between the seats and threw himself down on to the narrow bunk. Toni glanced around; the place was a clutter of empty take-away cartons and Coke cans. Like the driver it was repulsive and seedy, and Toni was as horny as hell. Grabbing hold of an overhead bar, she lowered herself on to the trucker's face. He stuck his tongue out greedily, lapping at her, and Toni ground herself onto him, not caring if he was suffocating. She was smothering him with her juices, pressing her clit against whichever part of his face was highest. She felt her climax uncurl as his tongue rode up deep inside her. She moaned as she rode his face, her nipples tight against his hot sweaty hands groping and squeezing her tits. She hung on to the bar above her head, thighs tense, gyrating like a rodeo rider determined not to be thrown.

The sound of him was gloriously disgusting, sucking and licking at her like a man possessed as her climax blossomed. Toni arched in ecstasy, her thighs quivering at the trucker's ears. His hot hands were on her ass now, holding her like a split melon as he gouged her out with his tongue.

Toni looked down at his face, smeared with her honey. 'Death by cunt, would you like that? Do you want me to suffocate you with my hot pussy?'

The trucker lapped at her more fervently and Toni felt sure that he would have happily died underneath her, smothered by her. His eagerness outweighed any lack of technique and Toni ground herself on him harder, her legs spread, rivers of pleasure flooding the banks of her pussy.

Sated, Toni sank into a corner of the cab, not wishing to touch his wobbling, sweating body. He lifted himself on to an elbow, his face slick with her juices, and looked sheepishly at his crotch. Around his flies was a large dark stain. Toni grinned in relief to know that she wouldn't have to go fishing for his cock now.

'Not to worry,' she said. 'At least we came together.' Toni stretched her long legs out along the bunk. 'Actually, I'm feeling pretty tired; it's been a busy couple of days. Do you mind if I doze here for a little while?' She did up one button on her blouse to hold it in place.

The trucker shook his head, eager to have her stay, and began a frantic clean-up. Toni didn't notice, and suddenly she was dog-tired. She'd had some pretty good sex these last few days and her body needed recharging. She laid her head back on some musty-smelling pillows and felt her eyelids droop.

The trucker gently placed a blanket over her and she murmured her thanks, tugging her skirt down to cover her naked backside.

'You're so beautiful. Can I watch you while you sleep?'

She felt the bunk sag as the trucker shifted his heavy bulk but she was too tired to answer. Eyes shut, she nodded slightly and let sleep pull her down.

* * *

She dreamt of her mother's Scandinavian painter standing bare foot on the porch back home. They had spent a few good years in a bleached wood cabin, poor but happy, before being forced to move into the city. They were the golden days.

He was dressed in just some paint-splattered jeans and his chest was bare. Tall and sinewy, his pale skin had tanned to a light golden brown. He was rolling up a cigarette as Toni's dream self strolled up towards the house, his pink tongue flicking out as he licked the paper. He raised a hand to shield his eyes from the sun and squinted. Toni shouted hi. She felt good; the stone lane was hot under her flimsy sandals, and her breasts jiggled beneath her thin cotton dress.

She waved from the rusty gate and the painter smiled, his blue eyes dancing with pleasure. Josh's eyes, and Josh's wide toothy grin. He dropped the cigarette in among the clutter of his brushes and paints and came towards her.

'All grown up now.' His accent was gentle, his words like falling blossom. The sound of it after all these years sent shivers up Toni's spine. 'No pigtails any more, huh?' He picked up a strand of her hair with a paint-stained finger and studied it. 'It's good to see you.'

Toni smiled serenely up at him. 'I want you to paint me.'

'Of course. Come.'

He took her hand and moved towards the house but Toni shook her head; she didn't want to go in there.

'Out here, in the sun.' The porch was a jumble, the same as when she was a child, a collection of painted pebbles, rusting bikes and thirsty plants hanging in macramé holders. Toni saw the old swing seat was still there – her favourite place to sit. 'There –' she pointed '– paint me there.'

The painter moved his easel and his canvas around to face the seat and looked for clean brushes. Toni slipped off her sandals and watched him; the worn wood of the porch was smooth beneath her feet. A breeze lifted and tugged at the hem of her dress, sending shivers over her flesh. She watched him in wonder; she had forgotten how golden, how beautiful, he was. Little wonder her mother had wanted his baby. His chest was smooth and hairless, his nipples small round pellets. On his flat stomach, a thin line of hair ran from his belly button down into his jeans – the front of which was bulging, Toni noticed. She bet he had a wonderful cock.

Without thinking, Toni slipped her thin dress down over her shoulders, letting it pool at her feet. The sea breeze ruffled her pubic hair. He was ready to paint her; his eyes followed her to the swing seat where she settled, supine, on the worn cotton cushions.

He dipped his brush into clean water and wet the canvas, his eyes studying her erect nipples and her relaxed limbs. She guessed he was used to nudes and this didn't shock him. Toni dropped a foot on to the floor and used it to rock the seat gently. She tipped her face up to the warmth of the sunshine and purred like a cat.

'Can you lift your other leg slightly, Toni?' the painter asked. 'You have such lovely dark hair, like a small puff of smoke between your legs. I would like to see it better.'

Toni obliged, her skin glowing with warmth, the gentle rocking soothing her almost to sleep. She lifted her other leg and hooked her ankle over the back of the seat.

'That's perfect; I can see you properly now, opened like a flower to the sun.' His words dropped tiny pricks of fire over her skin and she felt her sex lips open for him, unfurling like petals under the heat of his gaze.

His brush flew over the canvas. 'Such a sweet pussy, like an orchid, your lips are so pink and moist beneath your glossy fuzz.'

Toni tipped her head right back, aroused and drowsy, and closed her eyes.

'Can I touch you between the legs with my brush? I would like to mix your juices with my paint, it would be incredibly erotic for the painting –' he paused '– and for me.'

Toni nodded, her nipples puckering hard in anticipation. He padded across the porch towards her and knelt at her feet, his canvas on the floor beside him. Toni stopped herself from pushing her hips forwards. She wanted to appear relaxed when instead her sex was heavy with honey, dripping with lust for the touch of his brush.

'Touch me,' she whispered, letting her knees loll further apart. 'Touch me.'

He dipped his paintbrush lightly inside her so it was thick with her juices, and Toni whimpered with disappointment when he withdrew it. He painted it on to the canvas and returned for more, time and again, as she murmured in pleasure. The brush was gentle, tracing featherlight touches over the insides of her spread thighs and up to her open flower. Honey was pouring from her, and he was using it to cover his painting, working his brush over the insides of her sex lips and up inside her florid seam.

Toni moaned and writhed; the brush was too thin, too gentle. She reached down for the painter's hand; she wanted his fingers inside her. Toni's eyes flew open, her heart beating furiously when she realised that it was the trucker's finger inside her. Her legs were thrown wide, her skirt around her waist once more, her breasts escaping from her undone blouse, and the trucker was kneeling between her legs, dribbling with lust as he traced her moist quim with a forefinger – in and out of her growing warmth, his eyes fixed on her spread beaver, open wide for his full attention.

His finger stopped as he spotted her horrified glare. 'You said to touch you,' he stammered, fear creeping into his eyes.

Toni lay still, looking at the sweaty, jowly trucker looking over her. She had been dreaming of a beautiful golden painter and woke up to this. Nevertheless, Toni couldn't deny the heavy throb between her legs. There was no way she could continue on her journey without satisfying the craving there. She was weeping to be filled; the perfume of her arousal hung in the air around them as heavy and cloying as scented lily. She reached down for his thick, sweaty fingers and guided them up inside her hole, knowing herself to be a dirty, horny whore to allow herself to become so aroused that she didn't care who satisfied her as long as someone did.

She tipped her head back and shut the trucker out; her dream was ebbing away, she was losing the image of her lovely painter but the ache in her sex was still there. She pushed herself down on to the trucker's fingers, gasping for more. He hesitated and Toni grabbed his hand, pushing more of his fingers inside her. She used them to frig herself hard, plunging in and out of her wetness.

'I'm going to fuck you.' The trucker whipped his hand away and grappled eagerly with the zipper of his jeans. Toni looked on, horrified, visions of Al and the blonde leering up to mock her. 'No,' she forced the word out, but it died in her throat. She watched aghast at the trucker's wobbling chest and gut as he struggled to free his dick.

'Oh yes, I am. I'm going to fuck you, lady, and don't try telling me you don't want fucking, laying there with yourself spilt wide open.'

Toni mewled in horror and the trucker looked down at her, his fat face pink with excitement. 'I may not be the best-looking guy in the world ...'

Toni whimpered at the understatement.

'But I've never forced myself on anyone.' He paused with his hand on his zipper. 'If you don't want me, lady, you can get up and go now.'

Toni looked up at him. He meant it; he may not be the brightest or most handsome guy, but he was an honest one. A pulse throbbed painfully in Toni's head. She was so used to being in charge, how the hell did she manage to get herself into this situation?

'I think you're the most incredible lady I've ever met. You've got a fantastic body.' He dipped a finger back inside her and Toni yelped with pleasure. 'And the sweetest pussy ever. You'll make a fantastic dancer and I'll be proud to come and watch you.'

Toni groaned as his fingers sneaked back inside her. With his other hand he stroked the vulnerable skin on the inside of her thigh and worked his way up to her clit, rolling it with his finger like a ball of chewing gum. 'You don't want to be shy about showing off this body, baby.'

Toni moaned in frustration and bit her lip. He was giving her a pep talk for chrissakes! As if she needed approval off a big smelly hog like him. She wanted to laugh at the irony of the situation. A loser of a truck driver was tormenting her, Toni Marconi, the bitch who had chained up Inspector John Bradley and fucked him into submission. He was delving around inside her like a demented gynaecologist. However, she had to admit that he was driving her wild.

'Now, lady, do you want me to fuck you or not?' He withdrew and made for his zipper again. Her pussy felt empty and cold.

Toni nodded, her disbelief pushing her beyond words.

'Tell Uncle Pete the truth now, baby, you can say it, come on.' He looked kindly down at her as if she were a terrified virgin.

Toni's voice shook; she was finding the reversal of roles perversely arousing. 'I want you to fuck me.'

'Are you sure now? Uncle Pete will do it nice and gentle.' His cock sprang out between them and Toni looked at it in relief. She had been expecting a horrid white specimen but it was thick and solid, ready for action. 'Open up now, baby, and let me in.' The trucker was about to talk her through the entire thing. He prodded ineffectually at her hole, bracing himself for entry.

Toni ground her teeth in frustration. 'Listen, you fat prick,' she spat up at him, 'I want you to fuck me good and hard! Is that good enough for you?'

The trucker gaped in astonishment, but to his credit didn't lose his erection.

'Now!' Toni barked, and the trucker did as he was told, jamming his stiff prick into her. Toni sighed with pleasure as she felt her muscles opening around his thick shaft. The trucker's face contorted in pleasure and he froze for a moment, savouring the sensation. Toni was beyond niceties. She wanted shafting – now. She pushed against him, tipping her pelvis for deeper entry. He slammed into her, his fat wobbling with his exertions. Toni lifted her knees and then her ankles, throwing them over his shoulders so he could pump way up inside her.

'Fuck me!' she commanded, clasping his rank bedding and arching in pleasure. She came in huge spasms, gasping and screaming, clawing the sheets into a huge pile, and pressing her clit tight against him as her orgasm engulfed her.

Such text as they unwittingly dispose of anyway and the design around to their sundry that seem somehow shadows. from over everyone's of an and they think the wouldn't reptile with go it have needed remaining that angery way before now two in wall.

11

Up to her neck in bubbles, Toni soaked the dust of the road and the truck driver's sweat away. The deep bath was bliss and she smiled to herself; it had taken all her powers of persuasion to convince Uncle Pete that, no, she really didn't want to marry him. Poor deluded guy. If she'd had a bit more time she could have really indulged in a bit of power play with him; she was sure he would have loved it.

She stretched out a leg, checking for stubble. Tomorrow was her big day and she didn't want to blow it. Toni turned the tap for more hot water and the ancient plumbing creaked and groaned. She had been forced to book into a crumby motel; she needed to appear down on her luck. It really went against the grain, probably because it hadn't been that long ago since she really had been. She and Josh had spent a long time drifting before they hit LA. They'd done their share of shitty jobs in little towns to raise the money to move on to the next place.

Still, she didn't have that problem now. Her bath oil had cost three times as much as her room for the night and that was because she and Josh worked well together. He would have to understand that she was here on business, pure and simple. Toni braced herself for the thin scratchy towel the motel provided, and checked her cell phone. No calls – he could be infuriatingly stubborn at times. Well, she wasn't chasing him tonight. She wanted to check out the town and get something to eat; she was ravenous.

She chose a little pink skirt and white cut-away T-shirt. She slipped a pair of strappy high heels on to her feet. She needed to find the exact location of this club and didn't want anyone thinking she was a police-woman. The evening was balmy and warm and Toni made her way to Main Street. It wasn't a bad little town and was clearly used to tourists. There were lots of shops with a line in souvenirs and a couple of bars. Toni chose the seediest-looking one, where the locals obvi-ously drank, and ordered a beer. She struck gold: the bartender was young and male and his eyes lit up when he saw Toni enter. She didn't take it as a huge compli-ment, however – the fact that she was female, under fifty and not carrying a paunch probably put her leagues ahead of his usual customers. She wanted information, and the local bartender was a good place to start. The bar was pretty quiet and most of the men were watch-ing a baseball game on the television. There was a crowd of youngsters playing pool at the other end of the bar.

She climbed up on to a bar stool and gave him an eyeful of cleavage. His Adam's apple bobbed convul-sively as he asked her tits what they would like to drink. Toni resisted the urge to laugh as she ordered her beer. He looked very young to be serving alcohol; she bet it had taken him ages to grow his goatee. She sipped her drink and waited for him to speak first, but nerves had obviously got the better of him and he had polished almost every glass on the long shelf behind him before Toni decided that she would have to put him out of his misery. She caught his eye in the mirror behind the bar and beckoned him over with an index finger.

'Same again, ma'am?'

Toni's heart tripped; he looked so cute with his dark hair all ruffled, like he'd just got out of bed. His lips were set in a permanent sulk and were extremely kissable. She reached out and tipped his chin up with her finger so he was forced to look her in the eye. He looked terrified.

'Yes please and I need some help.'

'S-sure thing.'

She leant towards him. 'I'm looking for a club called the Sphynx. Do you know it?'

The bartender looked nervously around the room, as if he half expected his mother to be listening in. His lips pouted and he shrugged his shoulders.

Toni persevered, 'Only I'm hoping to get a job there.'

He slopped her beer on the counter and mopped at it with a cloth. 'Dancing?'

'Actually, I was hoping they needed an accountant.'

'Oh.'

'Yes, dancing.'

He blushed and Toni bit her lip; he was so sweet. 'Well?'

'It's the next town over. This is Verdeville. You need to head out on the old reservation road and it's probably half a day's drive.'

'Thanks, you've been really helpful.' Toni slipped a couple of bills on to the bar and slid off her stool. She watched the bartender's face fall.

'It's a pretty rough place, you know. Be careful.'

'I will, thanks.'

'Have you got a car? Do you need a lift?'

Actually she did. 'I'll be OK. Can you recommend somewhere to eat?'

'Sam's Grill does the best ribs in town. I'd take you there but I don't get off until twelve.'

Toni paused at the door and smiled at him over her shoulder. 'That's a shame because I'm ravenous now.' She gave him a cutesy little wave. 'Bye now.'

The night air was still warm and the sun was beginning to do down behind the distant hills. An old man watched her from a shop doorway and she felt a ripple of loneliness run through her. The bartender had reminded her of Matt, and it would have been nice to have some young hard flesh to press up against tonight. She felt a long way from familiar territory. Toni hugged herself as she examined the darkening sky over the edge of the town; for the first time she really considered the expanse of the desert and how far she was from a friendly face.

She stood on the narrow sidewalk and dug a cigarette out of her purse. She felt vulnerable in her thin top and short skirt; the cotton barely grazed her buttocks. The desert air blew in an ancient mystery with it, and Toni embraced it. Where was Caron Crossley? Buried out in the desert somewhere? Or was she living as someone else now? Toni knew that millions of people did that all the time.

The smell of garlic and charcoal wafted by from the nearby restaurant but Toni was lost in thought. What were her real chances of finding the missing girl? Undercover as a dancer they were far better than just flashing a photograph about and asking a few questions, but she had to admit to herself that it held a certain thrill as well. Josh was right of course – working as a stripper and getting hooked up with a biker chapter was living as close to the edge as you could get without really going over; and Toni's blood raced at the thought of it. She thought of the photo of Red. There wasn't much vulnerability about him, but a tough, brooding sexiness that had attracted Caron and turned Toni's nipples hard at the thought of him. Toni's stomach growled; she had to eat before she could indulge in any more sex.

12

Toni woke early. She had a long day ahead of her and had arranged for a hire car to be left outside the motel. She needed her own transport for the rest of her investigation; you never knew when you might have to leave a place quickly and quietly. And while she loved taking a risk, she had no intention of leaving herself stranded and vulnerable.

Toni picked up a few provisions in the local supermarket. She had decided to breakfast behind the wheel and make some headway before the harsh desert sun was up. The girl behind the till yawned widely, obviously not relishing her early start. Toni watched her from behind her dark glasses as she packed her grocery bag at a snail's pace and marvelled at how boring some people allowed their lives to be.

Before she left the town, Toni called into the giftshop where she had seen the old man the night before. Luckily it was already open. The bell over the door tinkled as she let herself in. She chose two soft leather Stetsons, one for her and one for Josh, and some beautiful pieces of hand-crafted silver and turquoise jewellery. You were never too far out in the sticks to shop. For good measure she threw in a leather belt with a chunky silver buckle but drew the line at cowboy boots. Paid for, she said goodbye to the silent old man and stepped outside to put on her new things. She grinned at herself in the shop window from beneath her new hat and threaded her belt through the loops in her denim shorts.

The buckle hung heavy just above her crotch and she liked the sensation. She slipped the bracelets on to her wrists and the silver shone brilliantly against her tanned skin. She was reminded of her mother's slender wrists, always jangling with colourful bangles. She quickly suppressed the thought and jumped into the car.

She kicked off her shoes so she could drive barefoot, and she opened the packet of bagels and the carton of orange juice on the seat beside her. Satisfied that she could now drive and pig out in peace, Toni left the town at high speed and headed for the desert.

The drive was peaceful. She was a tiny insect in the vast red desert, and a long way from LA. She missed Josh and wished he was here to look daft in the other hat, but still, she wasn't gone forever. There was no one on the road for a good many miles until she spotted a convoy of silver cigar-case trailers, which she guessed had probably been parked up for the night. A line of washing flapped from the door of one and Toni tooted her horn as she past by.

Toni found herself a room in a rundown motel on the edge of the town. She wrinkled her nose at the austere surroundings and decided to spoil herself in the shower with her most expensive soap, followed by an exquisite body oil. She sat on the edge of the little hard bed and massaged the oil into her aching calf muscles. Her instincts were sending frissons of excitement up and down her back, telling her that she had found the right town at last. On her way in she had noticed it was bigger and busier. There were casinos and bars but she hadn't noticed the Sphynx; that would be her next mission.

The town was buzzing, even this early in the day. The streets were crowded with tourists and gamblers and

Toni took a little backstreet until she found a sleazy-looking bar. These were always the best places for information and gossip. Toni was suitably disgusted; even by backstreet LA standards this was cheap. A middle-aged woman turned heavily kohled eyes towards her and narrowed them suspiciously as Toni entered. Her midriff rolled over the waistband of a satin miniskirt, the hem of which was unravelling. She turned back to her drink and sipped it carefully, as if trying to pretend that this wasn't her fifth of the day.

Toni smiled and lowered herself on to a rather greasy-looking stool. The woman ignored her. Finally, a man emerged through the plastic strip curtain at the back of the bar. His beady eyes lit up above a pockmarked face.

'What can I get the lady?' He flashed a gold tooth at her. His question, Toni knew, was an insult to the lush sitting next to her, probably his girlfriend, and Toni hated them both instantly. She could guess at the type of sordid relationship they had.

'Just a soda, please.'

He looked disappointed, hoping for a secret drinker, and placed a tall glass in front of her. Toni refrained from drinking from it – if he had polished it with the stinking cloth he had hanging from his waistband then it wasn't going anywhere near her lips.

'How can I help you then, lady? You clearly don't want to drink.' He removed a cocktail stick from an opened jar of lemon slices and began to pick his teeth.

'I'm looking for a bar called the Sphynx.'

That stopped him in his tracks; his glance flicked to the girlfriend and back to Toni.

His toothpick swapped sides and back again. He grinned again, and pointed a finger.

'Journalist, right?'

Toni forced a smile, though her flesh was creeping.

'I'll tell you everything you need to know about the place . . . for a price.'

Toni shrugged. 'No problem.'

'Do we have a deal?' He leant on the bar.

'Tell me the price first.'

'Threesome. You, me, her.'

Toni laughed in his face. 'Drop dead, mister.' She grabbed her bag, dropped from the stool and stalked from the bar. She liked a thrill but not one that cheap. She had taken three strides down the dusty backstreet when she felt a tug at her handbag from behind. Toni turned, her heartbeat going into overdrive. The barman had followed her. He stood in front of her now, his dark eyes burning with anger at her refusal.

Toni backed away. 'Get lost, mister. I'm not interested.'

He grabbed her and pushed her against a wall. 'Who the fuck do you think you are, lady, walking into my bar like you own the fuckin' world and then insulting me and my wife?'

Toni laughed; he was as offended as if she had used the wrong protocol, or not used some social nicety. Her laughter sent him into a rage. He slapped her face so hard that her ears rang and then he started to drag her back to the bar. But Toni didn't work as a private investigator without some self-defence training at her disposal. Fighting the panic that had began to bubble in her throat, she forced herself to roar and, at the same time, brought the heel of her shoe down hard on his shin. He yelped and lost his grip on her. Toni should have ran but he had really pissed her off. She braced herself and punched him hard in the face. She aimed for his nose and felt his cartilage shatter under her fist. His wife had come running out of the bar and started screaming at the sight of his blood.

Toni was breathing hard. 'I said no and I meant no, you greasy shit,' she gasped.

The barman lunged for her again but was caught from behind by a tall black man.

'What's going on? ' He looked at Toni's torn clothes and she knew that he had guessed the situation.

'Just a lover's tiff. Butt out.'

'I don't think so.' The black man dragged the barman by the scruff of the neck back inside the bar.

Toni watched, shaking with anger and relief, as he was forced backwards over his own counter. His wife had stopped screaming and watched in horrified silence as the black man drew a gun and jabbed the barrel into the other man's neck. 'Time to apologise to the lady.'

The barman was dragged back out and garbled an apology. Toni nodded her acceptance, eager to leave all this behind her. Her protector was putting his gun away. 'Any more shit like that and I'll be sending the Cobras round to sort you out.' He brushed dust off his immaculately ironed shirt. 'In fact, I think I might ask them to call in anyway. They could teach you a lot about how to treat a lady.' He turned to Toni. 'Let's get out of this dump.'

When they were back on the main drag, Toni looked up and held her hand out. 'Thank you so much.' she winced as a pain shot up her neck. The bastard must have hit her harder than she realised.

'You're welcome.' The man's voice was deep and calm. 'I'm not sure you needed it though. You looked as if you could take care of yourself.'

'I certainly gave it a try. But thanks, really. So many people would have just walked by.'

'Not this person. I often get accused of exploitation, but I know how to treat women. There's no need for that kind of behaviour. I would have had a bullet in him if that floozy hadn't been shrieking her head off.'

'I'm glad you didn't. I've only been in town a few hours. I would have hated to have witnessed that.'

'Why are you in town?'

'It's a long story but I'm looking for work. I'm a dancer.'

He grinned a wide brilliant smile. 'Well you just hit the jackpot, lady, because I own the classiest nightspot for miles. Come back to the club with me and I'll get the girls to clean you up and then we can talk business. What do you say?'

Toni's head ached, she had had enough trouble for one day. He sensed her hesitation and took a card from his jacket pocket, which he handed to her. On it she read:

The Sphynx Niteclub
Top Class Dancing
Proprietor Onyx Kane

Bingo.

'If you're sure, Mr Kane. That would be very kind.'

'All my girls call me Onyx and I'm always glad of a new girl who can take care of herself.' He held his arm out for Toni to take and she smiled.

13

Onyx took her to his apartment at the back of the club. It was spacious and cool with white tiled floors and lush pot plants. Large patio doors opened on to a swimming pool. The only sign that this wasn't a total fantasy was a high security fence, which ensured that that drinkers in the club couldn't wander in.

Everywhere she looked there were women wandering about in bikinis; swimming in the pool, sunbathing or lounging on the enormous zebra-striped sofa while watching MTV. Toni felt as if she had wandered back into the seventies.

'Could I use the bathroom?'

'Of course. Get yourself cleaned up in the hot tub. I'll send Coral in to give you a massage and then we can do an audition, OK?' Phones were ringing urgently in a nearby office and Onyx excused himself to go and answer them.

Toni found a sauna and several bedrooms before she found the bathroom. It was all marble with a king-size tub and glass shelves stacked with fresh towels. She shut the door behind her and examined herself in the mirror. She looked awful; her face was swollen, her hair mussed and her mascara smudged. Even though she couldn't have staged a meeting with the owner of the club any better than it had actually happened, Toni felt tears welling up. Delayed shock from the attack hit her and her knees began to tremble; she fumbled for the toilet and sat on the lid, fighting nausea.

Someone knocked at the door and Toni stared at it dumbly. Eventually, it opened a little and a girl with cropped dark hair peeked in.

'Toni?'

Toni sniffed and nodded. 'Coral?'

The girl rolled her eyes. 'No, I'm Edie. Coral is having one of her legendary tantrums. You'll find out all about those, if you stay. Can I come in?'

'Sure.'

Edie knelt in front of her and took her hands gently. 'You look as if you've taken a whack.'

Toni looked into the girl's unusual green eyes, so full with concern, and promptly burst into tears.

Toni never cried. Sex was her release. She was always in control, of her job, her men, but as Edie held her and gently stoked her back, Toni sobbed uncontrollably. The girl held her until she was finished and then gently drew back to find her a tissue, which Toni accepted gratefully. Perched on the toilet she blew her nose loudly and felt like a schoolgirl hiding in the john.

Edie stroked Toni's hair away from her face. 'Better?'

'Much. Thanks.' Toni gave a wry laugh. 'I bet I look gorgeous.'

Edie looked at her kindly. 'You look just fine. I'll run a bath and we'll soon have you fighting fit again.'

Toni watched Edie moving around the bathroom, collecting towels and switching on the taps. She wore a tiny pair of shorts and halter-top. She didn't look like a dancer; she was too boyish. She was tall and slender with small neat breasts. As she reached up for a jar of bath oil her top rode up, revealing the underside of each small breast. Toni's clit twitched.

'Let me help you out of those torn clothes.'

Toni rose to her feet. She felt sweaty and grimy. They were equally matched for height and Edie's touch was firm yet gentle. Toni felt unusually compliant, allowing Edie to undress her bit by bit. She watched as the girl undid her blouse and slipped it over her shoulders. Toni was aware that her touch was extremely sensual. She was alarmed; she had never been aroused by another woman before. Actually, that was a lie. Sid always sent her pulse racing but Toni denied it. She felt drugged by Edie's gentleness and stepped out of her skirt. She turned for her to unclasp her bra and slipped her panties off so that she was standing naked in front of her.

'You are beautiful. Onyx will go wild for you.'

Toni's nipples grew hard under her gaze but Edie didn't notice. She bent to unclasp each shoe and Toni marvelled at her beautifully shaped head. Her short hair grew into a small swirl on the nape of her neck.

'Step in. You'll feel like a different woman afterwards.'

Toni stepped down into the swirling fragrant waters and tried to relax. The jets of water soothed her aching muscles and she washed her face. She opened her legs so that the water bubbled over her quim and felt a sharp desire there for Edie. The thought terrified her. Toni had never had a woman. The water soon restored her and she watched Edie pad about the bathroom on bare feet. Toe rings shone on most of her toes.

'OK? Better?' Edie held out an enormous white towel. 'Come on, and I'll give you a massage.'

Toni stepped out of the tub and let Edie dry her like a child.

'You're very kind.'

'It's nothing. We all need a little TLC now and then. Be warned, not all the girls are so friendly. There's quite a bit of competition going on.'

Toni stared at her competent hands drying her all over, goose bumps raging over her flesh.

'Have you worked in many clubs?'

'A few. I'm looking for a fresh start.'

Edie raised one thin, dark eyebrow. 'Amen to that.' She dried Toni's calves and Toni's clit tingled at the close proximity of the girls face. 'You'll be OK here. There's no drugs or pimping. We dance, get paid, hang out here. It's a good life. There. Jump on the table and I'll oil you up. Have you got your costume?'

Toni lay face down on the table. 'They're all back at the motel.'

'No worries. You can fetch them later. Onyx will just want to see if you've got a good body and if you can dance.'

'OK.' Toni murmured. Her mind was nowhere near Onyx; all she could concentrate on was Edie's hands pushing her flesh in long slow sweeps. She kneaded her shoulders and Toni could feel her muscles relax beneath her touch. Edie worked her back muscles slowly, easing Toni's flesh with strong tanned fingers. She moved to her buttocks and Toni suppressed a moan, fighting the urge to push herself up against the girl's hands. Edie kneaded her buttocks and slipped her oily fingers in between her legs to massage the flesh at the top of each thigh. Toni inched her thighs wider, willing Edie to slip her fingers inside her hot crevasse, to oil her inside where she was burning with lust.

'OK, flip over and I'll do your front.'

If Toni had been a man she would never have hidden her arousal and she was grateful for the scent of the warm oil to disguise the muskiness of her desire. She watched Edie, fascinated by the play of the muscles in her slender arms as she bent over Toni to massage oil over her skin. Her small breasts just scraped Toni's stomach and Toni bit her lip, pressing her thighs together to dampen the throb. Edie had moved to her feet now, lifting her left leg gently and pressing her thumbs into the sole of Toni's foot.

A moan escaped Toni's lips involuntarily.

Edie smiled. 'Feels good, doesn't it?'

Toni nodded, desire forming a big lump in her throat. Edie put her foot down gently on the table and lifted the other one.

'You've got lovely feet. I'll lend you some toe rings if you like.'

Toni cleared her throat. 'Thanks.'

'OK, all done. You should feel like a different person now.' Edie helped her to her feet.

'God, I feel great.' Toni moved her head back and fore. 'That was brilliant, thanks.' She was perched, naked, on the edge of the table.

'No problem.' Edie didn't move and for the first time Toni wondered if there had been more to the massage for Edie too. Her green eyes watched Toni and she licked her full lips. 'Would you like me to brush your hair?'

Toni nodded, realising finally that Edie was prolonging the physical contact. It sent a rush of adrenaline pumping through her but still she held back. She was more courteous with this girl than she'd ever been with a man. She didn't want Edie to think she was brash or grabbing. Edie found a hairbrush and moved behind Toni to brush her hair. She was very gentle and Toni's scalp tingled as Edie brought the brush down in long soft sweeps. She tipped her head back and closed her eyes, totally entranced by the girl's attentions.

'You have beautiful thick hair.' Edie was running her fingers through it now. Toni opened her eyes and saw that Edie was watching her in the full-length mirror. Toni's heartbeat quickened, her eyes locked with Edie's and Edie tipped her head slightly to one side, as if asking a question. Toni opened her legs slightly and Edie read the signal. She moved up close behind Toni and traced her shoulders with her fingertips before moving her fingers down Toni's arms with a featherlight touch. Toni's large nipples, already aroused, hardened to pebbles and Edie watched them in the mirror as she reached in front of Toni to touch them lightly with the fingertip of each forefinger.

Toni's mouth opened and her breathing quickened as Edie traced her aureole with her fingertips. She could feel the girl's breath sweet on her ear as she watched herself play with Toni's nipples. The pupils of Edie's eyes grew huge and dark in the mirror. Toni's knees fell apart as she felt a hot rush of honey to her quim.

Edie was transfixed. 'I love your tits,' she murmured as she cupped each one, feeling its weight with each of Toni's nipples poking through her fingers. She released them and squeezed each nipple, hard, so that Toni flinched and clamped her teeth on to her bottom lip, but she didn't complain. Edie smoothed her hands down Toni's flat stomach and dipped her fingers into her dark pubic hair. 'I knew you'd be wet,' Edie whispered, 'because I'm soaking.'

Toni watched in the mirror as Edie stroked the cleft of her sex lips. 'Open your legs wider,' she urged and Toni, usually used to giving orders herself, complied without thinking. She opened them as wide as she could, affording Edie full view of her moist interior. Edie teased Toni's clit with a finger, rocking it slowly back and forth, firm but gentle. Toni had to remind herself to breathe, she was so aroused by the image in front of her and the sensations that the girl was causing inside her. With her other hand, Edie was twisting her left nipple, causing sharp pinpricks of pain. Toni wanted to drop her head back on Edie's shoulder and moan with ecstasy but she couldn't tear her eyes way from the vision of what she was doing to her in the mirror.

Edie was nibbling Toni's ear lobe but her eyes hadn't flickered from the mirror. 'God, you've got a fantastic body,' she was murmuring. 'Do you like that? Being stirred like that?' Toni moaned her assent, pressing her hands on to the table each side of her, allowing herself to be played like a cello. Every sinew in her body thrummed with arousal.

Edie's breath was hot and urgent on her cheek now. 'Have you ever kissed a woman before?'

Toni was still moaning in ecstasy. 'No.'

'Then I can be your first.' The fingering stopped and Edie moved around the table to stand between Toni's splayed thighs.

Toni felt suddenly nervous, a sensation she rarely experienced. She tipped her head up and waited for Edie's kiss. Edie's eyes were like dark green pools and her lips parted slightly as she placed a kiss, very tenderly, on Toni's mouth. Not even Matt could kiss that softly. Toni felt pole-axed with desire. Edie withdrew and Toni lifted herself slightly more upright so she could return the next kiss rather than just receive it.

Edie's lips fluttered over hers again but this time Toni lifted an arm and gently cupped the back of Edie's head to draw her closer. She moved slowly as if she were under water. Toni was so drugged with desire that her whole body felt heavy with lust. She opened her lips to Edie's and the two girls exchanged gentle butterfly kisses. The sensation was new and exciting to Toni; the softness felt exquisite.

Edie was kissing her harder now, pressing closer. Toni opened her mouth and wound her tongue around a female one for the first time. She tasted sweet. Toni remembered watching Edie's small breasts and felt for them now. As they kissed she pushed her hands up under the girl's halter but gently, still scared that she may be rebuffed despite Edie's obvious arousal. She felt like a teenage boy trying to cop a feel, praying that he would be allowed access to his girlfriend's tits.

But Edie wanted her hands on her, had probably been willing her hands to wander. She moaned into Toni's mouth and pressed her slender frame nearer. Edie's breasts felt surprisingly full in the palms of her hands. She kneaded them gently as they kissed and Toni felt a wave of tenderness and desire that she had never felt with a man. She wanted to touch Edie now, wanted to arouse her the way she had been. She withdrew and pushed up her skimpy halter so she could lick Edie's skin.

Her tongue skimmed her smooth flesh, tracing the outline of her ribcage and dipping into the hollow of her belly button. Toni's teeth grazed the emerald that glinted there and Toni wondered fleetingly if Edie's clit was pierced too. But it was her breasts she wanted to taste now. Toni's tongue flicked up until she found the full roundness underneath each one and she licked at the tiny droplets of perspiration and perfume gathered there. Edie's hands were in Toni's hair and she was groaning just as Toni had earlier. Her enjoyment sent a rush of wetness coursing through Toni's own pussy.

She sucked on one hard nipple and then the other. Edie was reaching up to undo her halter and scooped the garment over her head. Toni kissed each of Edie's collarbones and her neck until they were mouth on mouth once more. Toni wasn't thinking cohesively now, she just wanted to be in Edie and have Edie in her. She fumbled with the button of her shorts, pulling down the zipper as their mouths opened wide against each other, tongues entwining and teeth clashing in their battle to taste more, have more of the other.

Toni's hands swept over Edie's hip bones as she pushed her fingers around and into the back of her shorts. For such a tall, slender girl, Edie had a magnificent womanly arse. Toni's hands pushed her shorts down over her round, tanned buttocks and felt Edie reach around for hers. They stood, holding each other like that, for a long moment; kissing hard, breast-to-breast, bush-to-bush. Toni revelled in the sensation of another woman's skin on hers, another woman's nipples scraping hers, and the promise of another woman's wetness close to hers. Edie was pushing her back on to the table now and Toni allowed herself to be lowered. Edie stepped out of her shorts and climbed up on to the table with her. Edie kissed her softly and swept her hands over Toni and Toni felt herself lost to the sensation of female skin on female skin.

It felt as if she were swimming; Edie's skin was washing over her in gentle tiny waves. She slipped her hands down between Edie's smooth thighs and felt for her dampness, willing Edie to be as damp as her. She was, and Toni's finger slipped easily up inside Edie's hot pussy. Edie moaned and pushed her own finger up inside Toni so that one could mirror the other. The two women lay side by side, one leg hooked over the other's hip, and pushed another finger high up inside the other. Edie rotated her fingers slowly inside Toni and she gasped and moaned at the sensation. When Edie stopped, Toni did the same to her before pressing her thumb on to her clit in a soft vibrato. Edie writhed and moaned on the table next to her, stretching her legs wider and pushing her clit down harder on to Toni's hand. Toni eased another finger inside her and started to frig her hard. Edie's fingers slipped from inside Toni as her head fell back and she gave herself up to the climax that Toni was whipping up inside her.

Toni had never finger-fucked a woman before but she knew what she liked and she wanted to make Edie come – hard. She wanted to push her hand right up inside the other woman. Edie's leg was hooked up almost to Toni's shoulder and Toni's fingers frigged her hard and quick. Edie was almost screaming with pleasure and Toni dipped her head and sucked one of her dark nipples as Edie came, her cunt throbbing around Toni's hand and her entire body convulsing with pleasure.

Beads of sweat had gathered on Edie's top lip. She smiled at Toni, her full lips parting over neat, white teeth. 'That was pretty good for a beginner.'

'I just did what I would like.'

'What we lack in equipment, we make up for in dexterity.'

'There's nothing wrong with your equipment.'

'Or yours.' Edie had recovered now. She propped herself up on one hand and felt for Toni again with the other. Toni lifted a knee slightly and held her breath as Edie's finger slipped back inside her. Edie nuzzled her neck. 'You've got a divine pussy.'

'Have I?' Toni grinned but her smile soon faded as Edie began to slowly rotate her finger up inside her again. She moaned deep in her throat.

'Oh yes.' Edie's lips nibbled Toni's ear. 'I want to put my whole hand inside your wet pussy.' She slipped another finger in and Toni's sex stretched to accommodate it. 'I can feel you throbbing already. Do you want some more?'

Toni nodded but Edie persisted. 'Then tell me, or I'll stop.' Her fingers ceased momentarily and Toni gasped.

'No, don't stop. I want your fingers inside me. Frig me, frig me hard.'

'Good girl. Like this?'

'Ah, yes.'

'More?'

'Yes, more. Oh my God.'

'I'm right up inside you now, Toni. Does that feel good?' Edie's fingers were working up inside Toni's moist pussy and the ball of her hand worked against her clit.

'Tell me, is it good?' Edie panted into her ear.

'Yes, yes,' Toni shouted, but she was beyond dirty talk. She held on tight to the table to keep from falling off. She arched her back in ecstasy, and Edie sucked hard on one nipple. Toni's head tipped back as she called out her climax and felt her pussy convulse around Edie's slick fingers.

Edie really did know what a woman liked. As Toni came down from her orgasm she didn't whip her hand away but stayed by the side of her as Toni's breathing slowed. Pleased with Toni's reaction, Edie nipped at her lips, toying with them. Her fingers were still loosely inside Toni, and Toni clenched her thigh muscles to keep them there a bit longer, as her clit thrummed the last of her climax. She kissed Edie back, feeling her heartbeat quicken again.

'God, Toni, I could spend all day doing this with you, but this table is killing me.'

'And me.' Toni shifted awkwardly and Edie's fingers finally slipped from her.

The two women slid from the table and stretched aching muscles. Toni felt suddenly awkward and looked around for her clothes.

Edie hovered and cleared her throat, 'Toni, I –' Loud

knocking interrupted her and a stunning black girl poked her head around the door.

'Edie, when you've finished fucking the new girl will you tell her that Onyx wants her in his office.'

Toni's head snapped around and she felt her hackles rise. 'The new girl's right here so you can tell her yourself.'

The black girl looked Toni's naked body up and down slowly and tapped her long, decorated nails on the door. 'Consider yourself told, sweetie.' She disappeared.

Toni bent to scoop up her discarded clothes. 'Who's that bitch?'

Edie grinned. 'That's Coral. Don't take her personally, she's always wary of any new competition.'

'Yeah well, she'll have severe competition in the bitch stakes if she tries to rile me again.'

Edie wriggled her ass into her skimpy shorts. 'And there was me thinking that you were all sweet and vulnerable.'

Toni buttoned up her blouse and looked at Edie from under her lashes. 'I have to tell you that you are probably the only person in this world who has ever thought that.'

Edie swivelled for Toni to tie a knot in her halter-top. 'Well, aren't I the lucky one then?' She turned around and watched Toni smooth down her skirt. 'I'll look forward to seeing the fireworks fly.' She reached up under Toni's skirt and ran a finger over the cleft of her sex lips. 'In more ways than one.'

Toni grabbed her chin and kissed her hard on the mouth. 'You can count on it, honey.' Her heels clicked loudly on the marble floor as she left.

14

Onyx was stretched out behind his desk, tapping figures into a computer, as Toni shut the office door behind her. She hovered. There was nothing in this office to suggest that this man ran a strip club; no lurid posters of naked girls, no sleazy photos. It was plush and professional. Toni wondered what, exactly, his connection with the Cobras was. She couldn't imagine Onyx slumming it on a road trip. She guessed it was purely business. Bikers always liked girls of course. And girls were Onyx's business.

He swung away from his computer screen and grinned. 'Please, sit.'

Toni lowered herself into a soft chair and crossed her legs. Despite her rumpled clothing she felt calmed and pampered by Edie's ministrations.

'Did the girls take care of you?' His voice was low and deep.

In more ways than one, Toni thought, but answered a polite, 'Yes, thank you.'

'OK, here are the rules.' Onyx spread his legs and lent on his knees, hands clasped. 'However sleazy the men in the club are, I like my girls clean. No drugs, no booze equals no hassles. You dance for me, I pay you well. I employ bouncers in the club. They see anyone trying to harass you, they will remove the customer, no questions asked. You are welcome to hang out here during the day. I like to be surrounded by beautiful women and I have the best dancers and the sexiest women here. Any questions?'

Toni shook her head.

'OK, you show me what you can do and you can start tonight.' He sat back in his chair and brought his hands up to point into his chin.

Toni cleared her throat. 'Here? Now?' It all seemed a bit abrupt and businesslike. She felt suddenly very nervous.

'There's no room for modesty in this job.' There was a soft knock on the door. Onyx looked up. 'Ah, come in Steve, this is Toni.'

Steve was a six-foot bouncer, built like a Sherman tank. His head was shaved and his white T-shirt strained across the muscles in his arms. He turned and shook her hand politely. 'Pleased to meet ya, Toni.'

Toni swallowed, her mouth suddenly as dry as sand. Her hand felt limp as a wet rag in his huge grasp. She looked up into mirrored shades and knew that he sensed her fear. He smiled coolly.

'This is Steve, my front of house manager. He sits in on all the interviews.'

Steve perched on the edge of Onyx's desk and crossed his arms. He was hiding behind his shades, and she saw his head tip almost imperceptibly as his gaze drifted from her face to her breasts to her legs as he appraised her.

Toni's thoughts raced. Most men would give their right arm to sit in on 'interviews' which were based on the woman being able to give her 'interviewees' an erection. Or probably not their right arm, Toni thought, they would need that. Toni's head was reeling now. She was secretly trying to assess just how much control she had here, if any.

Being able to incorporate this little performance fantasy into her search for Caron Crossley had seemed like such a good idea while she had Piedro coming in his pants. Now that she was sat in an air-conditioned office being coolly appraised by two strange men who thought that she stripped for a living was, frankly, terrifying.

Toni knew it was put up or shut up time. If she told them to stick the job, she could still hang around and investigate the Cobras. If she performed for them now, it had to be because she, Toni Marconi, wanted to. She didn't *have* to do this.

Steve the bouncer cleared his throat and Onyx tapped his long black fingers together patiently. 'Do you have a tape, Toni? Or should I put some music on for you?'

Toni took a huge, deep breath. 'No, I have some.' She reached beneath her chair and took a tape from her purse. She stood, composing herself, and held the tape out for Steve. While he was fiddling with the tape player, Toni walked to the far end of the office, breathing slowly and deeply. As the deep throb of the bass filled the room, Toni could feel the men's excitement rising, though neither moved a muscle. She knew that they were both determined to retain a cool, impassive exterior and she was going to enjoy knocking it down. Toni slowly undid a couple of buttons on her blouse, thankful she had a sexy push-up bra on underneath and her own excitement started to rise. She'd get them both so hard, they wouldn't be able to think straight.

She turned and began to move her hips to the beat, licking her lips and staring Onyx straight in the eye. She shimmied a little nearer and inched her skirt up her thighs as she danced, opening her legs as she dipped. She rotated so that her back was to them and tipped forward, bending at the waist. Her skirt rode higher but not high enough for the two men to catch a glimpse of her ass. She wiggled it, teasing them. A good old-fashioned striptease, Toni thought, that would get their juices flowing. Her skirt was up past her thighs now as she bent and dipped to the heavy beat. Toni ran her hands over her breasts, a pulse throbbing heavily in her crotch. She was dancing in front of two complete strangers, and it was exciting.

She began to undo her blouse buttons in time to the music and danced slowly towards Steve. She could see his Adam's apple bob as she approached. He hadn't moved an inch since she began and Toni could see a large uncomfortable erection pushing at the front of his black trousers. She rotated her hips just inches from his knees and bent back away from him so that he was looking down the length of her stretched torso.

She rose and shrugged out of her blouse, throwing it at Onyx. Still moving to the music, Toni reached out and slipped the mirrored shades off Steve's face. If he was going to watch her, she wasn't going to have him hiding. His eyes were piercing blue and Toni held his look as she slipped his glasses on. His gaze wavered as she pushed down one cup, then the other, so that her breasts jutted over the top of her bra. He was riveted by them and uncrossed his arms, flexing his fingers in a bid not to reach out and squeeze them.

She danced away from him and moved towards Onyx, who watched her with dark, dark eyes. She bent towards him so that her breasts tipped out and slid her skirt down over her buttocks. She whipped it off and threw it smartly at Steve without looking at him. He caught it as a reflex. She writhed inches from Onyx's knees, gyrating in a mock sexual act, and feeling her pussy grow moist at the men's heightening arousal. She watched Steve over the rim of the mirrored shades and winked at him provocatively just as the music finished.

The silence hung heavy and awkward in the air. Toni caught her breath and the two men shifted uncomfortably. Toni handed back the shades and retrieved her clothes from the two men.

Onyx was the first to regain his composure. 'That was great. You can start tonight. I need your details for the payroll.'

Toni slipped her skirt back on. 'Sure.' That was no problem; she had aliases, which she used for just such an event. 'Would you?' She smiled sweetly at Steve and turned for him to zip up her skirt.

He grappled with it for a minute before succeeding. She could feel his arousal coming off him in heatwaves.

Onyx had noticed it too. 'I don't need to remind you, Steve, that the girls are out of bounds. You want pussy, you go into town for it.'

Steve cleared his throat. 'Yes, sir.'

Toni cringed inwardly, wondering if Onyx was a bit of a sadist, tormenting his bouncers with half-naked females and then forbidding them to touch.

Then again, there was a touch of the sadist in her as well. 'Actually, Mr Kane ... Onyx ... I would like the chance to dress up a bit more when I'm out there. I've got some black leather gear, crops, chains, that sort of thing.'

'Fine. You're in charge of your own look.'

'And ... how far does the floor show go?' Behind her Steve cleared his throat.

Onyx looked interested. 'How do you mean?'

'Am I allowed to ... touch myself ... intimately?' Toni looked at him innocently, trying not to grin as Steve muttered 'Fuck!' under his breath.

Onyx stretched out a well-manicured hand to lazily toy with the hem of Toni's skirt. His almond-shaped nails looked very pink against his long black fingers. She looked down at a gold signet ring that glinted on his wedding finger. Her heartbeat quickened when she saw the engraving on it, tiny but still noticeable, of a cobra entwined around an Eve-like figure. She looked back up, hiding her shock and biting back questions.

'I knew you'd be a hot little tigress when I saw you fighting on the street.' He idly stroked the outside of her thigh with a long forefinger. Steve had gone very quiet and still. 'It's up to Steve.' He looked at Toni but he directed the question at the bouncer. 'Do you think you can keep control of the hot-blooded men in the bar while this temptress plays with her pussy?'

'No problem, sir.'

'OK, then, you're excused.'

Reluctantly, Steve left the room. Toni wondered if Onyx's policy of look but don't touch included himself. His trailing finger was causing ripples of pleasure to run along her thigh.

'I bet you can be a real nasty little bitch when you want to be, can't you?'

Toni watched his finger move up under her skirt. 'Yes I can and you can get your finger from under my skirt unless it's invited.'

Onyx withdrew his hand and grinned. 'I thought so. I'll look forward to seeing you tonight, sugar.'

So will I, thought Toni, so will I.

'When do you start?' Edie was stretched out by the pool, dressed in a tiny red bikini.

'Tonight.' Toni lowered herself on a sunbed. It was baking out here, especially after the air-conditioned office.

Get undressed and have a swim. No one has any modesty around here.' Edie tipped her head up to the sun. 'Isn't this glorious?'

Toni admired her jutting hipbones and long slender legs. 'Yes, it is.' She started to undress.

Steve appeared at the foot of the sunbed. His huge, muscular bulk cast a shadow over her. 'Can I get you a soda?'

'I'd love one, thanks.'

He moved away.

Edie giggled. 'I see you've found a fan already.'

Toni stripped down to her panties. 'Aren't they tortured enough? How can they bear to hang around the pool as well?' She sat on the poolside and dipped her feet into the cool water. She squinted at the sun-pennies dancing across the pool.

'If Onyx catches the bouncers having an affair with a dancer, they're sacked on the spot. But he has to catch them first. Know what I mean?'

Toni looked at Edie over her shoulder. 'I must have been naive to think they wouldn't.'

'Two hundred and twenty pounds of quivering testosterone finds it pretty hard to keep its pecker in its pants for long, I can tell you.'

'They don't do much for you then?'

Edie smiled, her eyes shut. 'What do you think?'

'I think you prefer your fucks more soft and rounded.'

Edie crossed her legs. 'Mmm. And you are superbly soft and rounded.'

'Huh, not too much, I hope.'

Edie laughed. 'As if.'

Steve had returned with a tray of drinks for the two women.

Toni clambered to her feet and smiled gratefully. 'Thanks, Steve, just what I needed.' She gulped at the iced soda. 'No chance of anything to eat is there?' she ventured.

'Sure,' Steve's gaze followed a droplet of water as it fell from the rim of her glass to her right breast.

Edie had seen and rose from the sunbed. 'Here, let

me get that for you.' Steve looked on as Edie's hot tongue chased the freezing droplet down to Toni's right nipple.

'What would you like?' He stared, transfixed, as Toni's nipple puckered under Edie's lips.

Toni's clit was thrumming but she couldn't resist a tease. 'I think I would like a big ... hot ... sausage.'

'Huh, huh,' Steve muttered dumbly, unable to tear his eyes away from the two women in front of him.

Edie was quicker. Her dark head shot up. 'You witch!'

Toni laughed. 'What? I fancy a hot dog! So what!'

Edie's green eyes danced. 'I'm going to get you for that.'

Toni placed the glass down on the small table at the side of the sunbed. 'You'll have to catch me first.' She ran to the side of the pool and jumped in. Screaming with laughter, Edie followed. As they surfaced, they both laughed even harder at the sight of Steve standing, drenched, at the side of the pool.

'Thanks, Steve,' Toni called.

Edie rounded on her, her long limbs looking very tanned as they moved through the cool water. 'Fuck you, Toni, after all I've done for you today.' Her green eyes danced under lashes spiked with water droplets.

Toni pushed her own wet hair away from her face, enjoying the water rushing sensually over her bare breasts. 'Yeah, fuck me, Edie,' she replied, reaching out to pull her nearer in the water.

It was difficult to kiss and tread water at the same time. Toni kept getting mouthfuls of pool water instead of Edie's soft lips but the hit and miss of limbs gently bumping under the glistening surface was amazingly erotic. Toni struggled to release the knot on Edie's bikini top. Every now and then she would manage to brush the hard nubs of her nipples before having to move her limbs again to stop herself from sinking.

Edie resurfaced, almost choking after dipping her head under to suck on Toni's nipple. 'I suppose it's too much to ask that you were once the star performer in a synchronised swimming team?'

Toni grinned, and managed to sweep a hand up between Edie's scissoring legs. 'Yes it is. And I suppose it's too much to ask that you have a six-inch tongue?'

'You don't ask for much, do you? You'd never even kissed a girl yesterday.' Edie was unsure whether Toni was making a joke or a proposition.

'I'd never kissed you yesterday. Today I want it all.' The humour faded and Toni's sex pounded with lust.

Edie swam closer. 'I haven't got a six–inch tongue but I bet you'd like my tongue stud.'

Toni grinned. 'Race you to the side.'

Steve was returning from the kitchen and watched with lust as Edie and Toni pulled themselves out from the pool. Water coursed over their bodies as they padded hand in hand towards him. He stared at their softly bouncing breasts.

'Thanks, Steve, I'll have it later,' Toni muttered as she passed.

He watched them disappear into the apartment, sick with envy.

Steve had been given the task of driving Toni back to her motel to fetch her costumes and her own car. Onyx knew that her performance would have given the bouncer a semi-hard-on for the morning, but the bastard liked to test loyalties. The sight of Toni and Edie clambering out of the swimming pool dressed only in skimpy bottoms had made his blood pound. In fact he had lost all sensation in his body except for his boner and his balls, which ached like someone had inflated them with a hand-pump.

He knocked gently on the guest bedroom door, imagining what had been going on behind it. His job was the envy of all the boys he had gone to high school with but the frustrations weren't of the usual promotion and pay kind; the frustration was walking around with a stiffy when gorgeous women surrounded you all day and you weren't allowed to touch. There was always the Cobra Club, but he was stuck here until late tonight. Steve drew a deep breath and pushed the door open a fraction.

The two women lay entwined on the bed, the rumpled white sheet caught between them. They were dozing and Steve allowed himself to ogle at their pert breasts, still flushed from sex, and their trimmed pussies nestling between tanned thighs. Unconsciously, his hand drifted to the front of his pants, which were now stretched uncomfortably tight. Edie pushed one ringed foot outwards and stretched languidly. As she awoke from her doze she spied Steve, loitering in the doorway, from under her barely opened eyelashes.

She turned on to her side, pretending she hadn't seen him, and stroked Toni's right breast with her hand. Toni murmured and stretched beside her.

'Don't look now,' Edie whispered, 'but we're being watched.'

'Mmm?' Toni squirmed under her roaming fingers and pushed her hands up toward the headboard.

'I said –' Edie rolled half on top of Toni and kissed her on the mouth '– your fan is watching from the doorway.'

Toni was fully awake now but kept her eyes shut. 'What's he doing?'

Edie dipped her head to bite a nipple and looked to

see if Steve was still there. 'Well, at this moment, he's slowly undoing his zip.'

'Really? Naughty boy. Fancy spying on me while I'm still half asleep.'

'That's what I thought.' Edie rolled off Toni and lay by the side of her, drawing circles around her breasts while Toni closed her eyes, a sly smile playing on her lips.

Edie propped herself up on one hand and traced Toni's features with a finger. 'I wish you could see this,' she whispered. 'He's getting his cock out.'

Toni hid her smile and allowed Edie to roll each of her nipples under her moistened finger. The sensation of pretending to be asleep while Steve watched Edie fondling her was doubly arousing and her clit soon began to throb wildly between her legs. She opened her legs slightly, inviting Edie to dip her finger in between them and imagined Steve's excitement at seeing her bush.

Edie tormented her a little longer by stroking her finger along her ribcage and into her belly button before allowing it to stray into her pubes. She stroked Toni's soft curls, tantalizingly slowly, bringing her fingers up through the hair over and over. Toni bit her lip to stop herself from moaning and felt the honey begin to flow between her legs. She brought her knees up slowly and let them fall apart so her pussy lips were splayed like butterfly wings for Steve to gaze at and Edie to play with.

'You're driving him wild,' Edie murmured. 'His cock is purple with excitement.'

She continued her soft explorations with her finger, igniting the nerve endings on Toni's sex lips by stroking them softly and drifting inwards to stroke her tender inner lips. Toni was dripping with arousal by this time and her clit throbbed gratefully when Edie finally deigned to stroke it. She toyed with it, pressing it lightly as it pulsed with arousal. Then, agonizingly, she abandoned it and dipped her finger into Toni's moist hole, looking up at Steve for the first time as she did so.

Steve was too far gone to care that he had been spotted. He was stroking his cock in long slow sweeps and gawping at Edie's exploring finger as it dipped in and out of Toni's wet pussy. Edie smiled knowingly, revelling in the power of bringing such pleasure to two people at once. She concentrated on alternating between Toni's throbbing clit and her hot hole. Toni was squirming under her touch now, becoming more and more aroused. Edie's finger slipped in and out as it grew slicker and slicker with her love juices. She pushed her fingers deep up inside and Toni squirmed and twisted on the bed. Steve's eyes were riveted on her pussy. Toni threw her head back on to the pillows and lost herself in the sensation of Edie's fingers working their magic.

Steve grasped his balls with one hand and slid his other hand faster and faster over his rigid cock. When Toni bucked beneath Edie's hand he felt his cock pulse hard and explode. He came with a loud shout, shooting come over the edge of the bed.

Toni's legs slid back down on to the cool sheet and she watched the ceiling fan rotate as she caught her breath. Steve dabbed at his mess and tried to zip himself away at the same time, nearly giving himself a nasty injury in the process.

Edie sniggered. 'What can we do for you, Steve?'

'Boss says I have to take Toni back to your motel to collect your things.'

Toni turned, a twinkle in her eye. 'How long have you been standing there?'

Steve fiddled with the zipper of his jeans. 'Not long.'

Edie's hand slid over Toni's flat belly. 'I hope you haven't been invading our privacy?'

Steve held a hand out to Toni. 'Don't get me going again or we'll all have the sack.'

Edie was crawling beneath the covers. 'Well, I'm going to get some rest. For a beginner you've really worn me out.'

Toni accepted his hand and allowed him to pull her out of bed. His bicep bunched under the sleeve of his T-shirt.

She pulled the sheet over her breasts in mock modesty. 'I'll need to get dressed first.'

Steve shuffled back out of the bedroom doorway. 'Truck's out front. Don't be long.'

When he had gone, Edie sniggered from under the sheet.

Toni shrugged on her clothes. 'There was me thinking you were such a sweet thing.'

'He enjoyed it, didn't he?'

'It certainly seemed that way.'

Edie blew her a kiss. 'Better hurry, he's got the motor running.'

Toni pulled a face. 'I'll see you tonight.'

15

Steve drove her back through town to her motel. They sat in silence at a traffic light. She guessed that the bouncer was inwardly gloating at the little peep-show they had provided for him. She allowed him to stroke her thigh as the engine idled but her thoughts were on other things; for a biker town there was a distinct lack of bikers.

Toni chewed a thumbnail. 'A friend told me that bikers come through this place.'

Steve removed his hand to shift gear and pulled away from the lights. 'Sure do. They're in and out of this place all the time.' He paused. 'They're not your weekenders though, so be careful.'

'What d'you mean?'

'I mean they really live the life.'

'So?'

Steve pulled up outside the motel and removed his shades thoughtfully. 'You don't look like the type of chick who'd take kindly to being treated as no more than baggage on the bitch seat.'

'Are there girls like that then?'

'Oh, you'd be surprised.' Steve shifted his muscular bulk to face her. 'I could tell you stories about some of the girls I've seen pass through here.'

Should she ask him about Caron? 'Such as . . .?'

'Such as chicks that would pull a train with ten bikers just for the thrill of it.'

'They must really know how to party.'

'Yeah, they do, but they've had enough of journalists and sensation-seekers sniffing about their business.'

'I'm sure.'

He reached out a hand to stroke her cheek. 'Which are you then? Committed hedonist or interested observer?'

Toni shrugged. She wasn't sure any more.

'Or are you in it for the money? There are ways of making extra bucks around here if you're willing to take a few risks and something tells me that you're just passing through.'

'Oh yeah? How?'

Steve was tracing circles on Toni's tanned thigh. 'You would never have risked that fuck this afternoon if you'd really needed this job.'

Toni's blood pumped a warning. 'Onyx never said anything about sex with the other dancers.'

Steve shrugged. 'Didn't he now?' The circles were growing higher and Toni's skin tingled. She kept her thighs clamped firmly together.

'What are you after then, sweet thing? You being paid to inform on us here? You working for the cops?'

Toni removed his hand. 'I'm just working for myself, Steve. I was told that the Sphynx is a legitimate joint.'

'Well if you want to keep your job, you better keep quiet about this afternoon.' He handed her his card. 'Take my number, in case you're ever looking for extra work.'

'Yeah, right.' Toni let herself out of the jeep. His attempt at blackmail was pathetic.

Toni knew he was watching her all the way into the motel. She stayed calm until she made it into her room. Toni flung her purse on to the bed. 'Shit!' She punched the bed. How could she have allowed herself to have become so distracted?

She showered and changed and packed some outfits into a bag for the club. She checked her cell phone. There were a number of diverted calls from her apartment from Matt and John. Matt in particular worried her – she hoped he wasn't stupid enough to come and attempt to help her out. Nothing from Josh. She toyed with the idea of calling him and telling him where she was, for safety's sake, but dismissed the idea because it exposed her to the risk of his interference.

She slipped on a pair of shorts and a T-shirt and headed into town for something to eat. She hated to admit it but the thought of dancing in front of a packed room was pretty daunting. So far she'd danced for Piedro and then Onyx and Steve. Would it be harder or easier to dance for a whole crowd?

She found a restaurant with a good vantage point of Main Street and ordered herself a rare steak but, despite her normal healthy appetite, tonight's performance had her nervous and she picked at her food. She sensed that she really had something to prove. A ceiling fan whirred overhead and Toni tipped her head back against her seat, lost in thought. A waitress collected plates from an empty table.

Toni felt the low rumble of the engines before she heard them. Even from her distant booth, the waitress's excitement was tangible and so Toni followed her gaze through the flyblown window. First, there was just a cloud of dust way out on the old reservation road and then the sun hit them, thirty or so fenders glinting on the horizon. A swarm of low-framed, customised Harleys with their trademark high bars descending on Small-ville, Arizona. The waitress pressed herself hard against the Formica table in front of her, gazing open mouthed at the Cobras congregating outside the bar opposite. Toni curled her lip; any minute now she'd be running out of the café waving her panties over her head. And then she saw him, Alfred 'Red' Angelo, sitting astride his Harley-Davidson FXRT like he was king of the world. He was all muscle and sinew. His bare arms were bronzed and sweaty from his ride and his huge hands sported a collection of bulky silver rings. Toni shuddered. He was so not her type. Her crotch, on the other hand, was sending out completely different signals. She recognised the thrum. Fuck him or die. She crossed her legs and sipped her cold coffee, contemplating the biker. Maybe, but the beard would definitely have to go.

'They really are something else, aren't they?'

Toni jumped; she hadn't realised that the young waitress who had served her was hovering close by and, despite a room full of customers, was gazing at the bikers through the window.

Toni sipped her drink and stretched her legs beneath the table. 'They certainly are.' She loved working a case when there was a fanciable man involved.

The waitress had slipped into the chair opposite, clearly oblivious to the angry manageress who was dealing with a large party. 'I go all wet at the sight of muscle and engine oil. I love a man who's not afraid to be a man.'

'I know what you mean.' Toni watched the man she assumed to be Red, high-fiving his mates. His hands glinted with the chunky sliver rings. His chest was bare beneath his cut-off leather jacket and his legs were spread as he straddled his bike.

'See the one with the black bandana?'

Toni saw him. It was Red.

'He came in here a few months ago. Brought a crowd of bikers in with him.' The waitress licked her lips at the memory. 'He was chatting me up, you know. A lot of men do it but when I saw his hands, his knuckles were all grazed like he'd been in a fight.' She shuddered slightly. 'That just does it for me. Rough, mean men. It made my clit twitch, I can tell you.'

Toni looked at her clear pale face and her full red mouth. She guessed that they were coming at this from completely different angles. Toni loved tough men because they always submitted so beautifully to a strong woman – but this waitress, she obviously liked to do the submitting.

'Did you fuck him?' Toni lowered her voice, but only slightly. The guy on the table next to them was straining to hear every word.

The waitress shook her head. 'He asked me what underwear I had on, so I told him white panties and he asked me if I'd take them off and give them to him so he knew I would be serving him with no panties on.'

'And did you?'

'Yes, I did. When I went out to the kitchen with their order I slipped my panties off. I gave them to him on the tray with their drinks.'

'What did he do with them?'

'He thanked me and slipped them into his jacket pocket. While I was handing out the drinks he ran his rough hand up the back of my leg and stroked my bare ass. It felt divine.'

'Were you excited?'

'I sure was. And then more people came in, so I had to serve them, but the whole time I sensed him watching me, knowing I didn't have any panties on. My skirt is quite short and every time I had to stretch over a table, I knew he was looking.'

'Did he touch you again?'

'I wanted him to. I was very aware of my pussy, you know, because I was exposed underneath my skirt. It made me very excited. When I eventually went back to their table with their order he asked me if his friends could feel under my skirt while I served them.'

'What did you say?'

'I said yes.'

The guy on the next table was listening so intently, he had forgotten to eat.

'Did they touch you? How many were there?'

'There were five. They were really polite, not making fun of me or anything. Every time I had to stand next to one of them they would look up at me like I was the most gorgeous thing they'd ever seen and slip their hand up underneath my skirt.'

'Did they put their fingers inside you?'

'No, they just stroked me, really gently, running their fingers along the cleft of my pussy lips. But the first one, that guy, he was watching, like he knew I was getting excited.'

'And were you?'

The waitress bit her full bottom lip. 'I was so damp underneath my skirt and my clit was thrumming. But they just stroked me like they knew it was against the rules to go any further, even though I was squirming with pleasure at the touch of their fingers. I must have got everyone's meal wrong that night, I was so excited. I was moving from one biker to the other, willing one of them to go a little further. And the first one, the one with my panties, just kept watching his mates stroking my pussy underneath my skirt and me getting all flustered and frustrated.'

'Did he touch you again?'

'The other parties in the restaurant left without dessert. People get nervous around bikers; they don't like to hang about. So it was just the bikers and me again. I was quivering like a leaf and my pussy was throbbing with frustration, you know. So I told them we were closing for the night, and did they want anything else.'

'And did they?'

'Well, I certainly did. And that biker, he knew it.'

'What did he do?'

'Well, when I eventually gave them the cheque he ran his hand underneath my skirt and stroked the cleft of my buttocks. I stood there pretending to check the bill but I was waiting for his finger to finally push inside me.'

'And did it?'

'No, he said he wanted the other guys to see if I was aroused enough and would I mind if they tested me to see.'

'Did you?'

The waitress leant towards Toni, her pupils dark and dilated at the memory. 'I was so aroused; I think I would have agreed to anything. I'm not usually loose like that, you know, but it was so erotic. Anyway, the restaurant was empty except for me and them – the kitchen staff were clearing away – so I went around the table, from one to the other, and pulled up my skirt and opened my legs slightly and let them finger me, one by one, to see if I was wet enough and aroused enough.' Her gaze slipped back to the crowd of men on the road outside.

'What happened then?' Toni shifted in her chair; she was feeling pretty aroused herself.

'I asked if they could test me again as I wasn't sure if I was ready. No one was talking by this time. The atmosphere was thick with desire. They all wanted to touch me, in fact I know they wanted to fuck me, but the first biker was keeping them in check. It was like they had to show respect for me and respect for him. He was deeply aroused, I could tell, and I think I wanted to tantalize him a little further too, for teasing me all evening.

'I walked to the man on his right and pushed up my skirt. He looked up at me, swallowing hard, and I asked him, "Is my pussy wet?" He pushed a finger inside me, I was slick with juices, I could have taken four fingers, but he only inserted one. "It's wet, honey," he croaked. I let my eyes drift to the front of his oily jeans; he was more frustrated than me.

'I moved to the next, all eyes on me, and I asked, "Am I ready?" The next biker was licking his lips and gazing at my pussy. I inched nearer and he pushed two fingers inside me. It felt better than the last but still not enough. "Not yet," he answered, and I watched him hold his fingers underneath his nose to smell my pussy on his hand.

'I moved to the next. The men's arousal was all around me, they were desperate for me and I loved it. "Test me," I urged, my voice husky with longing, and the third man reached out a shaky hand to slip in one finger, then a second, then a third. I stood in front of him with my legs open and breathed a long deep breath, tensing my muscles to hold him longer, but he withdrew his hand slowly and I moved on to the next.

'I held my skirt up and shuffled my feet apart. "Am I moist?" I asked, feeling as if my blood was going to boil over. The fourth biker was red with frustration, but this was a test of loyalties and of power. They were only allowed to do as I asked, no more, and the first biker, I hoped, was going to get to fuck me. I'd never wanted it so badly. I stood with my legs apart and he slipped his fingers inside my hot, wet pussy. I'll never forget the look of concentration on his face as he pushed each finger inside until he had four fingers stretching me open. I lifted a foot on to his seat, revelling in the snug sensation of his hand pushed inside me. I bit my lip, wanting to work myself on them, but sensing that it was against the rules. He withdrew his hand and I turned to the first biker, desperate now for his cock inside me.'

'And?' Toni was enthralled by this time, oblivious, like the waitress, to the other diners.

'He handed me back my panties and said thank you for a lovely evening.'

'He said what?'

The waitress nodded. 'They all left, politely, and left an enormous tip, but not the type of tip I wanted. I was on fire.'

'I bet you were. What did you do?' Toni pressed her thighs together, feeling the waitress's frustration.

'Put it this way, my boyfriend got the best fuck of his life. But that bastard, I'd like to teach him a lesson.'

'Shit, I can't believe he left you frustrated like that.'

'It was a show of power, wasn't it? I wanted to sob; I needed to be fucked so badly. And his mates, they could hardly walk out of here, they were so hard. How did they release their frustrations? That's what I'd like to know.'

The guy at the next table threw down a handful of bills and left in a rush but neither of the women noticed. They were both staring out of the window, lost in their own thoughts. The waitress was wondering whether they'd come in again and whether she'd ever open her legs again for a table of bikers to poke their fingers into her moist quim as a test of loyalties.

Toni was wondering at the willpower of a man who could withstand that sort of temptation, and the sort of sexual appetite he must have. Her pulse was racing at the prospect of meeting him face to face. But the name Caron Crossley came to mind and the legend, 'Property of . . .' Was it just her perverse imagination, or was Caron Crossley someone whom five bikers could come home to at the end of an evening and fuck, one by one? And would Caron have waited, excited, all evening knowing that Red was testing them all, and their reward would be her – spreadeagled and waiting – if they succeeded? Knowing submissives as she did, she imagined Caron might even have spent the evening blindfold, in a dark room, stripped from the waist down, her senses alert for the return of Red.

He would go first probably, being highly aroused by the waitress and wanting Caron to be frustrated and highly charged too. He wouldn't bother with any pre-amble. His cock would be throbbing from the vision of the waitress asking his fellow bikers to finger her in a public restaurant. He would be heady with his own sense of power, that he was able to make grown men finger a strange woman's pussy in such a controlled manner.

One or two of them were probably jerking off, not realising that Caron was waiting for them, eager to be taken by more than one man; that her reward for waiting, frustrated all night, was being fucked by five faceless men in a dark room.

He would enter the bedroom, unzip his flies and pull her naked ass roughly towards him. She would be moist because she had been waiting for this for hours, and he wouldn't bother with foreplay. Pushing her legs apart, he would jam his cock into her from behind and gasp at the sweet release of hot pussy sucking at his cock. He would ram himself into her again and again, making her whole body jerk, her tits grazing the cotton sheet beneath her as her bound hands clasped the pillow beneath her for ballast.

The waitress made her jump for the second time that evening.

'What?' Toni was astounded by how far she had allowed her imagination to run away with her.

The waitress was clearing the table as if they had just been discussing the weather. 'Can I get you some dessert?'

Toni rummaged in her purse for her wallet. 'No, nothing thanks, I'm starting work in an hour.'

She left the restaurant burning with arousal and more than ready to perform in front of Red. She just hoped that the crowd of bikers she had been hearing about all evening would be at the Sphynx tonight. She was ready to meet Red and it was about time she found out more about Caron Crossley.

16

Toni arrived at the club around ten; she wanted to have a drink and suss the atmosphere before she went on. Steve fell over himself to greet her, and Toni felt like a movie star. She was surrounded by a handful of enormous security guys in tight white T-shirts and escorted to the bar where a tall drink was placed in front of her. The bar was expensively decorated; this was no seedy strip-joint off the Boulevard. Toni cast a glance around her and suppressed a smile. Except it was, of course, a strip-joint. Not five feet to her left she could see a man in a business suit hypnotised by a redhead in a zebra-skin thong who was scissoring her legs inches from his nose. Any nearer and he would fall right in.

Toni knew that a lot of women feared dancing because they felt that men would be abusive and disparaging. But when a place was run the right way, the girls held power – the power of holding men in sexual thrall. And that was what Toni wanted to experience. To be able to stand on stage and open her legs and thrust her groin because she wanted to sexually excite men. If only more women would realise the sexual power they had.

Coral was up on one of the stages and she looked magnificent. She was gyrating her muscular body like a gymnast. She was wearing a collection of beautiful pearl necklaces, which shimmered around her throat and between her breasts as she danced. She was obviously popular. A group of men were crowding around the stage, transfixed.

The bikers still hadn't arrived and Toni felt as if she'd been stood up. Sensing someone's eye on her she turned and saw Steve, hovering by the entrance, watching her. It was time for her to get ready.

Onyx had said that she could use 'the runway' – a long stage like a fashion catwalk where the girls could strut if they wanted to instead of being on the podiums. The girls would sometimes parade all at once. Some men found the sight of several dancers at once too much to handle and most of the security had been trained in resuscitation techniques.

The changing room was hot and clammy and electric fans whirred on the long dressing table, which was covered in copious amounts of make-up. Costumes hung from pegs on the wall. There were lots of girls in varying states of undress but she recognised Edie's butt immediately. She was wearing enormous silver stilettos and stood with her back to her. Toni carried her bag to a seat near her and was about to slap her buttocks when Edie turned and Toni gazed at her, astounded.

Edie grinned. 'Thought I would surprise you. It's about time you got ready, isn't it? We're on in half an hour.'

'My God,' Toni stammered, 'you look fantastic.'

'It's not quite so popular with men, but when I do girls' clubs, they go wild.'

'I'm not surprised. Can I touch?'

Edie's short hair was spiked and sprinkled with glitter and her make-up was silver and shiny, so she looked like a rebellious fairy. Like Tinkerbell on acid. Her body, too, was dusted with fine silver powder, not to excess but just enough to catch the light when she moved. The pièce de résistance was her chains. Toni had experienced the delight of her tongue stud but hadn't realised how many piercings Edie actually had. She gazed at the girl now, aroused by the sight of her nipple rings and her labia rings, all of which were joined together by fine chains.

'Don't they hurt?'

Edie shook her head. 'The sensation is exquisite. I get so aroused when I'm dancing I have to masturbate when I come off stage. Here, you can help with the last one.' She held out a silver collar for Toni to clip around her slender neck with yet another chain dangling from the back. Reaching between her legs she pulled it between her buttocks and clipped it on to her labia ring. She twirled. 'How do I look?' The delicate horizontal chain swung from her nipples as she turned and the vertical ones served to accentuate the smooth contours of her belly and back.

Toni swallowed. 'You look incredible. Good enough to eat. I'm creaming my panties just looking at you.'

Edie pouted silver lips at her. 'That's what I like to hear.' She nudged Toni with a polished nail. 'Come on, your turn to play dress-up.'

Toni turned reluctantly away and dug out her own costume. She felt aroused by Edie but there was another excitement thrumming away between her legs; it was the thought that maybe Red would be watching her tonight and she would finally start to make some headway into the investigation. She brushed her hair and lined her eyes with kohl. She had her best Miss Whiplash outfit and she was eager to try it on. First she slipped on skintight black plastic shorts, which only half covered her buttocks and had a zip that ran down the front. Then she wriggled into a half-cup bra to match. She joined these with thigh-high black boots and long black gloves. She pulled a black cap on to her head and pulled a short whip out of her bag. She was a dominatrix cliché but she didn't care.

She hadn't dared to look at Edie while she dressed but now that she was finished she turned away from the mirror and poised, glaring out from under the peak of her cap. Edie grinned. 'Ah, now I see where your heart really lies.'

Toni ran her fingers through the lashes of the whip and licked her dark-painted lips.

'You're on!' Steve was calling from the dressing-room door and the two of them turned towards him. 'Fuck! They're in for a treat out there tonight!'

Coral was making her way back from her performance and gave Toni the once over. She curled her lip disdainfully. 'Not very original, honey,' she hissed.

Toni bared her teeth in a mock snarl. 'We'll see, honey.' She turned to Edie, an idea quickly forming in her mind. 'Have you got any more chains?'

Edie's eyes flashed and she nodded.

'What do you say to a double performance then?'

'I'll go get them.'

Toni's pulse raced. She could hear the deep, sexy thump of the bass and the shouts of impatient men. Edie returned with the chain and Toni clipped it on to her collar. 'Follow my lead?'

Edie nodded again, too excited to speak.

'Let's go then.'

Steve had been standing open mouthed, slowly growing aware that Toni was no ordinary stripper and coupled with the knowledge of the chemistry that these two girls had between them, he knew that they were really going to blow them away tonight. He stood aside for Toni to lead Edie out by the chain, on to the stage.

The club seemed very dark after the glare of the dressing room and extremely hot. As Toni strutted down the length of the stage with Edie following, she wondered if the fat trucker had bothered to come see her.

The place seemed crowded and as Toni's eyes grew accustomed to the light she could see Onyx watching from a distance, the smoke from a slim cigar forming a halo around his head. She cracked her whip to show she meant business and the shouts of the men silenced. They weren't going to get a performance until they showed due respect. Toni paraded Edie up and down until she had a hushed, attentive crowd.

She wanted to see Edie dance and so she led her out on to the end of the stage, unclipping her lead-chain and cracking her whip as a signal for her to perform. She motioned to a bouncer standing by the stage that she wanted a chair and he passed one up. Toni placed one foot on it and watched Edie shimmy her glittering body to the music. She was magical, stretching and dipping so that her chains bounced and pulled around her body. Toni was transfixed by her small breasts bouncing as she danced and the sight of her pierced nipples carrying the chains made her hot and moist inside her tight shorts.

Edie twisted and twirled so that the back chain slipped up and down between her buttocks and Toni could imagine how the feel of it was arousing her. The atmosphere in the club was electric. More and more men were taking seats around the stage, and staring up, boggle-eyed at the shimmering dancer. Edie was dipping and opening her legs, teasing her audience with a glimpse of her pierced lips.

She pushed her booted foot away from the chair and advanced on Edie, clipping the chain back on to her collar. She led her to the chair and cracked the whip. Edie sat and Toni pushed the whip gently under her chin, so that Edie looked up. Her eyes were bright with arousal. Toni traced her breasts with the tip of the whip and brought it down between her legs, forcing them apart. Edie's rings glistened in the stage lights. She gripped the side of the chair, and remained with her legs open while Toni took her turn.

Toni danced for the men, who were watching slack jawed around the stage. The sight of their arousal sent hot shivers up and down her spine. One of them, a balding middle-aged man with a paunch and wearing a crumpled Hawaiian shirt placed a fifty-dollar bill on the stage. Toni bent to pick it up and could feel the heat emanating off him. Slowly she pulled the half-cups down so that her breasts sprang out. The man licked his lips and Toni dangled them just inches from the noses of the men nearest the stage. Carefully she rolled the bill up into a ball and flicked it back in his face. She adjusted her cap as she spun back towards Edie, still spreadeagled on the chair.

Facing Edie and with her back turned to the audience, Toni bent from the waist and slowly lowered her torso until she was watching the men from between the V of her legs. That was when she saw him, framed almost perfectly by the apex of her opened thighs. He was leaning against the back wall talking to Onyx but, as he brought a bottle of beer up to his lips, Toni could see that his eyes were actually on her.

Red. She felt that unexplainable tightening in her crotch as she rotated her ass and watched him through her legs. What was it that was so sexy about him? Was it the straight but over-large nose? His muscular torso crammed into a black shabby T-shirt? His dark tousled hair? Even upside down he looked dangerous – a fucker and a fighter.

Right, she told herself. I don't care how many women you've had, you're not going to forget this one. She straightened and knelt on the edge of the stage with her thighs spread wide and felt her nipples pucker tight. She lifted her pelvis slowly in time to the deep pulse of the beat. She leant back on one arm, her back arched, the hot lights caressing her pale torso in the smoky darkness of the club.

Toni's pussy throbbed. She felt so good, every muscle and sinew felt stretched and taut like the strings of a harp. She ran her right hand over her breasts and plucked at a nipple. Then, after glancing up to check that Red was still watching, Toni ran her hand down between her legs and felt for her zip. Slowly, she pulled it upwards. It ran right the way between her legs so that her black plastic crotch now split wide open to reveal her pussy lips. Toni smiled to herself. That was something which they didn't get every night. The men drooled and ogled. She had Red's undivided attention too. His bottle of beer hung by his side as he stared with dark, brooding eyes.

Spreading her pussy lips wide with her fingers, Toni stroked her clit, firmly and gently in tiny rotations, over and over. But she wasn't alone on the stage.

She rose, squeezing her breasts for Edie's benefit and walked towards the chair. Edie licked her lips, her breasts rising and falling and her sex glistening in the flashing club lights. She cracked the whip again and signalled for Edie to lie on the floor. Then, hooking the chain that joined each nipple ring with a finger, she pulled her slowly upwards. She knew it looked painful but Toni was careful not to really hurt her. Edie lifted her upper body with a dancer's grace until her head was just under Toni's crotch. Out came her tongue with its fabulous stud and she began to lap at Toni. Toni whipped off her cap and flung it into the audience, shaking her hair loose as she pressed her crotch down on to Edie's mouth. The sensation was unbelievable and Toni knew that they were causing a sensation. The excitement in the room was almost tangible. From the corner of her eye she caught sight of the bald man masturbating in his seat.

Toni noticed someone else watching them now, too. Curious, Coral had dressed and come back into the club to watch. She glowered, arms crossed across her chest, clearly furious at the sensation the two girls were making. Despite the glorious feeling of Edie between her legs, Toni was distracted. From the corner of her eye she watched her storm off to shout something at Onyx before walking out altogether. Red ignored her and slowly lifted his beer to his mouth but Toni noticed that Onyx went after her. She clearly didn't like competition. Well, it was tough.

She threw her head back so that her hair tumbled down her back and gave herself up to Edie's mouth. It wasn't quite enough, so she lifted one booted foot back on to the chair behind Edie and slipped the handle of her whip into her eager pussy. This was just for her now; she was oblivious to the baying men around the stage. It was the pinnacle of her performance fantasy. She worked her whip in and out of herself as Edie laved her clit. Her thighs tremored and the cries of her orgasm were drowned by the blaring music.

Toni felt shaky and stunned by how far she had gone with this one. She was, after all, on a stage in a club. Never one to give in to emotion, however, unless it was of the sexual kind, she calmly zipped herself up and cracked the whip for Edie to rise. As confidently as she had entered the bar she left, tugging Edie behind her on the chain.

Edie fell against her in the changing room, laughing. 'You were wild! I would just love for my friends in Phoenix to meet you. I'm soaking!' She tugged at the front of her shorts. 'Come on, you've got to do me now.'

Toni was trembling slightly, the rush of adrenaline she had felt on stage now making her feel weak. Edie lifted herself up on the shelf of the dressing table and pulled Toni between her legs. 'Hot bitch,' she was murmuring into Toni's mouth. 'Frig me hard.'

Toni felt her fingers guided into Edie and her thumb pressed on to her clit. Toni obliged, kissing her mouth and frigging her hard with her fingers. But her eyes were shut tight and behind her eyelids she could see Red, dark and brooding and dangerous. Edie was jerking on to her hand and Toni frigged her quicker and deeper, just like she wanted Red to do to her. She bit into the girl's neck and savoured her hot climax as her legs wrapped around her back.

17

Toni showered quickly in the dressing-room's functional bathroom. It was a far cry from the opulence of Onyx's apartment. Toni grimaced at the mildewing tiles and thought that it was no wonder so many of the girls chose to use his marble and onyx bathroom. She stashed her costume into her bag and wandered out into the warm night air to enjoy a cigarette. Her shoes crunched on gravel as she walked away from the club, putting a little distance between her and the thump, thump of the music. She walked to the far end of the car park and gazed out over the silent, empty desert.

Her orgasm on the stage tonight had left her feeling drained. She had wondered over the past few days how much of this investigation was about realising her own fantasies. Now that she had fulfilled one, she needed to concentrate on finding Caron. She blew a long line of smoke out into the air and smiled, wondering if Ms Crossley was pulling a burnt pot-roast out of an oven somewhere and wondering why her man was so late coming home. It was a possibility, wasn't it? Not every investigation had to have a sleazy ending.

'You're looking very pleased with yourself.'

Toni spun round at the sound of a husky voice. Her heart leapt as the flick of a lighter illuminated the familiar angular features.

'Josh!' She slumped against the fence. 'It's so good to see you.'

'And you.' Josh took a drag on his cigarette.

Toni threw hers away, disappointed that he hadn't greeted her with their customary bear-hug. She watched him in the darkness. 'How did your divorce case go?'

'Same old, same old. Bitter, twisted.'

'Oh.' Toni's hopes of a cheery reunion plummeted; she detected a deadness to his voice. Her throat constricted. She had a horrible feeling he was bringing bad news.

He got straight to the point. 'How far are you going to take this, Toni?' He ground his cigarette butt out with undue force and concentrated on his dusty toecaps.

Toni crossed her arms, goose bumps rippling her skin despite the warm desert air. 'As far as I have to, Josh. It's my job.' She stared into the horizon.

Josh hooked his thumbs into the back pockets of his jeans. Toni sneaked a look at him; he looked incredibly young and vulnerable.

'It's never just a job with you though, is it, Toni? There's always some thrill-seeking thrown in as well. I've come a long way to tell you that I don't want you to do this. It's too dangerous and too far from home.'

Toni barked with laughter. 'Home! Where the fuck's that?'

'LA. You and I have made our home there. I don't want you getting any more involved in this.'

Toni felt her hackles rise. 'Don't tell me what to do, Josh. I won't have anyone telling me how to live my life.'

'Well maybe it's time you took some advice from one who cares. You're going to take your sexual thrills too far, Toni, and end up wasted.' He dug out another cigarette and lit it with trembling fingers.

'Oh, for goodness' sake! I'd rather live on the edge than end up an emotional cripple and a twenty-five-year-old virgin!'

Josh rounded on her; she had never seen him angrier. 'Take a good look at yourself, Toni. You're so keen at barking orders you can't see what a bossy old harridan you really are.'

'Well, in that case you're better off without me, then!'

They stood in silence like too sulky children. But Toni's heart couldn't harden against him. 'You know how much I love you, Josh.'

Josh's eyes sparkled with unshed tears. 'I can't stand by and watch you live like this any more, Toni. It scares me too much.'

Toni's heart thundered with dread. 'Move on then; maybe it's time you did.'

Josh flicked his half-smoked cigarette on to the ground and scooped her up. She clung to his tall, rangy frame and drank in his familiar lemony scent. His breath was warm on her neck and she felt a hardening against her belly. She reached down and pressed her hand hard against his erection.

'Come on, Josh,' she whispered. 'Let's push some boundaries together.' The fence post caught her whack in the back as he threw her away from him.

'Get your filthy hands off me! I never thought I'd see the day you'd sink that low! You're my sister for fuck's sake!'

'Half-sister,' Toni corrected. 'Is that a no, then?'

'You want to do this thing? Well, you go ahead, but I'm not condoning it. Not any more. You're on your own, baby.'

'Well, maybe I've been wiping your ass long enough,' Toni spat back. 'You run along now and send me a postcard when you're all grown up.'

He towered over her, trembling with anger, but even now he was loath to leave her.

Toni rubbed her hand against her own crotch. 'You

know arguments get me all excited. I need to find myself a dick for the night and I don't mean a private one.'

It did the trick. Josh took one last disgusted look at her and clambered back into his jeep. Toni jumped to avoid the shower of gravel. He gunned the engine until he was well out of sight.

Toni stooped to pick up the remains of his Marlboro, which glowed like an ember in the dark. She brushed away a few grains of sand and placed her lips where his had been moments before. She pulled on it long and hard until she was sure that there would be no tears.

Josh was angry, sure, but he'd get over it. She would miss him like crazy but she'd done her job; it was time to let go. The cigarette tasted bitter in her mouth. Maybe one day she'd come to believe that. But if he had to move on, best he did it without looking back.

Toni took a deep breath and walked back towards the club.

'Toni, Onyx wants to see you in his office.' Steve met her at the door of the dressing room. If he had seen her talking to Josh then he gave no indication of it.

'Now?'

'Straight away.'

Irritated, Toni pushed past him. If he thought he was getting another floor-show tonight then he had another think coming – she felt completely drained. She grabbed her bag and made her way to the office, avoiding the bar. She had no wish now to see the gawking, salivating men there. Onyx was sitting in his chair and the air was thick with cigar smoke. Toni flung herself into a soft chair, awaiting praise for her stunning performance. Instead, Onyx remained silent and pushed a brown pay packet towards her.

She looked at it suspiciously. 'I didn't think I'd get paid so quickly.'

Onyx studied her for the longest time before speaking. 'You're fired.'

'Excuse me?'

'I said, you're fired.'

'Well, that was the shortest time I've been in employment. Except for the time I worked as a waitress and kneed the short-order cook in the balls on my first shift.'

'And how many of the other employees did you manage to screw in that time?'

Toni raised an eyebrow and kept her mouth shut; he had her fair and square on that one.

'The thing is, Toni, you're act is a little too ... lewd, shall we say, for this establishment.'

'Huh!'

'You and Edie put on a spectacular show tonight, there's no denying it. I see a lot of pussy displayed around here but you certainly raised a few eyebrows, not to mention a few cocks, with even the most jaded of us –'

'But?'

'Well, I can't afford to set a precedent like that. The girls here are dancers, not live sex acts. We're going to have to let you go.'

'That bitch Coral wouldn't have anything to do with this, would she?'

Onyx puffed on his cigar. 'My club, my decision.'

'Suit yourself, honey.' Toni grabbed the pay packet. 'Though I didn't really have you down as a guy who liked to be pussy-whipped. You can tell that cow that she shouldn't be afraid of a little competition.' Toni's self-satisfied exit was prevented by the appearance of two security guards in the doorway. 'Excuse me!' she grunted, but they stood, solid as rock, preventing her from leaving. She turned to hurl abuse at Onyx, but he was on his feet, and heading for her with a wicked glint in his eye.

'Close the door, guys. There's a few things I want to say to the lady.'

Toni wavered between fight or flight but there was no way even she was going to be able to fight her way through these three guys, and her heart began to beat an unpleasant tattoo. This was exactly the type of situation that Josh had worried about, and the fact that he had been right pissed her off even more.

'Spit it out, then, I haven't got all night.' She just about managed to conceal the tremor in her voice.

Onyx was breathing cigar smoke into her face – it reminded her of Al and a wave of nausea hit her. 'I knew you were a feisty one but I do wonder if it borders on stupidity. Don't flare your nostrils at me. You've enjoyed my hospitality here. I gave you a job. And what do I get in return? A real smart ass who breaks every house rule and then bad mouths my girlfriend when I have the audacity to fire her from my own club.' He gave a small nod to the men standing behind her and Toni felt both her arms gripped tight.

She pulled away from them but they held her fast. She winced as their fingers dug into her skin. 'Get your gorillas off me.'

'Uh, huh. I'm in charge now, honey. You're not the only one who likes to be boss, you know.' Onyx traced the line of her jaw with a fingernail and Toni's nerve endings prickled. 'Some women who've worked here would give their eye teeth to be held captive by two silent hunks and tormented into a state of sexual arousal by me.' He traced the outline of her nipples through her T-shirt.

'Get your fucking hands off me!'

'Now, now. That's not the attitude.' Onyx grabbed Toni's face hard. 'I bet if I felt up underneath your skirt right now, you'd be all moist and willing. Three blokes, what do you say? All in a day's work for a honey slut like you.'

His hand being slapped across her mouth smothered Toni's reply. His black eyes bored into hers as he handed his cigar to one of the security men to extinguish. No one relinquished his grip on her. She was held fast and was panicking, big time.

'You need to be taught a lesson, sugar.' He was nuzzling her neck as he talked and running his hands up and down her thighs. 'I could make you an honorary member of the Cobra Club, what do you say, guys? Fancy a piece of this little vixen? What do you say we hold her face down across the coffee table and take it in turns to give it to her up the butt? And when we've finished we'll give that bald guy in the front row a treat and call him in here to have a go as well. What do you say, honey? Fancy that? Want to join the Cobra Club?' He whispered in her ear as his hands wandered all over her writhing body. 'There are some women who positively thrive on it. The waiting, the humiliation, they love it. But not you; you like to hand it out. Why not take the time to find what it's like to surrender, to have someone else in charge?'

Onyx had pushed her skirt up to her waist and was fondling her cheeks, pushing her pants into the cleft of her buttocks. 'Ever had someone spank you till you cried and begged for mercy?' He kneaded her buttocks savagely with his hard fingers. 'Because this daddy thinks that's just what a bad girl like you really needs. A dose of discipline would do you good.'

Toni felt as if her head was going to explode, her blood pressure had soared so high. She liked to push things to the limits but she had surpassed herself with this one. What had she walked into here? Her arms felt raw and her thighs ached with trying to keep them together so that his hand didn't slither up between them. The strength of these men meant that she didn't stand a chance. They could have the entire audience forming a queue to fuck her and she wouldn't be able to prevent them.

A sob broke from her throat as terror engulfed her. Almost immediately, Onyx was signalling for the men to let her go. Her knees gave way with relief and she found herself supported by them instead of restrained. Onyx was returning to his chair. He took time to catch his own breath while Toni composed herself.

'Lucky for you, Toni, it's open to willing members only. We may have kinky sexual appetites but we are not psychopaths.' He flashed his brilliant teeth at her. 'Had you going there for a while though, sugar, didn't I?' He grabbed the front of his pants. 'You've got me all excited. OK, you two, you can leave now, and send Coral in here – she owes me a mother of a blow-job.'

Toni leant back against the door; afraid she was going to faint, nerves jumping in her groin. Onyx handed her a glass of water, which she sipped. 'I'm sorry I have to let you go. Really. But Coral is one jealous momma and she gives the best head ever. I meant it though – think about this little taster here tonight, see if you wouldn't like to dip your toes in again and let someone else take charge for a change. It could be a revelation to a control freak like yourself.' He brushed at a stray piece of cotton on his suit jacket. 'Perhaps you'd better leave before Coral gets here.'

Toni silently agreed. That was one confrontation she could do without tonight. She slipped out into the night, angry and shaken and, though she wouldn't admit it, heartbroken at Josh's decision to quit. What the hell, she told herself, he was a young man ready to make his own mark in life – she couldn't wet nurse him forever. She couldn't even think about what Onyx had put her through and pushed what had happened in the office to the back of her head.

She drove a good distance from the club until she found a bar that didn't advertise dancers and tidied herself up in the wing mirror before going in. Her eyes looked huge and dark shadows underlined them in the dusty glass. The country music swept over her as she walked into the warmth of the bar. A live band was playing and she found a table to collapse by. She lit a cigarette and inhaled deeply, letting the friendly atmosphere surround her like a cocoon. The waitress brought her drink and Toni sipped it gratefully, sinking deeper into her chair with relief.

Toni shook her head, irritated by the annoying voices inside her head. She loved Josh and didn't want to lose him, as a brother or as a friend. But she was working a case, wasn't she? She certainly hadn't made much progress on it so far. Deep in her gut there was an unquiet little stirring. Was there something else she wanted from Red, apart from Caron Crossley, she wondered. No man had ever been able to tell her what to do.

Would he?

And did she really want him to?

The next morning, the motel clerk handed her a wad of messages with a sly smirk on his face. Toni gave him one of her icy stares and waited to read them until she was in her room. There were three from Edie, worried sick about her, and two from Steve, wondering if they could get it together now that she'd been sacked. Toni grinned; she bet the clerk had had a field day taking these messages. There was nothing from Josh and nothing from Red. Toni seethed. She never chased men and these two were turning out to be real pains in the butt.

Toni was pissed, big time. She had really hoped to spend more than one night performing in the club. Her disguise as a dancer was over pretty quickly. Josh had deserted her and Onyx had turned out to be an asshole. She was on her own once again. She sat and brooded on her bed in the motel room, chewing on her third doughnut of the morning. Edie's messages were lying in the waste-paper basket. Toni retrieved one and punched out her number on her mobile. She owed her that at least. Edie sounded husky, like she'd just woken up.

'Edie? It's me, Toni.'

'Toni! I've been worried sick. The girls are all buzzing with the talk that that bitch Coral got you sacked because she's jealous of you.'

'I was too lewd, apparently.'

'You certainly were, kitten. My pussy's still throbbing with the thought of it.'

'Onyx humiliated me in his office before throwing me out.'

'Are you hurt? What did he do?'

'Nothing serious. Mind games more than anything. I think he just wanted to show me who was boss.'

'Bastard. I'll make sure to piss in his swimming pool.'

Toni smiled to herself.

'You wait till I tell the girls that I broke in a straight girl. They'll never believe me.'

'I'm not sure I believe it myself.'

'Keep in touch, yeah?'

'Sure.'

Toni fell back on the bed. She was bored and frustrated, always a dangerous combination.

Toni sucked the sugar off the fingers of her right hand and checked her cell phone messages with her left. Her beloved Corvette had been towed away for repairs. She was not to worry. It was in safe hands. Stan's ex-brother-in-law was taking good care of it.

She punched in the number.

'Stan?'

'Toni?'

'Yeah. Hi. Thanks for sorting my car out.'

'No problem. You got yourself an address yet?'

'Not yet. Where are you?'

'Cruising out on the interstate. You got yourself a rental?'

'Yeah.' She wasn't phoning to talk about cars. 'Is Nick there?'

'Sure is. Say hi, Nick. It's Toni. He's gone all red. What you up to?'

'I'm bored and horny.'

'Now that's a crime. You want two police officers to come round and sort it out?'

'I don't think there's time. Maybe you can talk me through the problem over the phone?'

'I can try but it's not something I've ever done before.'

'I don't think you'll find it hard after your performance the other day.' Toni's fingers edged down into her panties.

'What do you want me to say?'

'I want you to tell me what you'd do to me if you were here.'

'With Nick listening?'

'Especially with Nick listening. You're not going to be shy with me now, are you?'

'Baby, I'd give my pension to be there with you now.'

'With your head between my thighs?'

'With my head between your thighs – Whoa there, boy, you crossed the line then.'

'And your tongue in my slit.'

'Jeez . . .'

She could hear him clearing his throat.

'I'd have my tongue buried deep inside you, sugar . . . You just keep your eyes on the road there, boy . . . I don't know, I'll ask. Can I put you on speakerphone?'

'Yes. Now lick me.'

'I'm licking, baby. I'm licking real hard. What? . . . Nick says he's watching.'

'Oh, I like that, Stan.' Toni's fingers were stroking her cleft and lingering on her clit. 'I've got my legs open wide and you're tonguing my clit and Nick is by the door watching. Is he excited?'

'He says he's got a hard-on like iron. Hold on . . . he's pulling in.'

'So he can pull off?'

'Never mind him. You got your panties off for real, Toni?'

'Of course. My fingers are working on myself as we speak. I'm pretending that they're yours.'

'Can I kiss you now?'

'Yes. I can taste myself on your mouth.'

'I'm opening you up now. I've got my fingers inside you. You're all hot and sticky.'

'Yes, I am.' Toni's fingers were working faster.

'You're running like honey. My mouth is on your nipple and I'm sucking hard. My fingers are up, up inside and I can feel you clenching around them. Are you really touching yourself?'

'Yes, yes I am.'

'Can you feel me there?

'Oh yes. Your teeth are biting me hard. I'm squirming on the bed beneath you. Your thumb is working my clit.'

'I'm going to fuck you now, Toni. I don't care that Nick is watching. I've got to have you. Here I come. My cock is nudging your creamy slit.'

'Yes, I can feel it. You're big and hard inside me.'

'Oh yes, Toni. You feel good, hot and moist around my cock.'

'Harder . . .'

'Harder . . .'

Toni plunged her fingers up inside, hard and fast. She could hear Stan's heavy breathing on the other end. 'Fuck me, Stan.'

'Oh I am, baby, I am.'

Toni was coming; incapable of speech now, she moaned incomprehensibly down the phone.

'I can see you, baby,' Stan was murmuring. 'I can see you on the bed with the phone to your ear and your hand working furiously between your legs. I just wish I was there. Oh that's good.'

Toni drifted back to reality. 'Are you OK, Stan?'

'We're fine, Toni. Seen more of each other than most partners, I can tell you. I'll call you when the car's fixed.'

Toni yawned. 'OK.'

'And maybe we can get together?'

'Sure.'

'Bye, Toni.'

'Bye, boys.' They disconnected at the same time.

18

Toni parked up and wandered into town. What other choices did she have left, except to hope that she bumped into Red? She had been so convinced that she would meet him through the club that she was a little thrown. She knew that they hung out outside that bar and that made her think about the waitress, recounting her tantalizing encounter with Red and some of his gang. She had stared out of the window when she should have been working, frustrated and horny at the memory. That would be as good a place to start as any, and she could at least get herself a decent cup of coffee.

The restaurant was quiet this early in the day, and Toni was in luck – the waitress remembered her. She placed the steaming cup in front of Toni and slipped into the seat opposite. She leant towards her, her cleavage trembling with excitement. 'You're not going to believe this.'

Toni sipped her hot coffee and curled her toes with pleasure at the warm aroma.

'What?'

'The bikers are having a party up at the club house.'

Toni perked up; it was about time that she had a break. 'Really? Where's that?'

'I don't know yet, it's all a bit hush-hush but I heard it through the prison grapevine.'

Toni arched a quizzical eyebrow that the waitress dismissed with a flap of a hand. 'Oh, my brother, it's not important. But I do know that they throw the most tremendous parties; I know girls who've been. Girls who like a bit of danger, you know. I'm creaming my panties, I'm so excited – you don't get a decent fuck very often living in this town, I can tell you.' Her pupils were huge with excitement but she lowered her voice a fraction, aware of the manageress hovering nearby. 'I heard that some girls get taken on as chapter maids, so they get to travel around with the gang, and sometimes they pass you on to the next chapter, like you're their property or something. My brother told me of a girl from Frisco whose old man swapped her for a bike.'

Toni laughed. 'Shit, I'm not even sure who got the best deal.'

The waitress looked suddenly embarrassed. 'Sorry, it's just that when we spoke the other day I thought you were looking for, you know, a little –' she whispered the word '– domination. My mistake.' She edged out of the booth but Toni clasped her wrist, her mind racing as she thought of Caron Crossley 'passed on' somewhere, property of some other chapter.

'Don't go, I didn't mean to offend you.' The waitress looked doubtful, her pink cheeks clashing with her bleached bob. Toni persevered; she was too close to the prize to let go of it now. 'I make jokes when I'm embarrassed, that's all. I am interested.'

'Listen, lady, these aren't varsity boys you're dealing with here. Lots of them have done time and there are only three things to do in the can – work out, do drugs or dream about sex. If you like curling up on the sofa with a pizza and a bottle of wine on a Saturday, bikers aren't the guys for you. I don't want to get you involved in something you're not one hundred percent sure of.'

Toni's heart thundered. Domination. That was what she did, not what she endured. She didn't know if she could go through with this, not even for Caron Crossley.

And yet the thought of being manhandled by Red was perversely compelling. She took a deep breath. 'Honey, I've just had the sack from the Sphynx because my dance routine was too rude, so don't you worry about me.'

The waitress looked her in the eye, saw she wasn't lying and softened a little. 'That story I told you, the other day, well I've been looking for a little action ever since. That biker guy, the one in charge, he must really know what he's doing because he's had me revved up for months. But I really don't want to drag you into something that's too heavy for you to handle.'

Do or die, make or break, shit or get off the pot. It was Toni's choice. She could go back to LA that afternoon, make it up with Josh, tell Mrs Crossley that she hadn't been able to find her niece. She could take boring jobs that didn't involve porn actresses, or erotic dancers, or dangerous men. Shit, while she was at it, why didn't she just let her pussy heal over and join a knitting bee, or start making pickles? The thought repulsed her far more than stepping into a new sexual arena.

She scribbled her number on to a piece of paper and pushed it towards the waitress. 'That's my cell phone number. Let me know when it's on.'

The waitress glanced over her shoulder at the manageress, who was now bearing down on them. 'You and I are going to have such fun.' She quickly hid the number in the pocket of her uniform and slipped out of her seat.

Toni watched her hips sway across the restaurant and felt the hairs stand on the back of her neck. She wondered how close she was to finding Caron Crossley.

There was no way anyone was going to gatecrash this biker party, Toni thought. The guy in front of her had to be the most imposing front of house manager she had ever seen. Six foot seven and built like solid rock. Toni hugged her denim jacket around her despite the warm desert air. If that guy didn't let them in then she wasn't arguing. But more frightening still – what if he wouldn't let them back out?

He held a pool cue in one meaty hand. 'Invites, ladies?'

Carla batted her eyelashes. 'Are they strictly necessary if we tell you that we know how to enjoy ourselves?'

'I'm sure you do, ma'am, but it's my duty to only let in members of this chapter or their invited guests.'

Toni felt irritation churning in her stomach. She had trusted this halfwit waitress to get them in when she would have done better on her own. She thought of Red somewhere inside and felt as if she had been stood up.

'Do you accept blow-jobs as bribes?' Carla was stroking her finger up and down the greasy front of the biker's leather waistcoat.

The biker swallowed hard. 'Maybe.'

Toni swallowed her revulsion, wondering when was the last time he washed. This was seriously pissing her off. She felt like a C-list celeb bartering to be let in to some cheap nightspot. Caron Crossley, you owe me big time, she muttered under her breath.

'Well, let's not waste any time.' Carla was reaching for his zip.

'Hold on, I need someone to cover for me.' He used the pool cue to knock three times on the door.

It was Red himself who stepped out. 'What is it?' A blast of hot air and music came out with him.

'Got two ladies here who would like to party. This one's asking if we accept blow-jobs instead of credit cards.'

Toni felt humiliated and cheap and hated Carla for making her that way.

Red looked her way. 'What about the friend?'

'The friend's looking for a party but I'm not that desperate, sugar.' Toni shot him her iciest stare.

Red grinned. 'I'm sure you're not.' He didn't appear to recognise her from the club. But she couldn't be sure. He had an extremely self-satisfied air about him. Red spoke to the doorman but ran his eyes over her. 'Well, the feisty one can come with me and you can let the other one in when she's sucked you off.' He stepped aside for Toni to enter the building. She cocked an eyebrow and slipped past him. Out of the corner of her eye she caught Carla dropping to her knees in front of the bouncer and reaching up to unzip his fly.

Red must have seen the look on her face, a mixture of revulsion and interest. 'Something tells me that you two aren't looking for the same thing here tonight.'

'I'm certainly not looking to snag the knees of my stockings, giving head just to get into a party.'

'Neither is your friend, surely. She's hoping to sink a lot lower than that and she's come to the right place.' He pulled the door shut just as Carla was opening her pink lips around the doorman's stubby cock. 'I can't imagine what you are doing here. No lady comes to a biker party by accident. Or are you just looking to be persuaded to be a dirty biker slut?'

'Nobody persuades me to do anything. I was just curious.'

Red reached for the door handle again. 'This isn't a zoo, lady. We're not here to satisfy your curiosity.'

Toni's heartbeat accelerated. He was going to throw her out. She improvised quickly. 'I'm curious to see how far my bitch will go.' She turned and looked Red straight in the eye. 'I can make my own fun. But I do have to keep my eye on the little whore as you can see.'

Red's face broke into a sly grin. 'Best we get you a drink and give you a tour then.'

'About time.' Toni slipped her denim jacket from her shoulders as if it were a fur stole. Red found himself holding it. He scratched his goatee and grinned down at her, lines crinkling at the corners of his eyes.

'I'll hang this up for you then.' He threw it over the banister rail for want of anywhere better.

Toni smoothed her hands over her tight black dress and admired him from behind. He had a great body, lean and muscular. That tattoo disappearing into the sleeve of his T-shirt really turned her on. A quick image of him screwing her on the stairs flashed into her head. He turned back to her and Toni struck a haughty pose that allowed him to run his eyes over her body. She had picked the dress for maximum effect.

He ran his hand over his chest as he looked her over. It was a very masculine gesture and one that always turned Toni on. It also afforded her a glimpse of his grazed knuckles and silver chapter ring.

He flashed white teeth at her. 'Nice dress. I'm surprised I can't see your bush it's so tight.'

'All in good time.'

Red's nostrils dilated slightly and she knew he was turned on. His hand moved over his chest slowly, as if subconsciously he was feeling hers. Behind her the door opened and she could hear Carla's heels clipping across the hallway. Toni kept her eyes on Red as she barked, 'Go and clean your teeth. I don't want to smell his come on your breath all night.' She turned sharply with a warning look at Carla, which sent the waitress scampering upstairs in search of a bathroom. A warm hand was placed on the small of her back.

'Let's get that drink.' Red found her a beer in the enormous refrigerator in the kitchen. He was assessing her all the time. His eyes dipped to the arch of her throat as she drank from the bottle.

'That's good.' She licked the drops from her lips suggestively. Someone approached and whispered something in Red's ear.

'I need to go and sort some business. But I'll be back, OK?'

Toni shrugged. 'Sure.'

Red disappeared and Toni moved slowly deeper into the house, getting a feel of the place. Men in well-worn leather and greasy denim let their eyes wander lazily over her as she passed. There was no pretence at politeness. This wasn't a networking party. She cringed at the sexist badges and pins which covered waistcoats and jackets. A guy wearing a T-shirt with the logo 'Beg For It Bitch' was idly fondling a woman's ass but otherwise ignoring her as he chatted to his mates. The woman in question sported a mean dragon tat, which swept all the way up her right arm to her neck so that it looked as if it was nibbling her ear. She certainly looked as if she was more than capable of looking after herself.

There were plenty of women, most of them draped around a man, and Toni examined their faces without being too obvious. Could she risk showing around Caron's photo? She doubted that she would get anything but mistrust. It was warm and the music was pumping. Around her everyone was laughing and talking and drinking. It felt good. She felt the stares from a few of the men. There were plenty of appreciative glances but no one approached her. Perhaps she was losing her touch. Or maybe they had seen her talking to Red. Toni felt her blood begin to race. There was an awful lot of red-blooded male around her. She had never seen so many tattoos. She sipped her drink and smiled coyly at a beefcake with biceps like rocks and chipped oily nails. She would just love to have him begging for mercy. She imagined him chained to his bike and his stomach muscles tightening with pain as she dripped hot engine oil on to his sweaty chest.

'So much for girly chats in the ladies' room. You can be the real mean bitch, can't you?' Carla's minty breath was on her neck.

Toni turned. 'You said it. And in case you're wondering, I'm here as your mistress.'

Carla's dark eyebrows shot up into her blonde curls. 'Oh.' Her eyes were roving over the men like a child in a toyshop.

Red returned and Toni's pulse quickened. 'Seems like you've got a fan out there . . .'

'Carla.'

'Well, Carla, we've a little club within a club and, if your mistress allows, I was wondering if you'd like to come to a private party.'

Toni stalled for time. She wasn't sure quite what she was getting into here. 'How do we know it's safe?'

'It's OK. I have the last word in how far things go. The little waitress here knows I have good control over proceedings. We've met before.'

Toni could sense Carla oozing into her panties as they spoke. 'Will she be the only girl?'

'No, we have others. Some are visitors like yourselves and some are the permanent property of the club.'

'I'd have to watch.'

'Of course. I'm hoping that your pleasure doesn't come entirely from voyeurism; that maybe you like a little action yourself?'

Toni raised an eyebrow. 'Maybe.'

Red grinned and held out an arm. 'Then this way please.'

He steered them towards a staircase leading to the basement and Toni's heart hammered. She wasn't sure if she felt sick with excitement or disgust. Maybe a little bit of both. All she knew was that she wasn't able to let go of being in charge. Carla, on the other hand, was quivering in anticipation.

Toni turned on her. 'What are you so excited about?'

Carla looked confused.

'Don't presume that I'm going to allow you to be fucked. I'm still undecided.'

Red's eyes flicked from one to the other.

'Take your panties off.'

'Here?' They were standing at the top of the basement steps and Carla glanced nervously at the surrounding partygoers.

But Toni needed to be in charge. She would probably only have one crack at this and she didn't want Red to think she was playing at it. She slapped Carla hard on the cheek. 'Don't argue with me, bitch.' Toni held out her hand for the underwear.

Carla's cheek glowed from Toni's handprint and a curl tumbled over her eye, but she did as she was told. Toni wasn't sure if the brightness in her eyes was tears or excitement. Probably both. She slipped her panties down and stepped out of them, handing them to Toni in a shaking hand.

Toni took them, rubbing the flimsy material between her fingers. 'You are such a naughty girl, Carla. I shouldn't have to tell you twice.' She turned to Red. 'You first.'

As Red walked down the steps to the basement door, Toni whispered to Carla, 'If you want out, just say you want them back. I'll know what you mean.'

Carla touched her hot cheek with a shaky hand. 'I do need to be corrected sometimes.'

'I know you do. But if it goes too far, just ask for them back. OK?'

Carla nodded. 'OK.'

They stepped into a dark warm basement, the heavy door shut with a muffled thud behind them and Toni prayed that it would be OK.

19

They walked down a long dark corridor before Red unlocked another door and let them in to a square room. If Toni had expected candles and chains hanging from dungeon walls then this wasn't it. It was more of a retro seventies look with glass-topped tables and white walls. Onyx was sitting in a large black leather chair sipping a drink. He recognised her immediately but didn't speak. There were no bikers in evidence. Panic began to stir in Toni's gut.

Onyx's voice was a deep rumble. 'Two new little maids. How lucky.'

Red spoke from behind her. 'Only one. This one is the mistress.'

A cloud crossed Onyx's face. 'Not allowed, you know that.'

Toni could feel Red tense behind her.

'There's no room for sentiment in the Cobra Club, Red. Take her home.' Onyx's jaw was set with anger.

'I said she could come. I run this chapter.'

'But not the Club. What's wrong with you? This isn't a wife-swap in the 'burbs.'

'I liked her performance the other night and thought maybe she could do with a firm male hand.'

Toni's blood pressure shot through the roof. Red had known who she was all along. There was no way she was going to be allowed to be in charge here.

Onyx's dark face split into a wide grin. 'Oh, she most certainly could. I thought you were going soft on me there for a moment. Well you can take charge of her then.'

Toni's teeth clenched at being referred to as no more than a plaything but a bolt of excitement shot between her legs none the less. She spun on Red, anger in her eyes.

He looked slightly amused and pressed a finger on to her mouth. 'Ssh now and let me take care of you here, just for one night. I know you're dying for someone who's man enough to break through that tough shell.'

Toni's eyes widened in horror; she didn't think so.

'You don't think I bought that mistress shit, do you? However, if you don't like the rules you are both free to leave now before we start.' To prove his point he stepped towards the door and unlocked it.

Carla spoke up. 'I'm here to have some fun and I'll have my panties back now you're not in charge any more.'

Toni thought she detected a revengeful gleam in her eye. 'We're free to go.'

'Oh, I know. But I'm not going anywhere. I got you into this party and all the thanks I got was a smack across the face. I don't know why you're really here but you're not in charge, lady. Not here.'

Onyx was grinning like a Cheshire cat. Toni was rooted to the spot, confused and unsure.

Red was standing by the open door. 'If you don't like the rules, you really should leave now. If you stay then it'll be on the understanding that I will take care of you.'

Toni took a step towards the door and Red's stern face didn't change. A nerve jumped in his cheek. She should go. All the way back to LA. A heavy beat in her crotch held her back. Red was offering her a chance to explore a part of her sexuality she had never explored before – its vulnerability. She looked from Onyx to Carla and back at Red. He really was a sexy son of a bitch. It was double-dating with a perverted twist.

She looked up at Red and the words pained her: 'You promise to look after me?'

Red smiled. 'I certainly do, baby. You'll be my guest of honour.' He pulled her to him and Toni opened her lips for a kiss, but instead he whispered into her mouth. 'Take your panties off now. The same rules apply. If you ask for them back then it's over.'

Toni swallowed and did as she was told, slipping them down under her skirt and pressing the damp silk into Red's hand.

Red's dark eyes bored into hers. 'Good girl. I knew we could have fun.'

She wanted to fuck him, now, in the doorway.

Behind her, Onyx's deep voice boomed, 'OK, ladies, on your knees while I tell you the rules.'

Reluctantly Toni tore herself away from Red. Carla was already in front of the chair, looking up in anticipation at Onyx. Toni dropped to her knees with a look of distaste.

'Remove that look, lady; you are here through choice, not force. Remove it or you will be asked to leave.'

Toni dropped her eyes to the floor.

Onyx continued, 'We have many levels here in the Cobra Club. When you have completed a level you will be asked if you wish to proceed to the next. It is advisable not to begin a level if you think you may not be able to complete it. I promise you, ladies, we will open you up to experiences and pleasures you never thought existed. All we ask is submission and compliance.'

An involuntary grunt escaped from Toni's lips.

'I realise that it is more difficult for some than others. Some know why they are here while others find it difficult to admit even to themselves what their own desires are.

'Carla, I'm sorry to say that you have already completed the first level, so I'm now denied the pleasure, so I'm going to request that you remove your skirt and sit on the glass table while Toni undergoes her first task.'

Toni's face burnt. The bastard was going to get a blow-job out of her. There was no way. He was in no rush, however; both he and Red watched as Carla rose to her feet and slipped out of her skirt. The contrast of her neat black bush to her blonde curls excited Toni, despite the task in front of her. Now Carla was dressed only in her high heels and her tight pink blouse. Beneath her own skirt Toni's pussy clenched in arousal.

Onyx shifted slightly in his leather chair. 'Oh that's nice, Carla. That's a nice, nice pussy. Can you sit on the edge of the table there and open your legs for me, baby?'

Carla did as he asked. High heels set some distance apart; she lowered herself delicately on to the edge of the glass table. She perched her buttocks on the table edge but took most of her weight on her arms; her smooth thighs tensed as she opened them. Toni's throat grew dry as she watched Carla's neat black bush part. Toni glanced from her peroxide curls back down to the black line between her parted thighs. The contrast was intensely erotic and obviously the men thought so too.

'Suck me off while I watch this.'

Toni jumped when she realised that he was talking to her. Hypnotised by the soft thrum of Onyx's deep voice and the view of Carla's pussy, Toni shuffled forward on her knees until she was between Onyx's thick thighs. As she unzipped his trousers she watched Carla's pussy split open, the black hair separating to expose her pink inner lips.

Onyx pushed Toni's head down into his lap. 'Concentrate on what you're doing there or we'll throw you out.'

He made it sound as if it was he who was doing her the favour. Toni placed her hands on Onyx's spread knees, the expensive material of his trousers smooth beneath her touch. Toni opened her lips and took Onyx's thick black cock into her mouth. She didn't bother to be too gentle, she thrust her tongue into the hole at the tip and swirled it under the folds of his foreskin.

'Take it easy, you rough little bitch,' Onyx was murmuring above her. He grabbed her by the hair so that he could guide her head better. As Toni moved her mouth over his swollen cock, she tilted her head so that she could watch Carla, perched on the glass table edge, legs spread with her pink all gleaming. She couldn't see Red; he was somewhere behind her still.

'Don't move, baby, you keep that pretty pink pussy open for me now, you hear. OK, now you can swallow me further than that, I know you can. You'll get your turn to show off later – I know you like doing that.' His big black hand was still in her hair, holding her face into his crotch. 'Give me some more tongue, you little bitch. Ah, that's it. That's good. I think you could give Coral a run for her money. Oh, baby, that's nice.'

Toni could sense him begin to pulse but he held back. Her jaw ached but still she kept going down in him. Her own juices were running freely between her thighs; she could feel them all slippery. Her knees hurt on the hard floor.

'Slide yourself back on to the table, baby, I want to see those honey juices on the glass. I want you to show me that you're excited because I know this little bitch sucking my cock is getting hot for it.'

Toni worked her tongue for all it was worth, straining

to see Carla doing her thing on the table. She seemed a little self-conscious now but was still happy to obey. She moved back on to the glass tabletop and Toni could only guess at how cold the glass felt on her hot aroused pussy. Carla licked her lips and wiggled her ass on the table, rotating her pelvis so that her wet pussy smeared the glass.

'Oh, I like that, baby. I want to be under there watching you do that.'

In reflex to the suggestion, and deeply aroused, Toni sucked harder, swallowing his cock deeper than she thought she could and, despite himself, Onyx came, pulsing into her throat. He gasped in shock at the force of it and his jism flooded her throat, hot and bitter. He held her head so she couldn't pull away but Toni swallowed it all, eager now to please. Despite all previous reservations, she wanted to be on to the next step; her cunt was aching to be filled.

Onyx released her and Toni fell back on to her haunches, catching her breath, skirt riding high and come dribbling on to her chin. His cock showed no sign of collapsing and, as he stood, it pushed his shirt out like a tent pole. Carla sat on the table, waiting for her next instruction.

Onyx wasn't slow to issue one. 'On all fours now, baby, out here in the middle of the room. That's right. Red? You want one of these to give you some head?'

Red shook his head and Toni wondered at his reluctance; Carla had told her that he hadn't touched her in the restaurant that time either.

'Toni, take your skirt off, get your sweet little ass on to the other glass table and let's see that hot pussy you like showing off so much.'

She wriggled out of her skirt with her back to them both. Turning, she lowered her backside on to the table edge. It was cold and sensual against her bare skin. Watching for their reaction she spread her legs wide. She wasn't disappointed. Onyx gave a low whistle and Red's eyes darkened with lust. Toni thrust her breasts out towards them and inwardly smirked.

When Red spoke his voice was low and husky. 'Are you girls ready to jump a couple of levels now? I've got a great game we can play.'

Carla and Toni both nodded. Toni was ready all right; her pussy was heavy and dripping.

'I want them blindfolded,' Red continued, and Onyx grinned at the suggestion.

'I like your thinking.' He pulled out a drawer and took out two black silk blindfolds. Toni's heart careened as Red approached. Her skin was tingling for his touch and she felt dizzy with lust as his hands tied the blindfold around her head. She sensed him standing over her, looking at her and her sex ripened further. 'We're moving on a little quickly now, ladies, but I know that you are going to love this game.'

Toni wriggled on the table. 'I want you both to stay in your positions. You both look fantastic. I can see how aroused you are, but by the time I'm finished I'm going to have you both sobbing to be fucked.'

Toni certainly hoped so.

'I think we ought to tie this one to the table for good measure.' It was Onyx's voice and Toni tensed.

'Not without her permission. Toni, yes or no?'

Toni nodded. She wanted to scream at them to get on with it. Soon she felt her ankles being tied to the table legs, not too tightly but enough so she couldn't get up. Then her wrists were bound. She could lean her weight back on them but she was now held on to the table in that position, with her pussy exposed.

'What a sweet little muff, no wonder she likes showing it off so much.' Onyx was talking about her as if she wasn't in the room again.

'Bring them in, Onyx.' Toni could hear the arousal in Red's voice even more clearly now that she couldn't see him.

The room went quiet, she could hear the door being unlocked and opened. She felt suddenly vulnerable and naked. She wondered what or who was going to come through the door. Then the sound of footsteps, more than one person's, and muffled curses as men filed into the room. She could smell musk and fresh sweat. Her quim burned hot as she sensed several men gaping at it. How many she couldn't guess but she had a feeling she was about to find out.

'OK, guys, you know the rules. You only touch what I tell you to touch. Agreed?' More shuffling. Someone cleared their throat. 'See that table over there, it's smeared in love juices. You need to tell me which of these hot little bitches it belongs to.'

Toni heard a gasp and guessed it was Carla. She wondered if she was still on all fours. Her heart was banging in her chest and her clit was throbbing painfully.

'Who's first?'

Red was the only voice she heard. No one else spoke and she guessed that they had been told not to. Toni thought of the story Carla had told her, about Red's visit to the restaurant. He obviously got off on this – the thrill of manipulating his men, of allowing them to become aroused but unable to satisfy themselves. She wondered why they did it. The same reason as her probably. The anticipation of the unexpected was incredibly arousing. Something was happening; she strained her ears and her senses to guess what and then she felt breath, hot and heavy between her legs. Her knees jerked together as reflex but they were held apart by the ropes. Red spoke somewhere in the room.

'One taste of each. The table and then each girl in turn. Point to who you think the juice belongs to.'

Toni bit her bottom lip and suppressed a groan as a hot tongue touched her sex. It was tentative, probably nervous and flicked at her pussy as if it would bite. She wondered at how aroused the men must be, being led into a room where two half-naked females were waiting with their legs open for their love juices to be tasted. The flicking tongue was there again, delicate and ineffectual. Her pelvis strained towards it but she was held back again by the ropes. No wonder Onyx had wanted her bound; it was torture.

'I said one taste.' Red's voice again. 'If you can't do better than that then it's your own fault.'

There was the sound of scuffling feet and whoever had been between her legs went. They were soon replaced. Toni was straining to work out who was moving in the room. She heard Carla mewling in pleasure and agony somewhere near. Hot breath panted between her legs again. This one was determined to get a good taste of her. His tongue was warm and firm and dug into her slit with authority. Toni moaned as the tongue slipped up on to her clit. Her chest heaved with disappointment as it abandoned her. She couldn't do this. Her pussy felt cold and wet. It throbbed with arousal.

'That's enough,' she growled. 'I need a fuck.'

'You know the magic words, honey.' Red was standing behind her. 'Say them and we all go away.'

Toni was uncomfortable on the table, her legs and arms were beginning to ache, but it only made the ache between her legs all the more accentuated. She bit her lip and tensed as another tongue found its way into her creamy slit. Red's breath was in her ear. She sensed that he was kneeling behind her and that he was watching the men licking her out, one by one. She pictured his stern face watching dispassionately as her lips grew puffier and more aroused as each man tasted her. She would never know who they were. They were coming quicker now. She didn't know whether they were keeping up the pretence of the game or not. Every now and then she heard a little whimper from Carla and knew that she must be suffering agonies of arousal.

Another tongue moved over her clit and Toni surrendered, hanging her head back and moaning in agony. She was senseless with arousal, not caring how she looked or who fucked her as long as someone did.

'OK, all out.'

Toni wanted to cry. She'd had enough but if she bailed out now she would die of frustration. Her blindfold was removed and she blinked at the light. All was as before, just the four of them. Onyx was grinning but Toni noticed a fine film of sweat on his top lip. 'Are we ready to move on to another level, ladies?'

Carla didn't hesitate. 'Yes,' she whimpered to the floor. She was still on all fours. 'Toni?'

Toni couldn't bring herself to answer. She was aroused and angry at her compliance in their games.

Red spoke for her. 'I think this one needs a little more time to think.'

'Then she can watch her friend being punished instead.' Onyx moved to the drawer again. Toni watched as he took out a paddle. He tapped himself playfully on the thigh as he came to stand behind Carla. 'Move round so that your friend can watch your punishment.' Carla shifted position so that Toni could see her bare ass presented to her. Toni's groin pulsed as Onyx knelt by Carla and stroked her buttocks gently with his big black hand. The contrast was electrifying. Red was still close by, his breathing shallow.

'Do you want to see how aroused your friend is?'

Toni bit her lip and didn't answer but her eyes were glued to Carla's white buttocks. Onyx's hand slipped over her ass and slid down between her thighs. His fingers were glistening as he withdrew them. 'Dripping with honey and wanting so badly to be fucked. But I have to punish her because you are such an unhelpful little bitch.' His hand was still smoothing over Carla's cheeks. 'And this one is a dirty wanton little whore.' Without warning, Onyx drew up the paddle and caught Carla a viscous swipe across both butt cheeks. Her buttocks trembled with the blow and Carla screamed, more in surprise than pain. 'I really think she should have her panties back now and act like a good girl.' Another slap with the paddle. This time on the left cheek only and hard. Toni watched the white flesh turn red. She ground her teeth in pleasure.

'Put your panties back on, little slut,' Onyx taunted.

On her hands and knees, Carla answered, 'No.'

Another swipe, on her right cheek. Her flesh wobbled with the blow. 'What did you say to me?'

'No!'

Whack! 'You cheeky little slut, saying no to me.' Onyx brought the paddle down with such force that Carla squealed in pain. Her buttocks darkened to a deep crimson. 'What do you say now?' Onyx taunted.

Carla drew a shuddering breath. 'I said no.'

Toni flinched at the sharp blow of the paddle as Onyx brought it against Carla's raw flesh with all his strength. Toni gasped in horror and excitement as Carla's pale skin glowed from the blows.

Toni's throat was dry. Carla's knees seemed as if they

were about to buckle. Her thighs shook with the exertion of kneeling so long. She caught her breath again and cried out. 'No! No! No!'

Toni knew it was a challenge and a request. So did Onyx. Red was still behind her where she couldn't see his reaction. Again and again, Onyx brought the paddle down on Carla's raw buttocks. Carla whimpered and squirmed beneath the blows and Toni cringed at the sight of the tortured flesh in front of her, bright red and glowing with pain. She could almost feel the heat. Carla loved the agony but when Onyx slapped her with a particularly viscous swipe she collapsed on to her front and sobbed.

Toni swallowed hard. Red came from behind her and stood over Carla. 'Shit, Onyx, she won't be able to sit down for a week.'

Onyx was flexing his hand. 'That's one tough little honey. Get up, girl, and sort yourself out.'

Carla staggered to her feet, wiping at her tears.

'What do you say?'

Carla sniffed and wiped her cheeks with the back of her hand. 'Thank you.'

Onyx softened slightly. 'There's a mirror in the corner – go and admire my handiwork.'

Toni watched as Carla moved tentatively across the room. Her buttocks must have been on fire. She stood with her back to the mirror and gloated over her marked buttocks. Toni watched in fascination as Carla touched her cheeks with trembling fingers, admiring the red welts over her shoulder. It was clearly exciting Onyx too, he had a dangerous glint in his eye.

'Come and kneel over here, you naughty little slut.' He caught Carla by the elbow and shoved her on to the floor. She knelt up, keeping her scorched buttocks from coming into contact with the ground. Her breathing was shallow and excited. 'Do you want your panties back yet?'

Carla shook her head.

Toni was growing angry. Both men's attention seemed to be concentrated solely on Carla and Toni's groin was aching for some attention.

'Put your hands behind your back then, slut.' Onyx stood over the kneeling waitress and pressed her head to the floor with his hand so that Carla's left cheek touched the floor and her arms stretched out straight behind her. Carla was unable to move now and her ass and quim were entirely exposed. Toni could see that Carla found the bonds thrilling, while she felt a flutter of panic deep in her gut. Carla was revelling in her vulnerability; it was the sex to her. Face down, ass up, hands tied. She was property now. This was how you earned your biker-slut colours.

Toni flicked her gaze to Onyx. A fine sheen of perspiration coated his upper lip; otherwise he seemed completely composed. Surely he was going to fuck her now? Instead he went back to his drawer and took out a double dildo. He forced it unceremoniously at Toni. 'Suck it so it's slippery for your friend.'

Toni's mouth opened in reflex and she sucked on the rubber dildo until she thought that she would gag.

He knelt behind Carla. 'Oh, baby. You have such a sweet pussy.' He offered the dildo to her sex and Toni squirmed, wishing it was her. The look on her face told her all she needed to know; her mouth gaped and her eyes slipped shut. The dildo slipped in further and with it the butt-dildo slid in too.

'Is that nice, baby?' Onyx's long fingers slid the dildo right in so that Carla's two holes were plugged. 'I'm going to leave you here until you're cooked and then I'm going to come back and eat you all up. OK?'

But Carla had slipped off the planet and was floating.

Red came from behind Toni and undid her bonds. Toni sagged in relief. She was glowing uncomfortably and her arms and legs were aching and sore. Red pulled her to her feet. She could see that he had a king-size boner but still he didn't touch her. Toni pushed down her skirt and rubbed her cramped calves.

'Fancy riding with the Cobras? You want to be my property? My Bitch?'

Toni knew that was against the grain – big time – but nodded anyway.

'Just so we know you're not a cop or a journo, we start our little road trip right now. My bike's out back.'

Toni's mind was racing. To find Caron she had to win Red's trust. And if this was the way then so be it. But she would be on her own – no going back to her motel room for her gear. She'd paid in advance, so her room would be safe for a week. But clothes, toiletries, food? She guessed this was the way it was done – you stuck your thumb out, you got a lift and you hopped on the back.

She followed Red out on shaking legs. This could be the biggest mistake of her life – or the biggest thrill. She glanced at Carla as she left the room. Onyx grinned his crocodile grin. 'Parting is such sweet sorrow.'

Fuck! Did she just leave Carla here? Numbly she allowed herself to be led through the party and into the night. The massive biker on the door smirked and licked his lips at her. She got the message and the insides of her thighs tingled.

The desert was alive with cicadas. Red stepped over the low chopper and kick-started the engine, the scream-ing-eagle carburettor thundered in the night air. He flexed the throttle and moonlight caught the sheen of sweat that coated his bare arms. The engine settled to a low thrum and Toni's quim hummed in unison.

He looked almost demonic in the half-light. 'What d'you say, baby? You want to be free?'

Toni swallowed. She was aware of Caron's image stashed away in her purse. She had never gone in quite so deep before. She was stepping into a world she knew nothing about and all she had to do was be compliant, the horny girlfriend, the bitch on the back. The night suddenly felt chilly. She didn't do any of the above.

Red spat on to the ground. 'Get on the back. You know you want to.'

Toni cocked her leg over. Red watched her in his mirror and scowled. Toni adjusted her purse so that it was on her back, rucksack-style. The sissy bar dug into her backside and her knees hugged Red. As the bike pulled away Toni's arms shot round him and she clung on tight. The chopper accelerated and Toni felt as if her butt was dragging in the dirt. The wind took her breath away and she was suddenly scared. She held on as the bike cut a track through the desert. For fuck's sake! What had she done? Screw Caron Crossley. She hated this thing. Her bones rattled, the wind clawed her hair, her butt ached. Her fingers bit into Red as she held on for dear life. She could hardly breath. It was like a funfair ride, without the fun. If she hadn't been way out in the Arizona desert she would have been begging to be let off. But it was this or walk. Actually she would rather walk. The bike slowed and Toni's grip loosened. She gasped with gratitude.

'For fuck's sake, you're clawing me to bits.'

'That's because I can't breathe.'

'Can't you find the sweet spot?'

'The what-spot? I'm having enough trouble just staying on.' Arrogant bastard. He didn't seem quite so attractive close up and there was a definite whiff of manly odour about him.

'Tuck in behind me. Use my back as a shield and the wind will go over you. Shit! I didn't know you were a virgin.' He looked disgusted.

It had been a long time since she'd been accused of that.

'If we're going to ride two-up down to the coast then you'll have to do better than that or I'm kicking you off.'

Toni swallowed her scorn. At this moment she didn't want to ride two-up anywhere, but she had no choice. The bike sped off once more and Toni dipped her head down. It worked. She could breath. She couldn't say that she was actually enjoying it but at least she wasn't panicking so much. When they eventually stopped outside a trailer in the middle of nowhere, Toni was physically and emotionally drained and slid off the bike in relief.

'Go and make yourself at home. I'll put the bike away.'

Toni didn't argue. She dragged herself up the trailer steps and let herself in. The trailer was surprisingly neat, but good housekeeping was the last thing on her mind right now. She flung open cupboard doors until she found a bottle of bourbon and poured herself a double. Her throat burnt with satisfaction as she gulped the dark, sweet liquid. She backhanded her mouth and poured another. She was asleep at the kitchen table by the time Red came in.

20

Toni woke with a jolt, completely disorientated. She lay still, her heart beating wildly as she sussed out her surroundings. Her arms and legs ached. Shit! She sat bolt upright. Like she'd been tied to a table and tongue-fucked by a queue of strangers.

Red must have put her to bed because she didn't remember getting here. And where was here? Her dress had rolled up under her chin but at least she had panties on. She smelt a man on the bed but she was alone in the mussed up sheets. It was early. The sun wasn't quite up and out. The window was a cold grey square.

Toni's stomach flipped as she recalled last night's party and the way she'd left Carla. What had she been thinking, leaving her there trussed up and alone with Onyx? Hey, a little voice between her legs whispered, Carla had got exactly what she wanted, while she'd been submitted to the world's most uncomfortable ride on an outdated mode of transport. Hadn't Red ever heard of shock absorbers? These bikers and their love of the good old American machines – give her Jap crap any day. At least they looked like they had a comfortable seat.

Sweat pricked under her armpits. They'd ridden for miles over the desert and her buttocks felt as if they'd been used as a punch bag. Her clit was uncomfortably alert though. Despite the vibrations of the Evo engine between her legs, Red had left her high and dry when they got back. The way he stood by and watched last night led her to believe that voyeurism was indeed his thing. She also knew now that they had a club within a club.

Fuck. Her head ached. She didn't seem any closer to Caron now than when she first met her aunt. But, boy, was she stubborn, and she wasn't about to give up yet. She swung herself out of bed and peeked through the bedroom curtains. The view stunned her. The trailer was parked on a patch of scrub overlooking an expanse of desert and the sun was just beginning to warm the sand with an orange glow. Several bikes were parked beneath a gnarled Joshua tree. She guessed it would provide ample shade later.

Toni took a deep breath and scanned the tiny bedroom for clues. There wasn't much in here; a quick rummage through the fitted furniture only provided a glimpse of tatty men's clothing – jeans, biker boots and T-shirts bearing the instantly recognisable bar and badge. She stirred the contents of the bedside cabinet drawer. Rolling papers, lighters, biker magazines and make-up. Toni felt the tell-tale gooses bumps – Lancôme – Layla Crossley's brand and a bit outside the price range of your average biker slut. Still, it didn't prove anything. She knew plenty of women who had expensive taste in make-up and really cheap taste in men.

The place smelt stale and musty, her throat was dry and she needed a coffee. She pushed open the bedroom door and froze. Red and five others were sitting around the tiny Formica table speaking in hushed voices. The air stank of tobacco. She was still dressed in last night's clothes but the need for coffee drove her forward. She padded to the sink to fill the kettle and lit the gas cooker with a match. She cringed as her bare feet touched dried-up food bits and patches of grease on the floor.

'Hey, doll, if you're making coffee we'll all have one.'

Red was looking even seedier and grubbier than last night. A hank of hair hung limply over one eye as he counted a pile of money on the tabletop. 'Come and get the mugs.'

Bags of tablets and a brass scales covered the table. The men watched her with wary eyes as she approached.

'This the new squeeze, Red?' A biker with gold teeth looked up from the bag he was filling with a scoop. 'Or is she for us all to share?'

Toni was leaning across the table for the mugs and froze. She had woken in the middle of nowhere with six complete strangers and was beginning to realise that this was a step too near the edge even for her. She slid the mugs towards her and headed back to the sink. Red hadn't answered. She filled the bowl with warm water and scrubbed the mugs with a grubby cloth she found dried up on the edge.

'A piece of that would certainly get your motor running first thing in the morning.'

Toni bit back a retort. She found the coffee and scooped it into the pot. The aroma reminded her of home. Her fingers shook as she stirred the boiling water.

Red spoke. 'Come and meet the men who run the Cobras.'

Toni's head was spinning with ways she could get out of there. She advanced, nonetheless, with the mugs and the coffee pot, feeling very exposed in her skimpy dress. The men's eyes were all over her and her nipples puckered under their scrutiny.

Red's heavily ringed hand pointed out each man. 'My Treasurer, Enforcer, Vice-President, Sergeant-at-Arms and Road Captain. There's not a cop either side of the state line wouldn't give his pension to find us all in the same room.'

Toni fleetingly thought of Stan. She forced a smile

and went back for more mugs. The men were packing the bags of tablets into saddlebags.

'I hope she fucks like she makes coffee. This is great.' The Road Captain eyed her over the rim of his mug and, despite herself, Toni's pussy grew heavy.

She gulped at her coffee and helped herself to a cigarette from an open packet. Road Captain held out a light for her and examined her face with very clear blue eyes. She took a drag and surrounded herself with a halo of smoke. She knew she must look rough. Her hair was all mussed, her mascara was probably very panda-like and she could smell her own armpits. Still, last night had driven her to the edge with frustration and Mr Road Captain here was one mean-looking son-of-a-bitch. His chest was bare under a denim waistcoat and her eyes dipped to admire his tattoo. His neck, chest and muscular arms were a mass of monochrome swirls. He wore ancient leather chaps over his grubby denims. He looked every inch the one percenter

Toni sipped her coffee and edged away but Red wasn't letting her go that easy. 'Hey, sweet thing, where you going? Come and sit on my knee here.' He stuck out one jeaned leg from under the table, his dark eyes daring her to refuse. Toni perched on it primly, knees together. 'Don't be shy now, sugar. You ain't got nothing my boys haven't seen before.'

Toni's blood ran chill at their leery chuckles. She couldn't be sure if he was making reference to last night or not.

'Shit, Red, I thought that was Caron you had tied up down there.' The Treasurer looked shocked.

There was an uneasy silence for a long moment. Toni's senses were on red alert for clues but no one spoke. Was it her imagination or were the men waiting for Red's reaction?

Eventually Red broke the hush. 'Keep up, college boy. I can't believe I trust you with the club's revenue.'

Toni's heart thundered, it sounded like forced joviality, like he was hiding something, but she supposed it would to her. She should have spoken up, asked questions but the temperature had dropped below zero.

Except between her legs.

Tattoo-Road-Captain was rolling a smoke, picking at strands of tobacco from the pouch on the table in front of him with large oily fingers. She shifted on Red's thigh – her pussy was in danger of turning her into a whore.

His pink tongue moved slowly along the paper edge. Toni watched him, a pulse beating in her throat. He rolled the tube of tobacco slowly until it was perfect. His ringed fingers manipulated the cigarette carefully, deftly. Toni's Marlboro was burning away between her fingers, forgotten.

Toni's breathing quickened and he caught her looking. He tapped the cigarette on the tabletop, as if considering whether to smoke it or not. He met Toni's look and a spark leapt between them. Smoothing back his dark hair with one hand, he placed the cigarette behind an ear with the other. A silver skull hung from his lobe. Toni licked her lips nervously.

'Can I fuck her, Red?'

It had been years since anyone had made Toni Marconi blush but she could feel her cheeks tingle now. There was nothing like the direct approach.

'Shit, I think you better, she's making my jeans all damp. I want to clear up this lot first though.'

It was true. Toni was soaking her panties. She didn't want to be turned on but she couldn't help the moistness down below.

Red slapped her buttocks playfully. 'I know he does it

for you, baby, but if I let you fuck him, you have to do me a favour later. OK sweet thing?'

Toni couldn't answer but he took her silence as consent. She took a last puff and ground her cigarette out in the overflowing ashtray. She was appalled at herself; she was acting like a sex-starved puppet. But the wall-to-wall testosterone, together with last night's big tease, was making her crazy. She squirmed on Red's thigh. Her clit was pulsing like mad. She squeezed her thigh muscles tight and knew Red could feel her movements on his leg.

'All in good time,' he growled. 'I want this lot to the dealers by tonight. We've got the big drop coming over the border next week and I don't want this lot still hanging around. We've a few matters to take care of in the next few days. Be ready. Toni here can help us out with San Pinto now that Caron's gone over the side. Anything else need taking care of?' Red scratched his beard thoughtfully. 'Go on then, Neb. She's twitching like a whore with crabs.'

Tattoo Neb slid out from behind the table. His arousal was prominent and accentuated by the cut of his chaps. Toni stood up, embarrassed by the dampness she left behind, and wondered at Red's reluctance to fuck her yet again. Neb was keen enough, however, and she led the way back into the stuffy bedroom.

Neb seemed huge in the tiny room. He slipped off his waistcoat and Toni admired his tats. She traced a swirl from one nipple to the other and down his hard belly.

Neb caught hold of her hand. 'You got any tats you'd like to show me?'

Toni swallowed. Though she loved to watch in Happy Jack's, she'd always declined when it came to having her own skin tattooed.

'Thought not. You're one sexy chick, but I don't have

you down as a biker slut.' He slid one hand under her dress to feel her smooth belly and slipped it down into her panties. His chapter ring snagged on her pubes but he continued to slide it down between her legs. 'You're soaking wet though, you're not faking that.' Roughly he tugged her panties down to her knees and slid his hand back up her thighs. Toni opened them to allow him easier access. His finger moved along her moist crack before slipping inside.

Toni gasped, opening around his finger. He rotated it gently and Toni moaned, sinking gratefully on to it.

'Tell me what you're doing here, honey, all alone in a trailer in the desert. Are you all wired up and waiting for your pals to come arrest us?' With his other hand he pushed her dress up under her throat. 'Oh no. Nothing here.' His huge hand felt her breasts. 'Only some firm little titties.' He pushed another finger inside her and Toni sucked on it greedily. 'You must be just another horny slut looking to get laid. Well you've come to the right place. I hope you like it rough and ready 'cos that's all you get around here.'

Neb unplugged his fingers and Toni fell back on to the bed as her legs gave way. 'Slip those panties off and open wide for the biggest Cobra of them all.' He unbuckled his leather chaps and slung them across the room. He unzipped his oily jeans and pushed them down his hairy thighs. His tats ran down into his pubic hair.

Toni's eyes widened. It wasn't an empty boast. They could have named the gang after him for all she knew. His cock sprang out, thick and long.

'You can sit up and suck it first.'

Toni's mouth was already open in awe. He slid a hand behind her head and guided his cock into her mouth. Her eyes slid shut and she swallowed what she could. Her tongue laved his swollen head. She reached round and clasped his tensed buttocks with her nails.

'Shit, you vicious little bitch.' He kept pumping into her mouth and she dug her nails in harder, gripping the flesh on his buttocks as she worked her mouth up and down his cock.

Neb grunted in pleasure and pain as her nails broke his skin. 'Fuck!'

Hot creamy spurts shot into her throat. Toni swallowed and spluttered, come running down her chin and on to her chest. She looked up and Neb frowned down at her. 'I can see you're a tough little bitch. Well you're going to need to be if you hang out with the Cobras, baby.'

Toni eyed him hard. 'Don't worry, I'll get what I want.'

Neb tucked himself back into his jeans and winced at the cuts in his behind. 'I don't doubt it.' He retrieved his chaps and slung them over his shoulder.

Toni was buzzing with frustration as he left. She caught college dropout Treasurer staring at her through the open door. She opened her legs in invitation and tweaked a nipple. He looked terrified, his eyes huge in his white face. College Boy looked away, but Red had seen him looking. He nodded for him to go next. Toni bit her lip to suppress a giggle as he strode manfully but reluctantly towards the bedroom with a huge stiffy in his jeans. College Boy shut the door behind him and cleared his throat nervously. Toni stretched out on the bed and opened her legs wide. He knelt down and fumbled with his denims.

'Look at me,' Toni ordered.

College Boy's face was ashen. It must have been his head for figures that had got him into the Cobras because it certainly wasn't his tough line with women.

Toni reached out and tipped up his chin. 'If you're going to fuck it then you can look at it.'

College Boy gazed between her legs anxiously. His terror set her bush on fire.

'Fuck me hard,' she commanded, and gasped as he stuck his firm young cock into her. She edged down to angle herself better but it was too late. It was all over in a flash.

Toni ground her teeth. 'You better send the next one in then, hadn't you?' She shot him a look of contempt but he slunk out without looking at her. Matt had spoilt her; she'd forgotten how pathetic some of the young ones could be.

Toni used the sheet to wipe herself and crawled on to the bed on all fours. She didn't look up as the door opened and shut. She felt the bed dip and rough hands stroking the left of her buttocks. She reached under for the cock on offer and guided it in. It felt good and hard as it slammed into her with long, measured strokes. She reached down for her clit but again it ended before she was ready.

She was hungry for more and the next cock found her eager and straining for her climax. She ground herself back on to it, grabbing his hand and working it on to her clit, frigging it hard. Oh it was good, here in the squalor, not knowing where she was or who with or how many cocks were ramming into her. She throbbed and climaxed, howling like a mating cat.

They hadn't finished yet. One cock still hadn't had her. She raised herself back up, still tingling with climax but spreading her legs anyway. A finger smeared her juices upwards, lubricating between her buttocks; a finger tested and then the cock nudged her anus. Toni's throat ached, her pussy was sore but the pain was sublime, sharp and sweet on top of her orgasm as her ass was opened. Her legs trembled and collapsed; she grasped the sheet. Her ass was pulled upward. Her mouth opened, her cry too intense for sound. The cock was deep inside her, fucking her over and over.

It was late afternoon when Toni awoke. The room stank of sex and she flinched at the ache in her groin but smiled with satisfaction none the less. A shadow moved in the doorway. It was Red.

'You didn't waste any time, did you? You're worse than the last one I brought here.'

Toni immediately snapped awake. 'Would that be Carol or Caron, whatever her name is?'

He remained in the shadow. 'Why would you be interested?'

Toni yawned and stretched but her heart was thundering so loud she was surprised he couldn't hear it. 'Someone mistakes my pussy for someone else's, I'd like to know who she is.'

'I wouldn't have thought you were the jealous type.'

Should she push it? 'Was she your last main squeeze?'

A pause. 'No one for you to worry about.'

'I'd like to be told if there's any danger of some bitch scratching my eyes over my man.'

Red snorted disparagingly. 'One things for certain, sugar, there ain't much danger of that. Anyway, which man would that be? You didn't seem very choosy this morning.'

'I didn't have you down as the jealous type either.'

'Face it, sugar, we don't know anything about each other and that's how we like it around here. You chicks are all the same. We offer you a free life and you can't wait to tie us back down. She's gone and that's all you need to know.' He threw something on to the bed. 'Have this, you've earned it.'

Toni sat up and fingered the well-worn denim. It was the waistcoat Caron had been wearing in the photo, or one very much like it.

'Put it on.' Red's voice was deep and low but she couldn't read his expression from where he stood in the corner of the room.

Toni slipped her arms into the frayed armholes. Red pulled open a door to reveal the cracked mirror inside for her to see herself. Toni knelt up on the bed, naked except for the waistcoat, and looked over her shoulder.

So she'd earned her colours, had she? 'Property of Cobras' was emblazoned across her back. Cold ice ran through her belly.

Red knelt on the bed and grabbed a handful of Toni's hair. She felt cold metal against her stomach and realised with horror that he was pressing a gun flat against her skin.

'You're Club property now, sugar. Property of. Is that what you've been looking for?' He opened his mouth over hers and Toni's tongue tasted his. It was the first time that he had touched her. 'You are one hot little bitch, but being property is about more than pulling a train or two. You'll find out soon enough.' Red bent her backwards and nibbled each nipple in turn. 'Now get some sleep.'

Toni sank back down on to the churned-up bed as he released her and stared at the bedroom door long after he had closed it. She knew the road she was taking was a dangerous one but she was close to Caron now and she needed to take it just a little bit further.

21

Toni squeezed into the miniscule shower early the next morning. She revelled in dirty sex but grotty showers made her skin crawl. She guessed Red and his gang weren't the types for long hot soaks. Still, there was warm(ish) water and she did what she could with the soap. From the tiny window she could see Red wrenching out front. While the kettle boiled Toni checked the contents of her purse. She always kept an emergency wallet tucked into the lining for occasions such as these. It meant that she could leave as she stood and still have change, a Visa card and a mobile on her. There was no way she was going on a road trip in that dress. She got off on flashing herself all right but she didn't want it frozen solid at 110 mph. First chance she got she'd duck into a shop and buy herself some denims. She already had the waistcoat.

Toni looked at it on the bed; she couldn't explain why it gave her such a perverse thrill. She shivered in the threadbare towel and pondered her underwear – inside out or back to front, she wasn't going to find a comfortable way to wear those without a boil wash. She'd go without first. And the way her sex life was going, they were off more than they were on anyway. She pulled on her dress and poured coffee for her and Red.

The sun wasn't long up and the day was just starting to warm. In the shade of the trailer, the red desert earth was cool beneath her feet. Only islands of sage brush and cactus broke the monotony of the desert around them; they could have the only two people on the planet.

She paused when she saw the bike he was wrenching. His old Harley chopper was tucked in at the side of the trailer and this beast, the FXRT, was the one in the photo of him and Caron. Red was in front her, larger than life, but what had happened to Caron? Had she moved on to another biker?

Red was crouched by the side of his bike, stripped to the waist. Lost in his work, he didn't notice her admiring his tattoos. There was his One Percenter mark high on his shoulder and a majestic eagle across his shoulder blades. His hair was kept back by a grubby red bandana. Toni's eyes dipped and noted an old bullet scar low down near his waistband. He sensed her presence and turned.

'Coffee?' She offered the mug.

'Thanks.' Red swiped at his sweaty forehead with the back of a wrist. His torso was rippled with muscle.

Toni sipped her coffee. 'You work out?'

Red downed his coffee in two gulps and gave it back. Backhanding his mouth with an oily hand, he knelt back down.

'Nothing else to do in the pen. Used to use weights everyday. They eventually put a maximum weight on how much we could lift; we were getting so bulked out.'

'You been in much?'

'Enough. That's why I like to have this base way out here. There's no one to keep an eye on you between runs.' His muscles bunched as he worked at a tight nut. Toni curled her toes into the earth.

'Nice bike.'

'She's a beauty. I've had her a while now but I can't bring myself to part with her.'

'Will I get to ride her?'

'Shit, yes. Couldn't stand you bellyaching about the chopper all the way to the coast. This one's built for comfort.' He smoothed the long leather seat with the palm of his hand. 'Hop on.'

Toni hesitated, suddenly wishing she'd put her underwear on.

Red misread her hesitancy. 'Complain about this baby and I'm dropping you off in town.' He admired his handiwork as he wiped his hands on an oily cloth.

Toni put the mugs down on the sand. Red grinned, his teeth white against his dark beard. He threw a leg over and sparked the ignition. 'Purring like a kitten. Get your ass behind me.'

Toni did as she was told. Her skirt immediately rode up and her pussy caught fire as the vibrating machine sent ripples up her thighs. She clenched her thighs and clung on to the princess bar at the back. Red revved and set off. He was slower than last night, or the ride was more comfortable; either way Toni didn't want to scream to be let off. In fact, the way this baby growled against her bare pussy, she'd be proposing to it soon. No wonder chicks got addicted to this. Who'd drive a car when they could straddle one of these machines?

Red accelerated and Toni whooped – this was more like it – this was flying, this was freedom. The bike climbed a dune and Red stopped at the top, admiring the desert lying beneath them. Toni's pulse raced. She clung to the bar as the bike plummeted downhill. The wind pushed her dress against her breasts, her pussy thrummed on the seat. She turned her face up to the sun and felt her breath being swept away. She didn't know how long they jammed the wind, but by the time they returned to the trailer she was a convert. She was also as horny as hell but Red wasn't taking the hint. He was too busy twiddling with his twin head to be twiddling with her. Toni wondered exactly why he had brought her here.

If she couldn't fuck then she needed to shop because if anything was going to break her spirit it was lack of retail therapy. You could stick your LA shrinks and your New Age spiritualism – a gold card and a choice of labels was all a girl needed. And in this case, a change of underwear and a pair of denims would suffice.

'I need to get into town before we leave on this road trip.'

Red took two beers out of the refrigerator but ignored the comment.

'All I own is what I'm standing up in and a pair of panties soaking in the sink. I need some clothes.'

Red gave her cursory once over. She looked like dirt-poor trailer trash in her grubby dress and bare feet. 'I'll take you in this afternoon.' He threw her a beer and clomped back out to his bike, letting the screen door slam shut behind him.

A posse of Cobras was hanging out on the street opposite the restaurant. Stripped to the waist in the heat, covered in tats and wearing shades, they were a pretty scary bunch. The general population of Smallville thought so too and gave them a wide berth. Toni looked around but couldn't make out any she recognised. She felt very naked. Though their eyes were covered, the tilt of their heads told her that they were looking her over. No one spoke to her. The way they all ignored her made her hackles rise but their respect for Red was palpable. She expected a certain amount of rowdiness – rape and pillage wouldn't have surprised her – but they were pretty quiet. She sensed they were waiting orders, like foot soldiers. Before Toni could sneak off to shop, Red caught her arm.

'You won't get far without money.' He handed her a roll of twenties. 'Kit yourself out nice now, honey.'

Toni tamped down her reply.

'You've got an hour. If you're not here, we leave without you.' He turned his back on her.

Toni dug her nails into the palm of her hand. He was treating her like a simpleton, but she'd have her own back by the time she was finished. When she was satisfied that she was some distance away, she ducked behind a row of buildings to ring her mobile and check for messages. There was a curt message from Josh telling her that two LA police officers had been looking for her. Those two assholes would finish her business if they couldn't keep their noses out of her affairs. She sent a text saying that they were only to contact her if they had info on Caron. There was no way any biker would pack her on the back of his bike if they knew she was sleeping with the law. While she was at it, she left a message with Sid, telling her she was on the road and to contact her ASAP if Anthea remembered anything else. Best to keep all avenues of information open. You never knew what sometimes bobbed to the surface after interviewing someone. Before she kitted herself out she wanted to check on Carla. The thought of her trussed up in the clubhouse had niggled at her since the night of the party.

Toni avoided the bikers hanging out on Main Street and slipped into the restaurant. A family stared at her as she entered. She ordered waffles and coffee and caught sight of her reflection in the mirror behind the counter. Her hair was wild, there were dark smudges under her eyes and her lips were swollen. She looked like a hooker. She was suddenly aware that she was still dressed in her skintight party dress and that her legs were bare. Little wonder she was being stared at. Her stomach flipped in relief when Carla brought her order.

The waitress gave a low whistle. 'Wow. I thought I could party. Look at you.'

Toni poured a generous amount of syrup on her waffle. 'Can you talk?'

'Sure.' Carla slipped in beside her.

Toni noticed that she held herself slightly off the seat. 'I just wanted to see if you were OK after the other night.'

'I should say. Those guys really know about sex, don't they? I've spent years putting up with pathetic fumblings in the back of trucks but that night . . . it blew me away. Why the concern?'

Toni shrugged. 'I'm going to be riding with the Cobras for a while and just thought I'd check you were OK before I left.'

'Decided that you like a bit of rough action after all?'

Toni forced a smile. She had no idea how much.

'Don't you dare let them leave without me. The sooner I can get out of this dump, the better.' She was being called from across the restaurant and flapped a hand in reply. 'Yeah, yeah, I'm coming.' She turned back. 'Don't forget. I'm always up for a party.'

Toni nodded. She checked her watch. Shit! They would be leaving without *her* if she didn't hurry. She threw some of Red's money on the table, took a quick gulp of her coffee and left.

The streets were lined with typical small-town bargain stores and Toni wished she had transport to pop back to her motel and grab her stuff but time was marching on and as much as it grieved her she had to keep up with the Cobras. She found a wooden-fronted store and, ignoring a clutch of dentally challenged rednecks out front, proceeded to grab enough clothes to serve their purpose while she was riding two-up. The storekeeper watched her closely, especially her legs as her dress crept up her thighs when she reached for the higher shelves. He didn't offer to help, just chewed on his tobacco lazily. She put the small pile of Ts and denims on the counter and went back for a rucksack to keep them in. The storekeeper's eyes crept to her breasts as she pulled out her roll of bills to pay.

'How long did it take you to earn that little lot, lady?' He rung up the total on his old-fashioned till.

Toni ignored him and pulled off the required number of notes. She was aware now of the minutes ticking by. She'd never find the trailer in the desert if they left the town without her and as tenuous as Red's link with Caron was, it was the only one she had right now. She drummed her fingers on the counter impatiently.

'Got some boys outside willing to pay for a bit of fun, if you fancy it.'

Toni gave him her best chilly stare. 'No thank you.' She grabbed the bag.

'You don't look as if you're usually so fussy, lady.'

Toni headed for the door where the men were gathered in the shade of the shop canopy.

'Bet your legs are usually opening and shutting like automatic doors. Parading yourself round town like a slut and then complaining when you get hit on.'

Toni gave him the finger and pushed her way out into the sunlight. The men catcalled and whistled as she shoved her way through. There seemed more of them than when she'd gone in. One of them grabbed her ass.

Toni spun round angrily. 'Keep your fucking hands to yourself, mister!'

The men had closed in around her and Toni was

growing frightened. She didn't need this shit right now. She had enough men on her plate to last a lifetime and she didn't need a bunch of sex-starved in-breeds chasing her pussy as well.

'What do you say we have ourselves a little party? We've had a collection and we can pay.'

'I say you've got the wrong woman, now let me through.'

'Heard you weren't so fussy the other night.' A short stocky guy with yellow teeth was pressing his gut up close to her. 'Heard that you were letting anyone have a taste of that hot sweet pussy.' Toni froze as a sweaty palm inched up under her dress. Where the hell had he heard that? It could only have been Carla bragging about town. The men pressed in around her. The stench of body odour was nauseating. Toni's mind was racing with the best way to tackle them. She heard the roar of a bike somewhere in the distance.

'We're not animals. We're just looking for a party, same as those biker creeps who blow in as if they own the town.'

'Fine, let me know where and when and I'll be there.'

The men jeered. 'Oh, we were thinking right now.'

'Fuck off.' It wasn't wit but it was the best she could come up with.

'She's got a right filthy mouth on her. Best we fill it up so she can't talk back.' He was reaching for the zip of his jeans and Toni snapped. She wasn't going down on anyone without a fight. She brought her head back and butted him right in the nose. She heard it crack and the men were stunned just long enough for her to make a break for it. She ran smack into Red and three other bikers.

'Whoa. Slow down, sugar.' He steadied her and took

in the situation – the crowd outside the store, the man with blood streaming down his face, Toni's ragged breathing. 'You've just touched club property, citizen.'

'It was only a bit of fun. Tell her to lighten up.' The crowd of men were dispersing quickly, eager not to tangle with the bikers. Red and his men had other ideas and bikers were closing in from all directions.

No one was more eager to leave than Toni. 'I'm OK, let's just go.'

Red was grinning at the men, a mad look in his eye. She was forgotten. It was club honour that had been insulted, not her. She took a step back and her heart beat wildly at the sight of the man in front of her – tall and muscled, filthy, sweaty, tattooed and so fucking sexy – he took Toni's breath away. She watched him clench his fists. Time stood still as the two groups held their ground, and then the bikers moved in and there was mayhem.

It was a baptism by fire and Toni watched in awe as Red and his men waded in to defend their badges. Toni had covered her face but she couldn't hide from the sound of the fighting and that was the worst. The crunch of knuckles meeting cheekbone, the snap of fingers beneath metal toecapped boots made Toni light-headed with nausea. When the bikers were satisfied that the crowd of men had been suitably roughed up they jumped on their bikes. Red had thrown her an old-fashioned half-helmet and she had clung to him in terror as the bikers gunned their engines and did a lap of honour up and down Main Street, their brakes screaming, before roaring out of town.

They hadn't stopped to pick up Carla. They hadn't stopped to pick up anyone or anything. Main Street, Smallville, had been trashed and more than a few limbs broken by the time the Cobras had finished teaching the residents not to mess with their property.

The bikers had hightailed it out of there in a cloud of desert dust. They headed in the opposite direction to the club and the trailer, in case the cops decided to follow. There were none and Toni had clung on to Red for dear life, terrified at first and then learning to settle into the machine and move with him. She had to lay all her trust in him, which wasn't something she had ever done with a man before. But he knew what he was doing. He lived the life. A rumble with an angry mob was part of the action. He steered the massive bike as if it were an extension of his own body.

Two hours on the back of Red's bike dressed in a skintight dress and a denim waistcoat told her all she needed to know about being a biker chick – it was hard fucking work. She had nearly turned blue by the time they had stopped to refuel and pick up some supplies. Toni ducked into the bathroom to quickly change, building up layers to keep out the wind.

Terrified travellers at the truck stop stared at the bikers, and Toni had to concede that if they'd looked menacing before then they looked one hundred percent worse now that they were bloody and bruised. The girl behind the till served them with a trembling hand as they formed an orderly line to pay for fuel and cans of soda.

By the time they reached San Diego, Toni's legs were quivering like a tuning fork. She was tired and aching and more than ready for a hot bath and a clean bed. The Cobras had no such ideas. They cruised the outskirts of the city, turning heads on every street they took. When they stopped at lights no one bad mouthed them or threw insults. Toni realised that Harleys and their riders commanded respect. As she sat behind Red waiting at a cross-over with the engines roaring all around her, and thirty bulked-out men ready to kick ass at any given moment, Toni felt her primal self rear up inside her, she felt like a queen of the road and as horny as hell.

A black Road King drew up alongside them and a grinning Road Captain signalled hello with a black-gloved hand. He shouted over the roar of the engines, 'What's going down?'

Red eased the throttle. 'It's been sorted. No worries. Thought we'd check out the Bulldogs a bit earlier than planned and do some deliveries at the same time.'

'Good idea. What do you say we party on the beach later?'

'Sounds good.'

Neb flashed her a devilish smile. 'See you later, sweet thing.'

Toni couldn't help but grin back. An image of his fantastic cock immediately sprang to mind. Then the pack took off once more. Toni's stomach somersaulted as the bike roared away from the kerb and she whooped with exhilaration. It was a heady moment – like deciding to have sex for the first time. The sun glinted off the narrow fender of the Panhead in front. The sea air rushed by with the scent of pine and salt and the engine threw out the heady tang of diesel. Red's muscles tensed beneath her clasp as he guided the Harley out on to the freeway and Toni slipped her hands up further beneath his jacket. The bike thrummed between her thighs, whetting her appetite for the party tonight. She could feel the excitement building down there and grinned into the rushing wind. A horny man, a customised bike and around her a mass of testosterone-charged bikers, all swarming towards the coast. Did life or investigations get any better than this?

22

Word must have gone out that the Cobras were in town. Other Harley riders joined the winding snake of thundering bikes at every turn. They left the city and headed along the Bay Road until they reached, what Toni presumed to be, a sister chapter clubhouse. The bikes pulled on to the gravel car park, the riders getting off to greet the men who had rode in with them, stretch their limbs and take a piss behind the bushes lining the driveway.

Red removed his helmet. 'Here, give me that skidlid. I'm done with these for a while.'

Toni dismounted, her legs weak beneath her. Bikers were pouring out of the clubhouse to welcome them.

'Red! Good to see you, man! We didn't know you were riding in so soon.'

Red clasped the big, grizzled man who greeted him. He was wearing a Bulldog badge and looked as pleased as punch to see the Cobras arrive.

'Neither did we until three hours ago. We had to sort out some assholes down Arizona way and thought we'd hang out here while the dust settles.'

'Great news, man! I'll send the ladies out for booze and food and we'll party here.'

'Any chance I can get word out to my men that we're here?'

'No problem. Go right in and use the place like it's your own.'

'Thanks, Mac. This is Toni by the way. Toni, meet Mac, he runs the Diego Bulldogs.' Red left them to it and strode into the building. Toni noticed that there were women hanging out here and the place had a friendly feel to it. It was a far cry from the lonely trailer in the desert where the committee carried out business.

Mac shook her hand. 'It's nice to meet you, Toni. Red always did have good taste in women.'

Toni tossed her hair and smiled at the biker from under her lashes. 'He's a bit quiet about his last one.'

Mac pulled a face. 'Bad business that.'

'What happened?'

Perhaps Toni had looked a bit too keen. Mac's expression closed. 'Let's just say his pride was badly hurt.'

Toni looked knowing and sympathetic. 'I thought as much. It comes down to trust in the end.'

'It's all very well doing business with these people but if they don't ride ... you can't trust them.'

Toni opened her mouth to ask another question but Mac had spotted Red coming out of the clubhouse and was already turning away. 'Hope you enjoy your visit to the Bulldogs. We'll have a party tonight. Show these Cobras how it's done.'

The two men exchanged words but Toni couldn't hear them in the chaos of the car park. Excited biker chicks were already draping themselves over any man they could find, making sympathetic faces at the cuts and bruises on show.

Red nodded towards the beach. 'Come on, let's wash away the desert.'

This was a stretch of sand untouched by body-builders or tourists. Toni bet the bikers had it all to themselves with no arguing. Red was stripping off his clothes, throwing them on to the sand as he ran towards the sea. Toni looked around but no one here was about to be embarrassed. Red dived into a breaker and swam some way out. The turquoise water was too inviting to ignore and Toni began to unpeel the layers she had used as wind protection on the bike. The sun felt good on her naked flesh and she closed her eyes to appreciate its warmth on her face. Her cheeks burnt from the rushing wind. The roar of the bikes was all she had heard for so long, it was good to have a moment's meditation to savour the deep rumble of the ocean. Dropping to her knees, eyes closed, Toni immersed herself in the sounds of the beach and the rising heat of the sand. She lay down on its warmth. It was smooth on her belly and her breasts. Turning over, Toni reached above her head and arched her back, burrowing her buttocks into the sand's fire. Her sandy nipples pointed skywards like miniature minarets. Boy, but it was good to be off the bike.

She must have slept right there, naked on the beach and sprinkled in sand, because when she opened her eyes, a crowd of bikers were lighting a driftwood bonfire nearby. Red was sitting drinking. He was wearing just his jeans, which were slung low on his hips, and had swept his damp hair back off his face. Trails of salt had dried on his skin and glistened against the dark colours of his tattoos. Everyone had respected her space, besides which there was plenty of other half-naked females wandering down from the clubhouse with barbequed ribs and packs of cold beer.

The party had begun.

Toni's belly rumbled at the smell of barbeque. She raised herself up on her elbows.

'I thought you would have joined me for a swim.' Red fed a hunk of driftwood into the growing flames.

Toni yawned. 'I certainly meant to.'

'You attracted quite a crowd while you were asleep. The boys decided to bring the party down here to watch you.'

Toni squirmed in embarrassment. Thank God the sand had covered her, otherwise she would be burnt to a crisp. 'I think I'll go and wash the sand off.'

'I'll fetch us some food.'

Toni wandered down to the sea edge. It felt glorious to be naked and unencumbered by clothes. Her skin rippled with goose flesh as the waves lapped at her sandy skin. She stepped in and slipped under. She floated in the waves for a while before returning to Red and the others. The bikers watched her with interest as she searched for clothes in the light of the bonfire.

Red sunk his teeth into a rib and spoke with his mouth full. 'We've decided that we like you better naked.'

Toni snatched the rib from him. 'Fine by me, honey, just so long as I get fed and watered.'

The men laughed. Someone threw her a jacket. 'Sit on this, Toni. Don't deprive me of the view of your tush now.'

Toni shrugged and settled down. Everyone was half undressed anyway. She tucked into her ribs and beer and basked in the warmth of the fire. Nearby, a biker chick was smearing her nipples in sauce for Neb to lick off.

'Only do that in front of me, Suzy, if you promise me a taste later,' someone called across.

'Don't worry,' the girl quipped back, 'there's plenty to go around.'

From the Bay Road, Toni could hear bikes racing in the darkness. She could just make out a topless female holding out her T-shirt as a starter flag. There were other bonfires lighting up along the beach and someone had brought music. Good old-fashioned rock and roll was pounding out. Beers were passed around and Toni's head was beginning to get muzzy. She licked her fingers clean and staggered to her feet.

'Who's dancing?' she asked, and she was swamped with partners. The beat was making her want to shake her thing. It felt good to be naked in the warmth of the flames. She must have danced with every biker there and if they snuck the odd feel of her titties or a squeeze of her buttocks then that was fine. She felt alive and tingling all over. Lots of girls were dancing; everyone was getting drunk and getting down. She danced a whole number with her butt in someone's face and was applauded afterwards.

The biggest cheer went up when a drunken Suzy staggered across to ask Toni to dance. They writhed against each other, teasing the men by rubbing their bodies together and giggling like schoolkids. When they finished, Suzy fell on her knees in the sand. She crawled on all fours towards a spliff, which was held out for her, and took a deep toke. One of the bikers was quick to take what was on offer; unzipping his flies, he soon had his erection nudging between her thighs. Suzy's eyes shut as he slipped in from behind and the others watched.

Neb had his hand up some girl's top, lazily stroking her breasts as he watched Suzy being taken from behind. The excitement fizzled through the group and they were soon a mass of entwining limbs. Toni realised that someone had her head buried in Red's lap and meandered towards him, her eyes narrowed as she tried to focus. She was determined to have a piece of him tonight. Toni pushed the girl away. She gazed up at her, looking confused for a moment, but then she shrugged and rolled over to the biker on her other side.

Toni stood over Red, licking her lips at the sight of his cock jutting from his open flies.

He grinned up at her. 'Climb on, sugar. I know you've been dying to.'

'Egotistical bastard,' Toni muttered, but she straddled him none the less, opening on to the moist cock that had been laved by the other girl's tongue.

He didn't disappoint. Red drove his hips against her, pushing himself high inside her hot pussy. His callused hands held her buttocks tight as he held her pinned on top of him. He was determined to control the rhythm of their lovemaking. He wasn't going to let her rush this and Toni rose and fell, grinding her clit against him as her climax built. He was close now and a fine sheen of sweat broke out on his chest as he nuzzled her breasts. Toni pounded herself against him, driving deeper and harder until they both climaxed and he shuddered long and hard inside her.

Side by side in firelight, Toni and Red enjoyed a spliff and watched the party spin out around them. Eventually, Toni found her pile of clothes and dressed before stretching out on the warm sand. Pulling someone's jacket around her, she used her rucksack as a pillow. Along the beach, Cobras and Bulldogs were beginning to wind down. Some left the sand and staggered up to the clubhouse. Others stayed and slept where they fell. Now and then a drunken laugh or a sexy giggle broke the night's dark silence but by the time the bonfires had burnt down to embers, those who were left had passed out or fallen asleep.

Despite being bone weary, Toni lay for a long time listening to the surf pulling at the beach just below them. Red lay beside her snoring heavily. Toni examined his profile, wondering if she could ever get him to part with the beard. A bonfire crackled and Toni turned her face to its dying warmth. Tomorrow she would start asking serious questions about Caron.

23

It seemed as if she'd only been asleep for seconds when Red nudged her with his boot the next morning. His face was still crumpled from sleep.

'Get up,' he was ordering. 'There's a problem I need to sort.'

Toni shivered. Sleeping under the stars was not quite so romantic the morning after. She tried to roll over but Red was having none of it. A handful of seawater soon had her attention and Toni groaned with disgust.

Red put his half-helmet on and jumped on the bike. Reluctantly, Toni followed suit, just remembering to bring her rucksack as the engine ripped through the early morning quiet. One of these days, perhaps she'd get to look in her compact mirror again. She shuddered to think what she must look like. Toni clung on to Red as the bike climbed up on to the Bay Road. Despite her aching limbs and sleep-filled eyes, the sea air was magnificent. Riding two-up on the back of the Harley certainly woke you up. The bay at this time in the morning was awash with amber and gold. They soon pulled away from the sea and the fishing ports, however, and headed north-east.

Toni's buttocks quivered at the thought of another long run. They already felt as if they'd been flayed. Still, at the end of this investigation, she'd have the tightest buns on the west coast.

The morning ripened as they rode. They stopped once to refuel. They were heading inland and by early afternoon they reached a big housing estate, which sprawled on the edge of the desert. Red seemed to know exactly where he was going, despite the fact that every road and every house looked the same to Toni. Someone must have been warned that they were coming; the garage door was open for Red to park the bike off the street. When he cut the engine the garage was dark and silent.

Red didn't speak. His face was grim. Toni followed him through the garage door and into the house. They walked straight into an untidy kitchen. The first person Toni noticed was a very scared-looking Cobra Club Treasurer sat at the kitchen table. Two burly bikers sporting Father Christmas-type beards flanked him. Toni didn't need to be told that prettily wrapped gifts and acts of charity were not on their list of priorities right now. College Boy turned terrified eyes first to her and then to Red.

Red didn't have time for niceties. He stripped off his jacket and T-shirt and stuck his head under the faucet, letting the cold water run over his head and neck. Shaking himself like a dog, and spraying the kitchen window with water, Red then rubbed his face with his bruised hands before turning to address the men in the kitchen.

'Get me a beer,' he barked, and it took Toni a moment to realise that he meant her.

The atmosphere was too tense for her to argue. She got one for Red and one for herself; it looked as if she was going to need one.

Droplets of water glistened on Red's beard as he slugged from the bottle. When he had finished, he placed the bottle carefully on the table and looked at it as if for inspiration. No one spoke. One of the big bikers toyed with a nasty-looking blade, turning it over and over on the tabletop with his meaty fist. Red's chest was heaving with barely controlled temper. He curled his knuckles and pushed the silver rings on each hand together before resting them on the table in front of College Boy and resting his weight on his arms.

'OK, Sonny, you've got about a minute to tell me that these guys have got it wrong and you haven't just made a major fuck-up.' Red's voice was low and calm and all the more terrifying for it.

College Boy cleared his throat nervously. 'I thought you were still an item, Red, honest to God I did. No one told me it was over. The other night in the Cobra Club –' his eyes flicked to Toni and back again '– I thought it was Caron ... like I said. She'd been coming to me for stock ... I thought we were still doing the pen deliveries.'

'Don't tell me you've been taking her on the prison visits.'

'She said you were too busy –'

'And the money? Do you have all the money? For the stock, which you have allowed my lying, cheating dyke of an ex-girlfriend to smuggle into state pen up her pussy?' There was a dreadful silence. 'How many times?' Red's eyes were gleaming with a mad sheen.

The huge biker continued toying casually with his knife and held up four fingers of his other hand.

'Four times. OK, that's about four thousand dollar's worth. Do you have it?'

Sonny shook his head.

'And why?'

'She, she said she was giving it to you.'

'Oh, that's so sweet, Sonny. Helping me out in such a kind way. Letting that bitch stick my stock up her cunt every week and smuggle it in to Sticky Ken. Do I pay you for that? Do I? You fuckster. You're going to pay for this. That bitch has been laughing at me for weeks. Stealing money from right under my nose.'

Red marched the length of the kitchen, clenching and unclenching his fists, like a tiger prowling its cage. The two big bikers looked on with interest and Toni stood very quietly by the back door, momentarily forgotten, and listening with bated breath to the story of her latest runaway.

'I bet she's had you eating out of her hand, hasn't she, you naive little bastard? Haven't you ever been around pussy before? What did she do for you, Sonny? I hope it was good, man, because you're going to be very fucking sorry you let this happen.'

College Boy looked ready to faint.

Red hadn't touched him yet, however. He was working on a plan. 'Does she know you're on to her?'

College Boy shook his head.

'When were you going to tell me, for fuck's sake? She must be laughing fit to bust at us. She's got my Club Treasurer supplying her with speed and she's cleaning up.' Red took a deep breath and calmed himself. 'OK, here's what we do. It's San Pinto we deliver to today, right? Got the visitation order?'

College Boy nodded.

'And the warden is still on our payroll?'

Another nod.

'Where are you meeting Caron?'

'We're meeting on the west side of Torodecko Bridge.'

Red frowned. 'How does she get there?'

College Boy's face grew even paler. After a painful silence he mumbled, 'Steve from the Sphynx brings her.'

Red pointed with the knife. 'I want his gizzards when this is over, OK? Here's what we do. You meet Caron on the bridge as usual. You give her the tube, but the drugs will be dummies. Get Nifty Frank to fax me over another visitation order straight away.' He snapped his fingers and the biker rose to his feet. 'Tell him to make it out for Hal Burrows, that old-timer would just love a visit from a hot broad like Caron. While you're at it, make it out as a conjugal visit. Thirty minutes locked in a trailer with Halitosis Hal will teach Caron a lesson or two about fucking with me. When she comes out I'll have Neb waiting. That bastard was always dying to get his hands on her. OK, get to it.' Red turned to the other biker. 'You watch asswipe here and don't let him out of your sight. I'll settle the score with him once I've sorted that double-crossing bitch out. You . . .'

Toni had been pressed against the wall, her mind spinning. She jumped when she realised that Red was talking to her.

'Time to show us what you're made of. Get your pussy shaved; you're going to get the delivery into San Pinto while Caron's giving Hal the only sex he's had in fifteen years. Don't look so worried. It's a straight in and out – the warden's have been paid to turn a blind eye.' He turned back to the quaking boy. 'Haven't they?'

College Boy nodded furiously.

Red continued. 'Well, they may want to watch, sugar, but you won't get arrested for it. Don't pretend to be shocked. You've never been shy about using your pussy before. This time it'll be doing me a huge favour. Have you still got the butt-skimming dress that got us all thrown out of Smallville? Then wear it. You can open your legs with that on and Sticky Ken will have his consignment out in a flash. Don't worry; he used to be a doctor.'

He ignored Toni's ashen face.

'Jump to it! The bathroom's second on the right.'

Toni clutched her rucksack and headed for the

bathroom. After bolting the door, she sank on to the floor and took deep breaths. Her overriding emotion was panic and she took long deep breaths to calm herself. She envisaged a lengthy stretch of incarceration in Chowchilla, where the only fuck she'd get would be from a hairy, sweaty bull-dyke with a finely tuned sense of sadism.

She could make a bolt for it now; squeezing through the window shouldn't be a problem. She looked up and discovered that the window was barred. Panic pounded in her chest again. If she did that then she would have to leave Caron behind and the only chance she had of finding her now was to stick close to Red, or at least College Boy. Professional pride wouldn't allow her to leave Caron Crossley to the Cobras. She had a reputation for solving cases, and she wasn't going to let that reputation go.

If she did the delivery then could she rely on the Cobras for protection? They believed her to be a genuine biker slut, so she would probably be safe, though she couldn't rely on it. Boy, she could just see the look of supreme righteousness on Josh's face if she got arrested. Failing all else, she had to get someone to Caron before the Cobras took her into San Pinto. Steve could look after himself but Caron was next month's pay packet.

It was the longest twenty minutes of her life and she would be forever grateful for her emergency cell phone. Never underestimate the practicality of a woman's purse, she muttered, as she dug into her rucksack. She punched out numbers with shaking fingers, praying there would be someone on the other end.

Red was soon hammering on the door and Toni was only just struggling into her dress.

'Ain't you got that pussy shaved yet?'

'I couldn't find a razor.' Toni rammed clothes into her rucksack, burying her phone.

'Well, we haven't got time now. We have to get to Caron. Get your ass downstairs.'

'Can I wear my jeans to ride in?'

'Whatever. But make it quick.'

Toni pulled on her jeans, buying as much time as she could, but Red was too pissed to be kept waiting. The door crashed open and Toni looked up into the barrel of a revolver.

'That pussy's had plenty of fun, now it's time to put it to work for the Cobras.' Red signalled to the door. 'Move.'

Toni didn't argue. Downstairs, she exchanged terrified looks with Sonny.

'OK, College Boy, you get to ride two-up with Wacko here, just so you don't get any ideas about heading for the border. When we get to the bridge, all you have to do is take Caron in as normal.'

Toni didn't need to ask where she was going. They went out into the dark garage and Toni climbed on behind Red. The engine roared to life. If she got out of this thing alive, she promised herself, then she was never going to take these risks again. She'd take up charity work – maybe work with underprivileged kids.

She almost had herself believing it.

She squeezed her eyes tight as they reversed onto the road. Wacko rode in front with Sonny gripping the sissy bar. Toni wondered what would happen to him when this was all over. There was nothing she could do. Getting herself out of this mess was going to be hard enough.

24

The ride seemed to last a lifetime. Toni clung on tight, feeling more nauseous by the mile. They cut through wide expanses of desert and blue hills rose up on the horizon. The scenery was lost on her now. Her mind was racing. She remembered about Red's gun. Would he use it?

Her heart thundered when she caught the sound of the wail over the engine.

She mumbled a mantra under her breath. Let it be Highway Patrol. Please. She'd never quarrel with Josh again. The bikes slowed and the patrol car cut in front of them both. Red stiffened but he kept cool. Toni was nearly fainting off the seat.

The patrolman strode towards them, his eyes hidden by mirror shades; he was closely followed by his partner. They both seemed cool and calm.

'May I see your license please, sir?'

Red dug in a battered leather saddlebag and handed over dog-eared documents. The patrolman was close enough for Toni to see herself in his shades. Up in front, Wacko was cooperating too. Toni wondered how long Steve and Caron would wait before realising they'd been rumbled.

'And yours, ma'am?' He held out a gloved hand for her documents.

Red was watching her suspiciously.

Toni fumbled around in her rucksack. She had an alias document in here somewhere. The patrolman accepted it and studied it carefully. 'I'd like you to sit in the car, ma'am, while I check this out.'

Red's knuckles were white on the handlebars. 'What's this all about, officer?'

Toni slid off the bike and took a step towards the patrol car. She felt faint in the hot desert air. The road ahead was shimmering. Torodecko Bridge was just around the next bend.

Red gripped her arm. 'She aint going nowhere till I have a satisfactory explanation.'

'We've had instructions over the radio to check out all female bike passengers in this area. We've had a report of a Caucasian female answering your girlfriend's description, wanted for holding up a drug store a week ago.'

'Not this one. You've got the wrong girl, officer.' His hold was biting into her arm.

The patrolman smiled benevolently, enjoying the game. He glanced down at Toni's phoney ID. 'The evidence would strongly suggest otherwise, sir. Says here that Ms Hedges was born one Frederick Green. He, or should I say she, is wanted in more than one state for armed robbery and deception.'

Red's grip instantly fell away. His look was one of disbelief, but she knew he wouldn't take the chance on it being true.

Toni was too nervous to laugh. Red's face was a classic. She wished she had time to enjoy it more. It was an old ploy but the macho ones fell for it every time. It was the surest way of giving someone the brush-off. She made a bolt for the car, hoping the patrolman would get the hint that she was in a hurry.

He couldn't let it go, however. 'I'm sorry if that's come as a shock to you, sir. You wouldn't be the first man she's fooled.'

Red's jaw was working up and down but no sound was coming out.

Toni couldn't miss the opportunity to rub a little salt in. 'Hey, you couldn't blame me for showing it off, could you, Red? They'd given me such a beautiful pussy.'

Toni climbed into the car, praying the patrolman would quit dicking around before the shock wore off and Red decided to teach her a lesson.

Patrolman number two was walking back towards the car. 'You guys will have to turn your bikes around. There's a roadblock up ahead.'

Toni shrunk down low in the back seat and watched through the window. Wacko was angry and questioning Red. As predicted, Red didn't want the other bikers to know what the patrolman had said and was keen to leave. He was shaking his head and gesturing for them to leave. Toni breathed a massive sigh of relief when the bikes turned and roared back down the highway. Her dress was sticking to her like glue, she had sweat so much.

Nick turned in his seat. 'How did I do?'

Toni smiled. 'You were perfect. Just perfect. If you'll just help me pick up my friend, I promise I'll make your trouble all worthwhile.'

'It was worth it just to have the chance to fuck that biker off. Did you see the look on his face?'

'You did promise though,' Stan cut in.

'Only if we get to my friend in time.'

'We're on our way.'

Steve's jeep was parked off the road. Toni marvelled at their audacity. She couldn't believe that Caron had had the balls to pull the scam off as many times as she had and still come back for more. Toni waited in the car as the two patrolmen went to fetch her.

Caron was livid. Only someone as guilty as she could

act so indignant at being questioned. Steve was keeping his mouth shut; after all, it wasn't him they were after. Toni felt a stab of guilt. By the time the Cobras had finished with him, he'd be wishing he'd been arrested too. She had his cell phone number somewhere – maybe she could tip him off. She'd see. You never knew when you might need to call in a favour.

Today being a case in point.

Toni had dug the photo out of her purse. It was Caron, for sure. The girl was now being led towards the car. The spinning lights cast on odd glow on the sand.

'Fascist!' Caron spat as the patrolman pushed her down into the car. She turned and glared at Toni. 'Who the fuck are you?'

Toni took a deep breath. These runaways, they were always so pleased to see her.

'Caron Crossley?'

The girl's expression told Toni that she was right.

'My name is Toni Marconi and I'm a private detective, hired by your aunt to find you.'

The two patrolmen turned in their seats to listen.

'The good news, Caron, is that you are not under arrest. However, you and I both owe these gentlemen a rather large favour.'

Caron looked sceptical.

'You wouldn't believe the mess these guys have just got us out of. I'll explain while we drive.'

The car pulled away and Toni settled back in the seat.

Caron Crossley crossed her arms and pouted. 'I need to pee. I've been stuck waiting in the jeep with that gorilla for an age.'

Toni smiled and caught Nick's eye in the rear-view mirror. 'All in good time, Caron, all in good time.

'Now, Stan, about my Corvette . . .'

* * *

On the sidewalk outside Piedro's, Toni shook hands with a classy middle-aged socialite.

'Thank you so much for finding my niece, Ms Marconi.' Bony fingers slipped into her Louis Vuitton for the envelope of cash.

Toni accepted it and did a quick check. It was all there. 'She's waiting for you in the restaurant. I felt it should be a private moment.'

'I appreciate the thought.' Layla Crossley's face was impassive behind her huge dark glasses. 'But perhaps not quite the reunion I was hoping for?'

Toni didn't answer. She couldn't lie to her; she was far too perceptive and anyway getting involved in other people's affairs was against her religion. She'd got Caron to return and that was her job done. She stepped aside for Layla to enter the restaurant.

Layla Crossley gave a wry smile. 'Still, it will be interesting to see which carries the most weight – a life chasing cheap thrills or a more conservative one with the promise of a hefty inheritance.' With a haughty wave she disappeared into the restaurant.

Toni drew a deep breath.

Devious old bat. There was more than a passing family resemblance with those two.

It was good to be back. Toni took a stroll and paused outside Prada; the envelope in her purse was beginning to smoulder. She took a deep breath. Oh yes, for all its faults, LA certainly gave good retail.

Toni returned to her office weighed down with shopping bags and was feeling very smug indeed until she saw Josh's empty desk. So, he had kept to his threat. He had gone. She collapsed into his chair, completely deflated. There was an ivory envelope with her name on it but she didn't want to read that yet. Shit! She could not imagine her life without Josh in it. But she only had herself to blame. She expected puppy-like devotion from him while she completely did her own thing. Still, she had got it out of her system now and the whole biker thing had got a little out of hand.

A cold shiver ran down her spine when she thought of the corner she had painted herself into. She really needed to get back on the right side of the law. She spun lazily in the chair, wondering if Matt and John would be upstairs in Piedro's. Then again, word would soon be out that she was back in town – let them chase her.

She listened to her messages. The boys had been missing her by the sound of it and there was a number of requests to call back about assignments. Toni sighed. Was she wasting her time? A good portion of the people she traced didn't even want to be found. They wanted to be living on the edge. The final message cheered her up big time. It was an invitation from Sid to spend some time back in SF for carnival weekend. Now that was an offer too good to refuse. Sid would be amazed at the things she had learnt since she'd been away.

Stan's ex-brother-in-law had restored her Corvette to full health – thankfully. She didn't know how she would have got Caron back to LA otherwise. There was also a rather hefty bill on the doormat, along with an irate letter from the resident's committee with regards to her driving over the communal lawn. For fuck's sake, they were so anal. Toni threw her shopping on the bed and decided to run a deep bath. Heaven.

While she was soaking she read the letter from Josh and discovered that all was in fact not lost.

Toni was too nervous to appreciate the splendid bougainvillea draped around Josh's new front door. Cool jazz wafted out from an open window. She took a deep breath and collected herself before ringing the bell. She had primped and preened for hours. Despite the head-to-toe labels she was still unsure whether she looked OK. She smoothed the non-existent wrinkles on her skirt. She had been careful not to wear anything too low or too high. She looked respectable, just like Josh wanted.

He was branching out on his own as a photographer but he was offering an olive branch, and Toni was here to take it; at a dinner party to introduce her to his respectable, settled life.

There was no accounting for taste.

The door opened and Toni looked up. He looked fantastic. She had forgotten how tall and golden he was. She held out the bottle of Bollinger and grinned.

'Forgive me? Life is shit without you.'

Josh stepped out and hugged her. It had been a while since she'd spent time with a man who bathed regularly and he smelt and felt divine. From inside his apartment Toni could hear muted laughter and the tinkle of ice in crystal glasses.

'Clean slate?' Josh asked.

'Most definitely.'

'And you read my letter?'

'Yes I did.'

'No bikers, outlaws or other degenerates?'

'Definitely not.'

'And you've brought along a respectable law-abiding date?'

'Oh, Josh,' Toni purred, glancing back over her shoulder at the car. 'I've done much better than that – I've brought two.'

Visit the Black Lace website at
www.blacklace-books.co.uk

BLACK LACE

**FIND OUT THE LATEST INFORMATION AND TAKE
ADVANTAGE OF OUR FANTASTIC FREE BOOK OFFER!
ALSO VISIT THE SITE FOR . . .**

- All Black Lace titles currently available
  and how to order online
- Great new offers
- Writers' guidelines
- Author interviews
- An erotica newsletter
- Features
- Cool links

BLACK LACE — THE LEADING IMPRINT OF WOMEN'S SEXY FICTION

TAKING YOUR EROTIC READING PLEASURE TO NEW HORIZONS

LOOK OUT FOR THE ALL-NEW BLACK LACE BOOKS – AVAILABLE NOW!

All books priced £6.99 in the UK. Please note publication dates apply to the UK only. For other territories, please contact your retailer.

SNOW BLONDE
Astrid Fox
ISBN 0 352 33732 X

Lilli Sandström is an archaeologist in her mid-thirties; cool blond fisherman Arvak Berg is her good-looking lover. But Lilli has had enough of their tempestuous relationship for the time being so she retreats to the northern forests of her childhood. There, in the beauty of the wilderness, she explores and is seduced by a fellow archaeologist, a pair of bizarre twins, woodcutter Henrik and the glacial but bewitching Malin. And when she comes across old rune carvings she also begins to discover evidence of an old, familiar story. *Snow Blonde* **is also an unusual, sexy and romantic novel of fierce northern delights.**

THE HOUSE IN NEW ORLEANS
Fleur Reynolds
ISBN 0 352 32951 3

When Ottilie Duvier inherits the family home in the fashionable Garden district of New Orleans, it's the ideal opportunity to set her life on a different course and flee from her demanding aristocratic English boyfriend. However, Ottilie arrives in New Orleans to find that her inheritance has been leased to one Helmut von Straffen – a decadent German count, known for his notorious Mardi Gras parties. Determined to claim what is rightfully hers, Ottilie challenges von Straffen – but ends up being lured into strange games in steamy locations. **Sultry passions explode in New Orleans' underworld of debauchery.**

Coming in November

NOBLE VICES
Monica Belle
ISBN O 352 33738 9

Annabelle doesn't want to work. She wants to spend her time riding, attending exotic dinner parties and indulging herself in even more exotic sex, at her father's expense. Unfortunately, Daddy has other ideas, and when she writes off his new Jaguar, it is the final straw. Sent to work in the City, Annabelle quickly finds that it is not easy to fit in, especially when what she thinks of as harmless, playful sex turns out to leave most of her new acquaintances in shock. **Naughty, fresh and kinky, this is a very funny tale of a spoilt rich English girl's fall from grace.**

A MULTITUDE OF SINS
Kit Mason
ISBN O 352 33737 O

This is a collection of short stories from a fresh and talented new writer. Ms Mason explores settings and periods that haven't previously been covered in Black Lace fiction, and her exquisite attention to detail makes for an unusual and highly arousing collection. Female Japanese pearl divers tangle erotically with tentacled creatures of the deep; an Eastern European puppeteer sexually manipulates everyone around her; the English seaside town of Brighton in the 1950s hides a thrilling network of forbidden lusts. **Kit Mason brings a wonderfully imaginative dimension to her writing and this collection of her erotic short stories will dazzle and delight.**

HANDMAIDEN OF PALMYRA
Fleur Reynolds
ISBN 0 352 32919 X

Palmyra, 3rd century AD: a lush oasis in the heart of the Syrian desert. The inquisitive, beautiful and fiercely independent Samoya takes her place as apprentice priestess in the temple of Antioch. Decadent bachelor Prince Alif has other ideas. He wants a wife, and sends his equally lascivious sister to bring Samoya to the Bacchanalian wedding feast he is preparing. Samoya embarks on a journey that will alter the course of her life. Before reaching her destination, she is to encounter Marcus, the battle-hardened centurion who will unearth the core of her desires. **Lust in the dust and forbidden fruit in Ms Reynolds' most unusual title for the Black Lace series.**

Coming in December

THE HEAT OF THE MOMENT
Tesni Morgan
ISBN 0 352 33742 7

Amber, Sue and Diane – three women from an English market town – are successful in their businesses, but all want more from their private lives. When they become involved in The Silver Banner – an English Civil War re-enactment society – there's plenty of opportunity for them to fraternise with handsome muscular men in historical uniforms. Thing is, the fun-loving Cavaliers are much sexier than the Puritan Roundheads, and tensions and rivalries are played out on the village green and the bedroom. **Great characterisation and oodles of sexy fun in this story of three English friends who love dressing up.**

WICKED WORDS 7
Various
ISBN 0352 33743 5

Hugely popular and immensely entertaining, the *Wicked Words* collections are the freshest and most cutting-edge volumes of women's erotic stories to be found anywhere in the world. The diversity of themes and styles reflects the multi-faceted nature of the female sexual imagination. Combining humour, warmth and attitude with fun, filthy, imaginative writing, these stories sizzle with horny action. Only the most arousing fiction makes it into a *Wicked Words* volume. This is the best in fun, sassy erotica from the UK and USA. **Another sizzling collection of wild fantasies from wicked women!**

OPAL DARKNESS
Cleo Cordell
ISBN 0 352 33033 3

It's the latter part of the nineteenth century and beautiful twins Sidonie and Francis are yearning for adventure. Their newly awakened sexuality needs an outlet. Sent by their father on the Grand Tour of Europe, they swiftly turn cultural exploration into something illicit. When they meet Count Constantin and his decadent friends and are invited to stay at his snow-bound Romanian castle, there is no turning back on the path of depravity. **Another wonderfully decadent piece of historical erotica from a pioneer of female erotica.**

Black Lace Booklist

Information is correct at time of printing. To avoid disappointment check availability before ordering. Go to www.blacklace-books.co.uk. All books are priced £6.99 unless another price is given.

To find out the latest information about Black Lace titles, check out the website: www.blacklace-books.co.uk or send for a booklist with complete synopses by writing to:

Black Lace Booklist, Virgin Books Ltd
Thames Wharf Studios
Rainville Road
London W6 9HA

Please include an SAE of decent size. Please note only British stamps are valid.

Our privacy policy
We will not disclose information you supply us to any other parties. We will not disclose any information which identifies you personally to any person without your express consent.

From time to time we may send out information about Black Lace books and special offers. Please tick here if you do not wish to receive Black Lace information.   ❑

Please send me the books I have ticked above.

Name ....

Address ....

....

....

....

Post Code ....

Send to: Cash Sales, Black Lace Books, Thames Wharf Studios, Rainville Road, London W6 9HA.

US customers: for prices and details of how to order books for delivery by mail, call 1-800-343-4499.

Please enclose a cheque or postal order, made payable to Virgin Books Ltd, to the value of the books you have ordered plus postage and packing costs as follows:

UK and BFPO – £1.00 for the first book, 50p for each subsequent book.

Overseas (including Republic of Ireland) – £2.00 for the first book, £1.00 for each subsequent book.

If you would prefer to pay by VISA, ACCESS/MASTERCARD, DINERS CLUB, AMEX or SWITCH, please write your card number and expiry date here:

....

Signature ....

Please allow up to 28 days for delivery.